D1552873

# THE STUDY OF MURDER

A MUIRTEACH MACPHEE MYSTERY

# THE STUDY OF MURDER

## SUSAN McDUFFIE

**FIVE STAR**
*A part of Gale, Cengage Learning*

GALE
CENGAGE Learning·

Detroit • New York • San Francisco • New Haven, Conn • Waterville, Maine • London

**GALE**
CENGAGE Learning®

Copyright © 2013 by Susan McDuffie
Street Plan of Oxford, England by Paterson Simons of "simonsfineart
.com".
Epilogue: copyright © Susan McDuffie.
Five Star™ Publishing, a part of Cengage Learning, Inc.

LIBRARY OF CONGRESS CATALOGING-IN-PUBLICATION DATA

McDuffie, Susan.
    The study of murder : a Muirteach MacPhee mystery / Susan
Mcduffie. — First Edition.
      pages cm
    ISBN-13: 978-1-4328-2720-5 (hardcover)
    ISBN-10: 1-4328-2720-0 (hardcover)
    1. Colonsay (Scotland)—Fiction. 2. Scotland—History—1057–
1603—Fiction. I. Title.
PS3613.C396S78 2013
813'.6—dc23                                        2013014024

First Edition. First Printing: September 2013
Find us on Facebook– https://www.facebook.com/FiveStarCengage
Visit our website— http://www.gale.cengage.com/fivestar/
Contact Five Star™ Publishing at FiveStar@cengage.com

Printed in Mexico
1 2 3 4 5 6 7 17 16 15 14 13

This book is dedicated with love to my father, Bruce McDuffie, a professor of analytical chemistry. Growing up in a wonderful academic environment no doubt had a great deal to do with this book.

# ACKNOWLEDGMENTS AND AUTHOR'S NOTE

Thanks, as always, are due to so many people. Donna Lake and my mother, Wini McDuffie, read the manuscript and offered helpful suggestions, while my dad kept me at it. Fellow author Mel Starr suggested some wonderful research sources. Paterson Simons created a wonderful map of Muirteach's Oxford. Salvador provided emotional support to get the job done.

Donald, the son of the Lord of the Isles, actually did attend Oxford for a few years during the 1370s. His chaperones Muirteach and Mariota are of course fictional characters. Thomas Houkyn was the coroner of Oxford during 1374 and some fascinating coroner's records from that era are available online—at least I found them fascinating! Relations between the town folk and the schools were actually fairly calm during this era, twenty years after the Saint Scholastica Day riots of 1355. I have taken the literary liberty of introducing a little more unrest for plotting purposes. Also, so far as I know, none of the Balliol masters were ever murdered, and their characters and names are totally fictional, as are most characters in the book. DeWylton, however, was the university chancellor during this period.

The spark for this book came from my interest in the Voynich manuscript, a curious manuscript written in cipher that has never been deciphered, confounding many eminent cryptographers. There are many theories about this strange manuscript that now resides in the Beinecke Library at Yale University. Readers wanting to know more about it might refer to *The Voynich Manuscript,* by Gerry Kennedy and Rob Churchill.

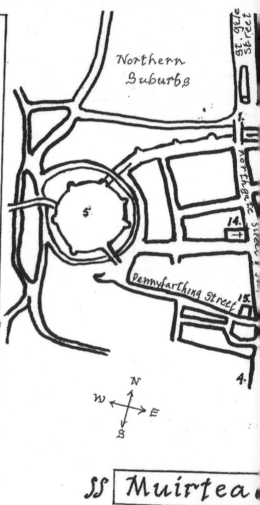

**Legend.**

1. North gate and Boccardo
2. Smith gate
3. East gate
4. South gate
5. Oxford Castle
6. Balliol College
7. Widow Tanner's
8. Anthony and Crispin's
9. Vintner Gibbes
10. Austin Friar's
11. Lecture Halls
12. Adam Bookman's Shop
13. The Green Man
14. Chapel
15. Torrilda's Lodging

Northern Suburbs

St. Gile Street

Northgate Street

Pennyfarthing Street

N
W ← → E
S

SS Muirtea

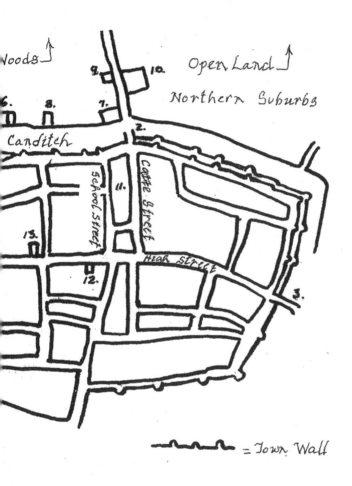

Woods↑

9.  10.  Open Land↑

6.  8.  7.  Northern Suburbs

Canditch  2.

School Street  11.  Castle Street

13.  High Street

12.  3.

〰〰 = Town Wall

's Oxford ~ 1374  n

# CAST OF CHARACTERS

**Muirteach MacPhee,** the Keeper of the Records for the Lord of Isles

**Mariota,** his wife

**Donald MacDonald,** thirteen-year-old son of the Lord of the Isles

**Master Abraham Jakeson,** proprietor of the Green Man, a tavern in Oxford

**Mistress Jakeson,** his wife

**Jonetta,** his lovely daughter

**Phillip Woode,** a senior student at Balliol College

**Anthony,** a first-year student

**Crispin,** another first-year student

**Master Clarkson,** master of Balliol

**Master Julian Delacey**

**Master Ralph Berwyk**

**Brother Eusebius**

**Widow Tanner,** a local landlady

**Rufous,** her small dog

**Adam Bookman,** a bookseller, and his wife

**Walter Grymbaud,** undersheriff of Oxford

**Ralf,** his assistant

**Torvilda Bonefey,** Ralph Berwyk's mistress

**Mistress Bohun,** Ralph's aunt

**Justin Penwarred and Vortigen Penwryth,** lodgers with Torvilda

# Cast of Characters

**Thomas Houkyn,** the town coroner

**Chancellor deWylton,** chancellor of the university

**Ivo,** the gatekeeper at Balliol

**Avice,** his young daughter

**Ruldolfo of Salerno,** a physician and teacher

**Richard deVyse,** another student

**Walter of York,** a chapman

# PROLOGUE

*Oxford, England, 1374*

The nymphs first. Images flowed onto the page and the writer struggled to get them all down, to convey the essence of the visions correctly. The expanding worlds, the interconnection between the spheres, the propulsion of the seed as it traveled. The feminine principle, bathed in divine liquor, dancing and playing in its showers. It was crucial that he record this as he'd been instructed, they demanded it. There must be no errors.

The light faded and the September evening grew chill, but the writer paid no attention until the darkness grew absolute. He then lit a tallow candle and continued working, stopping occasionally to stretch cramped hands. The flame wavered in the drafts that found their way through the cracks in the roughly plastered walls as he worked on, the only sound the scratching of quill on parchment. The autumn wind gusted outside, finding its way in through the wooden shutters of the small window, but the writer continued, at times adding color to the elaborate drawing.

It was a pity his last efforts had not been accurate. These must be correct.

The silence broke with a knock. The writer at first did not hear, so involved was he in his efforts. The door opened, the noise broke his concentration and he quickly tried to hide the papers as another man entered the room.

"Working late, are you not?"

"Some simple jottings merely, a few poor scribblings of my own. Nothing that need concern you."

"Can you take my lecture tomorrow? I've an appointment I dare not break."

"On *The Sentences*. Yes. I should be happy to assist."

The visitor departed, leaving the writer to his labors. He worked on feverishly, until the candle guttered out and the dark night sky outside showed a lightening in the east, along with the bright point of light that was the morning star. Then he secreted his parchment and went to deliver his lecture.

# Chapter 1

"That must be Oxford, there ahead."

I pointed out the city walls, glinting in the setting sun, to my traveling companions. Our horses neighed wearily. They too were tired of traveling.

"We must make haste, I'm thinking they'll lock the gates soon."

Our journey was ending but not our labors. They were just beginning.

Donald led the way. Indeed, on our journey so far Mariota and I had both often let him take the lead. His thirteen-year-old body, restless and impatient, balked at our pace. It seemed easier to let him travel ahead a bit, while we came on at a slightly more sedate speed. He galloped his horse down the road despite the crowds of people converging on the Northgate. Mariota winced, and I felt my own shoulders tense as we watched Donald nearly run down an old woman carrying a wicker cage of chickens.

"I suppose we were like that once," I commented, trying to make light of the lad's behavior.

"Perhaps. But I'm not thinking the monks at the Priory would have given you much chance to ride, let alone run down old women. I'm surprised the boy did not learn more restraint, those years the old king kept him hostage at Dumbarton for his father's good behavior."

I shrugged. "The lad was held there for two years. Perhaps

that is why he is now so wild and must have both you and I to be his nursemaids while he attends the college. And with his own grandfather sitting on the throne of Scotland perhaps he feels no need to watch his step any longer."

Mariota nodded and managed an exhausted laugh. She reined in her horse while Donald, now well ahead, nearly trampled a man carrying his little daughter, missing them by an arm's breadth. The man, poorly dressed, did nothing, for Donald's gear spoke of nobility.

"How can he have such energy?" she marveled. "And such arrogance? What kind of leader will he make someday? *Och,* there's nothing for it now. I want nothing more than a clean bed and some supper. And you must be tired as well."

Mariota and I had been married but a few months, and I still marveled at my good fortune. Although, to tell strict truth, this latest journey did not seem especially fortuitous. How was it, I wondered, that we were here so far from Islay, playing nursemaid to a spoiled and impulsive thirteen-year-old?

I didn't have to wonder long about it. Donald's father, John MacDonald, was the powerful Lord of the Isles and overlord of my own MacPhee clan. I served him as his Keeper of the Records, and His Lordship had ordered us to attend on his son at Oxford. And so here we were, after a journey of several weeks, nearing our goal. Both Mariota and I felt exhausted from the travel and our charge, but Donald himself appeared not tired at all by the journey.

Many travelers and townsfolk hurried into the town as the afternoon ended, and even Donald's youthful exuberance seemed somewhat dampened by the unfamiliar crowds. I heard a smattering of languages, some Latin but more of it the less familiar English tongue, and missed the soft lilting sounds of my native Gaelic, feeling every bit a stranger in this busy town.

The trip had given both Mariota and myself some opportunity to practice our rudimentary English, the dialects of which seemed to vary greatly as we made our way south. At least Latin was spoken in the schools, and both my wife and I spoke that language fluently.

We caught up with Donald somewhat before the gates, on a broad street where a large ditch circled the town walls and carried much of the sewage of the town away. After the quiet and clean air of the countryside, it was not a pleasant smell.

"Donald," Mariota reproached him in Gaelic, "did you not see those people you nearly trampled? You must have a care for their welfare."

"They should not be so slow. And I did not trample them. So all's well."

"No, Donald," returned Mariota, irritated. "No, all is not well. It is not well for you, a young lord, to treat poor people in such a way. Your father has put you in our care. And arrogance is a sin."

Donald flushed with anger and opened his mouth to reply. I intervened before he could speak. "Look you, they are getting ready to close the gates. We will have leisure to deal with this later, I think, after we've found lodgings and eaten a bit. Now, hurry."

And so we entered the town of Oxford, crossing through Northgate. Indeed, it was more of a narrow tunnel than a simple gate, as it passed under a two-storied building that I later discovered housed the town gaol. Inside the city proper, the broad main street was crowded, both with townsfolk frequenting the merchants, most of whom appeared to be trying to close up shop, and with many students. We passed a church on our left, then continued down Northgate Street and turned onto the High Street. I was glad we were on horseback as we crossed the drains that ran down the center of the roadway.

We found temporary lodgings without much difficulty, at an

inn on High Street. We entered through the gate that stood facing the street and into the inn yard. The groom took our weary mounts and we were led to the main hall, our baggage hauled to our room above.

Travelers busy eating and drinking crowded the dining hall. The innkeeper seated us at a table and sent his wife to see to our chamber. He took our orders and then rapidly brought us some spiced ale that went down well and helped wash the dust of the road from our mouths. Our food came soon after and tasted fine enough. As we finished the meal of eel pie, more ale, another typed of baked fish and some cooked apples, Donald was all for seeing the sights of the town. The thought made my head ache. It was with some difficulty that Mariota and I, both tired, sought to dissuade him.

"But there's still daylight left," Donald pouted. "Please, Muirteach. Let us go and perhaps Mariota could stay here and rest, since she is tired from the journey."

Eventually I gave in, despite my headache, and consented to go with him for a stroll. Mariota decided to accompany us as well, although I could sense she was a bit annoyed. We finished our meal and checked that our baggage was safe in our chamber, then the three of us left the inn and wandered the streets a bit. The side streets looked crowded with students. At least I assumed they were students, all young men of various ages, many of whom wore the clerical garb of minor orders. Most students took minor orders.

"Tomorrow we must find lodgings, and then you must go to Balliol and meet the masters there. But that will leave time to see a bit of the town."

Donald grimaced. "I could well have come on my own. Many students do, at my age."

"Aye," Mariota put in, "but they are not young lordlings. It would not be seemly, for your rank, to be unattended."

"Why not send me with a groom and a manservant, then?" Donald responded rudely. "I am too old to have a nursemaid."

"Had your behavior been better, we would not be here at all," I retorted, my jaw tightening as I spoke. "Your father was thinking that we would do well. And we are far from being nursemaids." I protested perhaps a little guiltily, as I had often had that same thought. "But we will have plenty of time tomorrow to get settled a bit."

"I'm thirsty," Donald announced as we passed a tavern. "Let's stop here and have some wine."

The tavern looked pleasant enough. The wooden signboard, well painted, bore a picture of a green man leering out from between two trees. I glanced at Mariota, who shrugged hopelessly and then nodded. So we went in.

It was a fairly large room with several tables and benches, busy already this evening with a clamor of students and others. The atmosphere smelled pleasantly of wine and the rushes on the floor looked relatively fresh. The tavern keeper, a stout dark-haired man, saw us seated and his daughter came to take our order. She was a lovely lass with curly blonde hair, large brown eyes and a shapely figure, which Donald seemed to appreciate. She gave her name as Jonetta, when Donald asked her, and said her father was Abraham Jakeson.

The noise in the hall grew louder when several more youths, with their heads tonsured in the style of clerks, entered, sat down with a collective swagger and demanded ale and claret. The tavern keeper filled their beakers and they drank quickly, then started to make advances on Jonetta, calling for her and joking with her. She laughingly fended off their attentions until one of the students, somewhat larger and older than the other youths, pulled her down beside him on the bench.

"Muirteach," Donald hissed, "yon's no gentleman."

"She seems able to manage him," I observed, as Jonetta

competently pushed him away and rose. "No doubt she's dealt with this type often enough. The town is full of clerks and students. And her father stands ready, should things get out of hand."

Jonetta had moved away from the students, but returned quickly enough with more wine for them. I noticed she sat next to the older youth again for a moment. He said something seriously to her and fingered a medal that she wore on a chain around her neck. She pulled away, with another laugh. But she did not seem angry.

A couple of the younger students, one with an untidy head of reddish hair and the other dark haired with a lean face, had been glaring across the tables at Donald, somewhat in the way of tomcats, and I saw the red-haired boy nudge the other with his elbow, pointing out our attire, and laugh. I prayed Donald would not notice this and rose, hoping to leave quickly and forestall trouble.

I was not quick enough. The room was crowded and as we made our way between the tables, the dark-haired boy stuck his feet out in the aisle, tripping Donald. Donald stumbled, but recovered his balance, and upset the red-haired lad's ale into his lap. I do not think that was an accident. In an instant the two lads were on their feet and Donald was swinging a blow at them, while the older of the students rose also and quickly tried to restrain the two younger boys.

"We beg your pardon, sirs. And lady, as well," the older man said, holding the red-haired boy back by his tunic. "My charges are clumsy oafs, and have no sense of the size of their own big feet." He spoke in Latin, and I replied in the same.

"And this young gentleman here should apologize as well," I said, my jaw tight, as I sank my fingers into the flesh of Donald's arm. "For spilling the ale all over this poor man's tunic."

"I shan't apologize," Donald hissed to me in Gaelic. "He

tripped me. It was ill done."

"Perhaps," I hissed back, restraining my urge to give the boy a proper clout, "but you'll solve nothing by starting a war with the English your first night in Oxford."

"It was ill done, indeed," the older man assented, almost as if he read our thoughts. "But perhaps we can buy you a glass of wine to atone for it. We are poor students. I am Phillip Woode, from Balliol Hall, and these two are called Anthony and Crispin. They are but bejants still and lodge nearby."

"Balliol, you say? That is fortuitous, as my young lord here has a letter of introduction to the master there. We will be visiting there tomorrow. Donald MacDonald is my lord's name. He is also a bejant, I believe, as it will be his first year of study. I am Muirteach MacPhee, and this woman is my wife, Mariota. We accompany him here from our home in the islands of Scotland."

Anthony and Crispin sullenly made room for Donald on the bench while Phillip seated Mariota and myself on his side of the table. The younger boys continued glaring at each other while Mariota and I conversed with Phillip awhile. He proved a pleasant enough man, a senior student, soon to take his final examinations. We shared a glass of wine, then took our leave and returned to our inn.

The innkeeper had provided the three of us with a private chamber. Donald took the bed while Mariota and I slept on a pallet on the floor. Still, it was passably clean and both Mariota and I were tired, my bad leg aching from the exertions of the day.

"How he expects to study for his examinations there at The Green Man, I do not know," said Mariota tartly as we spread our blankets on the pallet.

"*Och*, white love, I've done a fair share of similar preparation in my day. Don't be hard on the lad."

21

"Aye, well, it looked to me that he was studying Jonetta, and not the *Quadrivium*," Mariota whispered to me.

"Perhaps he was just admiring her necklace," I whispered back. "It was an unusual one."

"Oh, so you admired it too?" Mariota asked with a little laugh in her voice.

"Those two boys are great louts," Donald muttered rebelliously from his bed. "And they will be my classmates. What a mischance."

And so, amid such ponderings, we slept.

The next day dawned sunny, with blue sky. We rose with the sun and breakfasted at the inn, on porridge, cheese, apples and small ale. The innkeeper's wife served us with a smile that put Donald in a better mood, and we then set out on foot through the town of Oxford.

Balliol College had been founded over one hundred years earlier. The Scottish heiress Devorgilla, wife of John Balliol the Englishman and mother of John Balliol, the past king of Scotland, had herself endowed the school for poor scholars, all graduate students working on advanced degrees. But we had a letter of introduction to the master of the college and it was there that the son of the Lord of the Isles and grandson of the present king of Scotland would seek his tutor.

The college where the masters and a few senior students resided was located in some three houses just outside the northern wall of the town, near the old Jewish quarter, we were told. Most undergraduate students rented beds in student tenements unconnected with the college. However, Donald was not to lodge there, nor did he necessarily need to attend all the lectures required of the students. He would have a tutor, his father had instructed, and we were to find other lodgings nearby, more suited to his station. But first we went to see the college.

We arrived, still early in the day. The tenements that lodged the fellows and masters had been procured one hundred years earlier when Devorgilla originally endowed the college. It looked as though little had been done to the original buildings since, although there was a newly built chapel and all the buildings seemed in fair enough repair.

It seemed that one tenement housed the majority of the fellows, and was called the New Hall. There was a great room there where the fellows took their meals. Another hall was known as Old Balliol Hall, where the masters and a few senior students resided. The college also owned several lecture halls within the town walls, on School Street, where many of the masters gave lectures, and another tenement nearby, which rented rooms to undergraduates. It was there that Anthony and Crispin lodged.

The gatekeeper, an old man bent nearly double, demanded our identities, glared a moment and then refused Mariota entrance. Women, it seems, were not allowed in the school, for all that a Scottish princess had founded it. The gatekeeper bade her wait in the back garden while Donald and I were ushered inside one of the three houses that made up the lodgings of the college.

The fellows already had finished their first lecture of the day and were now at breakfast. We waited until the master of the college could receive us. I glimpsed Phillip Woode at a table with the other scholars.

"I am Master Thomas Clarkson, master of the college," came a voice in Latin. I looked up to see a tall man, well built, of about forty. He had a resolute face and dark hair with a few streaks of gray showing in his tonsure.

"I am Donald MacDonald, *filius* of John MacDonald, *dominus insularium*, the Lord of the Isles, and grandson to Robert Steward, the king of Scotland. My noble grandfather and father have required that I study here in Oxford, and I beg you to take me as a student. This is my letter of introduction," Donald replied, pleasantly in fair enough Latin. He handed Master Clarkson the folded parchment, sealed with his father's great seal. Apparently the lad had learned some manners during his years as a hostage at Dumbarton, after all.

Master Clarkson read the letter impassively, although I thought I sensed some pleasure as he read. It could only be good for him to have such a noble student. Finally, he finished reading and smiled an unctuous smile at Donald. "We will be honored. I shall be pleased to guide your studies. You will lodge elsewhere?"

I nodded. "We will find suitable lodging today and Donald can start his studies in the morning."

"This is Muirteach," Donald said, introducing me. "He and his wife have accompanied me here."

"You might speak with the widow Tanner. She has a fine house, rents lodgings, and lives nearby. Her house is just down Canditch, that broad street that runs along the town walls." I got the direction while the master continued speaking to Donald. "We have several other masters here, associated with the college. Master Delacey, Master Berwyk, and Brother Eusebius. All give lectures for undergraduates at our hall on School Street, inside the city walls. The first lecture starts before dawn, in the hall. These are the ordinary lectures, on the Trivium. Then there is breakfast, and then the extraordinary lectures are later in the morning. You are welcome to attend them if you wish, although I will be your tutor. I can instruct you individually should that be preferable."

A tall, gangly man approached. He had yellow hair going gray, somewhat curly, and walked with the stooped posture of one who spent much time reading. He wore a much-patched Franciscan habit of gray.

"This is Brother Eusebius. You have wax tablets? And books? Phillip Woode, here, will show you where the stationer is located. And he can show you the widow's house as well."

I greeted Phillip again, while Donald respectfully took leave of Master Clarkson, saying he would look forward to his instruction the next day. They made an appointment to meet after breakfast. Then we left.

Phillip seemed happy enough to leave the college for the morning. We found Mariota, examining some herbs in the garden next door to the houses, and set out.

The Widow Tanner's house was a commodious one, down a bit from the buildings that housed Balliol and facing the town's wall. It had a large central hall and two stories on either side. She had a stable to house the horses we had brought, although it seemed we'd have little use for horses here in the town. In the back near the stable was a fine garden, and somewhat further down the street was the tannery from which her husband had taken his name. She was pleased to let us have two rooms on the second floor of her house, although the rent was outrageous. The rooms were small, and only the front one had a window. But that may have been just as well, for scents from the nearby tannery, as well as the ditch on the other side of the street, wafted unpleasantly in through the shutters.

"You'll get used to it," Widow Tanner assured us. I thought longingly of my farm in Islay, and even my little cottage in Scalasaig, mean as it was, swept by the clean sea breezes.

My thoughts were interrupted by the barks of a small furry reddish-brown dog. It had followed Widow Tanner up the stairs and now yapped excitedly as we looked at our rooms.

"Eh, this is Rufous," said the widow, as she scooped the dog up into her arms. "Do not worry, sirs, he is quite friendly."

Mariota reached out to pet the beast, which licked her wrist and squirmed out of the widow's arms.

"He's taken a fancy to you, Mistress. He doesn't always take to everyone."

As if he understood her words, Rufous growled a bit at Donald, who was loudly tromping around the rooms.

"Behave yourself, pup," the widow admonished the dog, which quickly trotted downstairs with her.

We settled on our terms for the lodgings and sent a servant to the inn, with the message to bring our belongings and horses to the widow's house. We were just leaving for the stationers when I heard loud voices hailing Phillip. Looking down the street, I saw the two young students Phillip had been with the evening before, Anthony and Crispin, approaching. They saw us and stopped, glaring. Donald rolled his eyes and groaned when Phillip greeted the boys. Then Phillip led the way to the booksellers through the Smithgate, while the boys continued down Canditch to their tenement.

"Will I never escape those louts?" Donald muttered to me when we were out of earshot.

Adam Bookman had a small shop on High Street. At least they did not forbid women in the bookshops, and Mariota was elated as she viewed the volumes. Donald had brought a copy of Aristotle with him, but needed a copy of *The Sentences* and other volumes, as well as wax tablets, pen, and some used parchment that could be washed clean and reused. The smell of the parchment and the ink minded me of my days at the Priory on Oronsay. Of course his father had provided ample funds and Donald would not need to copy his books, sentence by sentence, from the lectures of his teacher.

Mariota looked longingly at a copy of Galen in Greek, oblivious to the scowls of Master Bookman. I had a feeling she would be back to purchase it soon. As we left the stationer's and returned to the widow's, Phillip Woode departed, leaving us to set up housekeeping in our new rooms.

The rooms were well enough appointed, and it took little time to unpack our belongings, which had arrived promptly from the inn. Donald's room had a small desk with a chair, for study, and a bed with hangings. Our room also had a bed with hangings, a chest, and a table and chair. The widow fussed in and out, accompanied by her little dog, bringing blankets and bedding, and airing the rooms. She seemed impressed enough with Donald's lineage and called him "my young lordship," which he seemed to enjoy. While the good widow dithered and my wife arranged our belongings, I wondered at what had brought us here.

It had been that July that I'd heard the first of it. We'd been at Finlaggan, on Islay. John MacDonald, Lord of the Isles, had completed signing a treaty I'd recorded, and then he drew me aside. "Muirteach," he had said, "I'm needing to get Donald out of the Isles. He's running wild here, and the latest is that he's been making sheep's eyes at that daughter of the MacLean, for all that the lass is betrothed to a MacKenzie, and her father is aye upset about it all."

"Yes, my lord?"

"Now I'm thinking that the MacLean had better send his daughter off to the nuns on Iona, if he cannot be controlling her better. But then she is a flirt, there's no doubt of that. And at the feast a few days ago, Donald was drinking and challenged that MacKenzie in the hall, and it came to blows. The lad—the MacKenzie it is that I'm speaking of—was knocked down and hit his head on a pillar. Your own wife's father is saying the lad may not survive the blow. He's lying senseless the now. You can see it was not Donald's fault, but the MacKenzie is in a high rage—that boy was the apple of his eye. But, just to calm the MacKenzie down a wee bit, I'm wanting to send Donald down to Oxford. It will get him away from here for a time, until things blow over. And it will be a good thing for him as well."

"How so?"

"He'll need more education than he can get here, and it would give him some polish, and experience with the English as well. He's of an age to go, just turned thirteen this spring. Let him make sheep's eyes at the English girls and knock some sense into the students there in the south."

"Yes, my lord?" I had repeated, feeling an uncomfortable sinking in my gut and a tightening in my chest.

"I'm not wanting to send him down there by himself. And, since he's spent so much time as a hostage at Dumbarton, there's no servant I'd altogether trust with him. He needs a firm hand."

"Yes?" I replied, carefully keeping my voice neutral.

"Well, you are close enough to him in age, but still a grown man. You can remember what it's like to be young. I'm not wanting to be sending him down there with a gray-beard."

"You want me to go with him?"

"Wasn't I just saying that?"

"But, sir, I've no desire to go. What of my wife?"

"*Och*, she can go with you. She's of a serious bent; no doubt she'll like to see the schools. She's a healer, is she not? There are doctors, and many learned men there. She'll enjoy it, Muirteach."

I tried one last time, hopelessly. "But I've no experience with children."

"He's not a child, Muirteach, the lad's thirteen. And close to making horns on the head of the MacKenzie's son. You're the man I'm wanting for this task, so go and tell your wife and pack your bags."

"But how long are we to stay with him?" I had protested. "Surely not for years. Won't you be needing me here?" It did not do to refuse a direct command of my overlord, but I had no wish to leave Islay. And I did not think at that time that Mariota would like to go, but in that I was proved wrong.

"I've clerks who can write up a treaty, so do not fash yourself over that. I'm not thinking he'll stay that long, there at Oxford, but perhaps the lad will surprise me. Perhaps he'll show talent for learned disputations. *Och,* perhaps you can both stay just a few months, you and your wife. Until the spring, that should be long enough. To make sure he's settling into his studies and all. Then, if all is going well, I'll send Fergus or someone down to stay with him. Although he is not an overly studious lad."

# CHAPTER 2

In that, Donald's father had spoken truly. Perhaps the boy had hidden academic prowess, but on the long journey down to Oxford he had seemed much more interested in the game we spotted along the road and in racing his horse at top speed than in practicing his Latin.

So that was how Mariota and I came to be in Oxford. Mariota had been eager to come along, excited by the great learning that such a town must exude. I'd been less impressed, and much less eager. We'd left Somerled, my dog, in Islay, but as we'd traveled I'd increasingly felt Somerled's four-footed company would have been preferable to the young lordling I was supervising. I was not sure how Mariota felt about it all, as we'd had precious little privacy on our journey. I found myself looking forward, at least, to our private room that night.

By now the afternoon was somewhat advanced, and Donald raced into our room.

"Now," he declared, "that's taken care of. We must go into town and see the sights."

So we set off. Although they say Oxford is not as crowded now as it was before the Plague days, it seemed busy enough to me. We walked through the walls at Smith Gate and down to High Street, then worked our way down to the cathedral of St. Frideswyde's. St Frideswyde was a Saxon princess, martyred for her faith. Her relics were displayed there in a rich golden casket. There was also a fine bell tower in the town dedicated to St.

Martin. We then headed back toward our lodgings, intending to walk down School Street. But on our way there we passed the sign of The Green Man and, it being a hot afternoon for September, stopped in for some refreshment.

Master Jakeson was wiping off the tables in the hall, and greeted us, although he seemed subdued. He professed to be glad when he heard of our new lodgings. His daughter was nowhere to be seen, much to Donald's dismay. I'm sure it was on the tip of his tongue to ask of her, but his pride would not let him.

We drank our ale and left, walking up School Street, then over through Market Street and back toward Northgate again. It was market day, and the streets of town were crowded.

The market stalls were beginning to close for the day, but still the variety of goods surprised me and delighted Mariota. There were cloth merchants, with all manner of materials—fine velvets and brocades, as well as linen and wool. Mariota bought some linen and some other fabric while I idly examined some silver pins at a nearby stall.

Shoemakers and tailors were just closing their awnings, as were the apothecaries, but the cries of street vendors still mingled with the chatter of the townsfolk. Spices from the east, the smells of cloves, cinnamon, and nutmeg, mingled with the less fragrant odors of butchered meat, offal, and the liquids running down the drains in the center of the streets. Despite the smell from the tannery, I was glad our lodgings were outside the town walls.

The town was crowded and noisy, elbow to elbow full of people, and I felt a sharp pang of homesickness for my islands. At least outside the walls of the city were green meadows and trees, even if our rooms stunk some from the tannery. Inside the town the first and second stories of the houses jutted over the street, nearly shutting out the daylight. It was altogether new to me, raised in the northern islands, and to Mariota as well; although we'd seen some cities as we traveled south, we had not tarried there or walked the streets.

Donald relished it all. He was more at home in towns, having spent some time in Edinburgh. As we passed the street that led to the Adam Bookman's we saw Master Clarkson leaving, walking rapidly as though angry, away from the stationer's. He did not see us in the crowd and strode quickly out through Northgate.

"Yon's your master," I jibed. "Don't you wish to go greet him?"

"*Och,* no, he seems busy," replied Donald, who seemed in no hurry to begin his studies. "I'm wanting a meat pie." He walked back a few steps to the pie man and purchased the treat. Then Donald turned, as though he saw someone he recognized.

"Who is it?" I asked.

"I think it was Jonetta, the tavern keeper's daughter," Donald mumbled, his mouth full of pastry. I turned, too, but the crowds were thick and I could not see the woman, just a gray robe disappearing behind a corner.

"Was she wearing a gray cloak?" I asked.

Donald shook his head and wiped some crumbs from his mouth. "Just the same green tunic she had on last night." He sighed, obviously love-struck. "She's a bonny girl."

"Doubtless she's on an errand for her father," Mariota put in. Donald looked disappointed, and I thought I saw Mariota hide a smile, but she said nothing else. I smiled back at Mariota and when I next looked round, Donald had vanished. "Where has the lad gotten to?"

Mariota scanned the crowd. "There he is, Muirteach. Oh, dear."

The reason for Mariota's distress became evident when I saw Donald making his way back through the streets with a large, bulky package.

"And what is that?" I asked him sharply in Gaelic, regretting the money I had given the lad from his father's funds before our trip into town.

"It is a lute, a beauty. I've always wanted one. A French musician had one on him at Dumbarton."

"And can you play it?"

"No, but I'll learn easily."

I doubted that but managed to hold my tongue.

We strolled with our parcels through the throngs and out toward Northgate. As we exited the town walls we saw Phillip Woode entering the town, heading toward High Street.

"I'm thinking perhaps he'll be off to The Green Man, to study his *Quadrivium* with Jonetta," Mariota whispered to me when Donald could not hear. I myself thought perhaps she had the right of it, but I said nothing.

We made our way back to Widow Tanner's, my own stomach growling as the shadows grew longer. She had a fine meal prepared for us, a roasted chicken and some manchet loaves, as well as some apples and cheese. Donald had an appetite, despite his snacks at the market. I had not tasted the pie man's wares and fell to with spirit, as did Mariota. After eating our fill, we retired, leaving Donald trying to tune and play his lute, and Mariota and I enjoyed the privacy of our chamber.

The next morning, early, we rose and rousted Donald from his bed. He had stayed up late and had much to learn about the lute, although he made up in enthusiasm what he lacked in training. Mariota and I had cringed as we heard him through the wall that separated our rooms. But this morning he was wanted at the college, for his appointment with his tutor.

It took but a few minutes to walk to the college. Donald went inside to meet with Clarkson, and I bided my time in the back garden behind the hall. A wooden bench near the house looked over the backlands. There was a vegetable garden, privies, and some open space, as well as a small cottage, a servant's I guessed. The gardener tended to the vegetables while I looked on.

Some of the fellows kicked a pig's bladder around the backspace, as breakfast was finished and they were between lectures. I idly listened to voices wafting out of an open window behind. It seemed they were arguing, about what I could not be sure. At least it was not Donald's voice, I thought, enjoying the moment of leisure and the rare September sunshine. My eyes closed, and I drifted off.

I woke as someone sat down next to me. I opened my eyes to see Phillip Woode.

"I am sorry," he said. "I did not mean to disturb you."

I shrugged my shoulders. "I am just waiting on young Donald. It is no disturbance," but I was not ready for what he said next.

"It is so unfair!" he exploded.

"What is?" I asked, recognizing his voice as one of the ones I had heard from the window.

"I have always wanted to be a physician. But I cannot attend lectures at other schools until I have my baccalaureate. And I have prepared, I am ready, but that man will not hear my disputation. He refuses to approve me."

"Why not just attend the lectures?" I asked, curious as to how these things worked.

"No, one must be matriculated. That is, the master accepts you and writes your name on his list of approved students. And the master at the other school refuses to accept me until Clarkson approves me." He glanced at me. "I know the work, I know the arguments, but when it comes to *disputio*, my wits leave me. I can think of nothing to refute the arguments, and my memory takes flight. I know I could be a good physician, but I shall never even get the chance to try."

He took a deep breath, struggling for control. "When I think of all my father has sacrificed, to get me here. And I am such a dullard, my wits leave me. Clarkson has said if I cannot dispute properly, he will send me away."

"And could you not then attend the medical lectures?"

Phillip shook his head. "No. The founder of the school here funds me. There are sixteen of us poor scholars." He looked at me and gave a wry grin. "You can see why it is that I prefer the tavern. Wine lends me wit."

"You could dispute when drunk."

"Perhaps that might be best. But I am sorry, I have taken your time with my troubles."

"It is no problem," I answered. "But here is my charge." Donald emerged from the hall and kicked at a clod of dirt on the pathway. "Let us see how his meeting with his tutor went."

"Ah, yes," said Phillip. "Well, I must be away to prepare for this afternoon's disputes." And he left.

"How did it go?" I asked Donald.

Donald appeared nonchalant. "He's very learned."

"Oh?" I said.

"He didn't like my Latin, and bade me study. I hate rhetoric. And grammar. It's dull, and there's no point. And I had to wait some time to see him. He wants me to attend lectures. Like a commoner."

"Well, that is why your father sent you here, is it not?"

Donald scowled and kicked at a clump of grass. "I might as well be back at Dumbarton."

"*Och,*" I said, "surely it's not as bad as all that. You're no longer a hostage, and your own grandfather is the royal King of Scotland." Donald didn't reply. "Come," I continued, for I was feeling hungry myself, "let's go into town, to that tavern. I could do with some food, and you've had nothing to eat today yet."

Donald assented, and we left the college and made our way into town and down to the tavern. It seemed unnaturally quiet, and Mistress Jakeson served us our ale with red eyes. Again, we did not see Jonetta, and now I wondered at it.

"Where is your daughter?" I asked, as she brought us bowls of stew.

Mistress Jakeson stared at me strangely, then rushed away from us back to the kitchens. Her husband, standing nearby, shook his head.

"She's taking it badly," he said.

"What?"

"Our daughter's gone. Run off, I'm thinking."

"Surely not," I said, thinking of the winsome girl who had served us two days ago.

"Well, she's not here. She's been gone since yesterday. And we've no idea where she might be."

"Have they searched?"

"I called the authorities, and they've put the word out. And searched, aye. We've all been searching. But no sign of her." He sighed. "She's a good girl. It's not like her."

"Could she have run off with someone? A man?" I felt a chill cross my heart.

"I'm not knowing who. I keep a sharp eye on her, for all that she serves in the tavern."

I thought about seeing her with Phillip Woode. Donald remembered too, for he blurted out, "I saw her here speaking with that Phillip. From Balliol. The student. That first night we stayed here. She sat next to him a moment, but he seemed insistent."

"Aye," said Master Jakeson thoughtfully. "He comes here and did often speak with her."

"But we have just seen Phillip," I pointed out, "at the school. And Jonetta was certainly not there."

"But then we saw her in the market yesterday," Donald offered. "After we left this place."

"I did not see her," I added quickly. "When I looked, she had disappeared."

"Still, I will tell the town constable," Master Jakeson said. "And the undersheriff, Grymbaud. Perhaps that Phillip has hidden her away someplace. I am sorry to say this, young sir, but students are often licentious, that is no secret."

"They are young, and many are on their own, away from family constraints," I put in mildly.

"No, no, it can be very bad, sir. Very bad. There were riots here some twenty years ago, I remember them well. My wife and I were but newly married. There was fighting in the streets for three days; the students took refuge in Saint Mary's of the Virgin and the townsfolk in another church. Many folk were killed. Many students. The mayor still must make penance to the university every St. Scholastica's Day for the town's part in it all. But it never would have come to pass if that student had not attacked the poor tavern keeper. He did not like the wine he was served. Such a brawl for naught, and folk dead as well. God rest their poor souls. I pray my poor girl be safe, and not lying in an alley someplace, unshriven."

I shivered as though someone had stepped on my grave. "Surely they will find her."

"They've not found her yet," Master Jakeson replied darkly, and he went to attend to some other customers.

"Muirteach," said Donald, "you could look into it." The lad was sounding a lot like his father, too much for my liking. My jaw began to tense as I listened to him. "I know you have solved many mysteries for my father."

"I am thinking the officials have it well under control."

"I am thinking not, for they haven't found Jonetta yet." Donald drained his glass. "And we were some of the last folk to see her."

"You saw her, I did not."

"Still, we must tell the authorities what we saw. And perhaps we can be of help."

A shaft of light shot through the dimly lit tavern as the front door opened and in walked a man, heavy-set, of middle years, wearing a hauberk. He strode over to Master Jakeson and spoke seriously to him for a moment. I suspected this must be the undersheriff, and my suspicions increased when Master Jakeson motioned toward us and walked toward our table with the stranger.

"This be a young lord from the north, here to study, with his man." I bristled at the introduction, but it was true. "Sirs, this be Walter Grymbaud, our undersheriff. The High Sheriff is often away in London and Walter is in charge in his absence. These men were saying they saw my Jonetta in the market yesterday."

Donald told the man what he had seen, and then blurted out, "My man, Muirteach here, has a good head for solving mysteries. He has helped my father, who is a great lord in Scotland. The Lord of the Isles."

I groaned inwardly, wishing my charge had kept his mouth closed tight.

Undersheriff Grymbaud did not look overly impressed, but Donald continued, undeterred. "He can be of assistance to you, I am sure. You are welcome to his services."

The man looked thoughtful; I strove to avoid this awkward situation. "I apologize, sir. The lad is somewhat forward. I do not seek to do your duty for you."

"No, you might be of some use," Grymbaud replied. "Since you are at the college, perhaps you can keep an eye on this

Phillip Woode for me. Just let me know if you see anything suspicious in his movements, or such. That would indeed be of help. Townsfolk are not overly welcome in the schools, and if a university man commits a crime the university chancellor has jurisdiction. But I will question him, all the same. Perhaps we will learn something of use." He gave orders to several of his men to go and fetch Woode to the castle to "assist in inquiries."

Donald and I finished our ale, although my throat was tight and I could barely swallow for all the anger that I felt. Phillip seemed a nice enough man, and now he would be painted with suspicion, and it seemed he was already not on good terms with the master of the college. And Donald himself had landed me in a difficult spot. For if I helped the authorities search for the missing lass, I would not be watching over my charge.

Donald, however, seemed pleased with himself. It was with bad grace that I threw a penny on the table for our ale and tried to hustle Donald back to our lodgings. He had schoolwork to attend to. We were not here to solve mysteries.

# CHAPTER 3

When we got back to our lodgings I found Mariota busily sewing with Widow Tanner, working on the linen she had purchased yesterday in the market. It looked to be a shirt. We told her and the widow of Jonetta's disappearance.

"What a sad thing. She's a bonny lass," Mariota murmured. The widow rushed off, saying she was away to church to pray for the poor girl. This left Mariota, myself, and Donald, and I found I did not much want to be spending the rest of the day with Donald, still annoyed as I was with him.

"Go and get that old parchment we bought yesterday. Take it out and soak it in some water, it must soften for a time. The widow's serving man will have a bucket. Or get one from the cook. We will have to scrub the parchment clean before you can use it, with bran and milk; and you must learn how to do it."

Donald opened his mouth to protest, but I gave him a glare and he shrugged his shoulders and complied, leaving the room with an unpleasant swagger.

I told Mariota what Donald had done, and how now I was to help the undersheriff search for Jonetta. "And I'm thinking Donald is pleased with all of this, for I'll not be there to chaperone him as much—indeed, that was probably behind his suggesting it," I fumed.

"You do not think he could be truly concerned for the lass?" Mariota suggested. "And was thinking you could be of help? You have helped his father, you know."

"Perhaps, but I had you to help me, *mo chridhe*," I replied, somewhat mollified.

"And am I not here now as well? For Muirteach, I cannot sit here and sew with Widow Tanner every day, I shall go mad."

"I do not want you to involve yourself, *mo chridhe*."

The set of Mariota's jaw did not look promising to me. We dropped the subject and spoke of other things.

Just then Donald entered the room. "I'm away to the college. I want to see if that Phillip has confessed to the crime."

"There's been no crime proved as yet. We do not know what has happened to the poor lass. Best to remember that before making wild accusations."

Donald scowled and I wondered whose company was preferable, his or my wife's. I went with him, leaving Mariota to fume at the widow's. It was not my fault that women were not allowed in the schools.

We arrived at the hall to find things in a bit of an uproar. The younger students milled excitedly around in the backlands. I saw Anthony and Crispin and asked what had transpired.

"The undersheriff came," said Anthony, breathless. "And accused Phillip of making off with that Jonetta. The girl from the tavern," he added unnecessarily. "With the tits."

"She's disappeared."

"Aye," Crispin said, "that is what we heard. But we were with him that evening at the tavern. He came back with us that night. And yesterday, he was gone in the afternoon, but back here with us in the evening, and no Jonetta with him."

"Where is Phillip the now?" I asked.

"They questioned him, but left him here. No one had seen him with Jonetta yesterday, there was no proof, and since he is under minor orders, he would not be subject to civil laws."

"He is a good man," said Anthony hotly. "He liked Jonetta well, but he would do her no ill. Who accused him of this?"

Donald said nothing and neither did I. I, at least, was grateful Phillip had not been taken to Oxford Castle for questioning. And Donald looked uncomfortable. Perhaps he would begin to learn some restraint.

"Where is he now?" I asked.

"He is closeted with Master Clarkson," Crispin replied. "They have been in the master's chamber for some time now, since the sheriff's men left."

Just then we saw Phillip emerge from the hall and walk quickly to the other building that served as the dormitory for most of the scholars at Balliol.

"I wonder what has happened," Crispin mused. "Come, Anthony, let us go and speak with him." The boys left.

"You see what your meddling has accomplished," I hissed at Donald. "I am sure he is not involved in Jonetta's disappearance."

Donald looked somewhat subdued, and we left the college and walked back to Widow Tanner's.

"Now, you'd best get busy scrubbing some of those parchments you left soaking before dinner. You can do it inside here, at this desk."

Donald sat down to the laborious task. I remembered days of doing this as a young boy, at the Priory, and sympathized somewhat with him. It was a boring job, scrubbing old parchments with a mixture of bran and milk.

Mariota was still sewing and I did not quite know what to do with myself. I felt hungry, but it lacked some time yet until dinner. I approached Donald's desk. He was working with alacrity.

"It's dull work," I said to him.

"No," Donald said, "It's no so dull. This is strange parchment. Look you, Muirteach."

I looked at it. Most old parchments are covered with lists— old court chronicles, records, and such things. But as this parchment had soaked, the original markings were revealed. It seemed covered with drawings of figures. One began to emerge—a drawing of a naked woman. We looked at more of the parchment and other figures became apparent, faintly visible on the surface.

"These are strange, Muirteach."

"Aye. But you're enjoying the task. I wonder what they're from?"

There was little writing on the folio, just the odd pictures. It looked to be a bathhouse or something. Naked women, all blonde, bathing in a strange apparatus, different pipes and vessels.

"Look at the other parchments we bought. Are they all from the same source?"

"They seem to be," Donald replied.

"It will be interesting to see if the other sheets are the same. Come, I'll give you a hand."

Donald and I examined the sheets in silence for a time, and uncovered more of the strange drawings on another sheet.

"I've never seen anything like this," I muttered, "certainly not in the manuscripts at the Priory."

"What is it keeping you two so quiet in here?" asked Mariota, entering the chamber.

"Look." I showed her the pictures.

Her brow wrinkled in that way I loved so much, the way it did when she was bemused. "I've never seen anything of the like. It could almost be a medical text of some sort, but there is no writing, no explanations, and it makes no sense."

"Well, it is strange. If nothing else, it will make a dull job more interesting."

Donald smirked a bit, but said nothing. Just then the widow called us for dinner, and we did not discuss it at table.

★ ★ ★ ★ ★

The next morning Donald rose early to attend the lecture. I was somewhat surprised at his industry, but did not dissuade him. His father had sent him here to be educated, after all. We heard chapel bells tolling the early hour, and he left. I did not accompany him. It was a short distance to the lecture halls on School Street, and Mariota and I dallied in our chamber until the light grew stronger. Then I left her to attend upon Donald and to see what had transpired with Phillip Woode.

"He's on sufferance," Donald announced to me when he emerged out of the hall into the backlands. "He's still here, but it is said that Master Clarkson nearly expelled him. They're not on good terms."

"Aye, he was saying something of the sort to me, just yesterday morning it was," I said, remembering our conversation of the day before. "And how was the lecture?"

Donald shrugged. As his father had said, he was not overly studious.

"Is Brother Eusebius an able lecturer?"

Donald shrugged again.

"Did you stay awake?"

"Of course. Well, most of the time."

That seemed fair enough. There were no other lectures that morning and so we returned to our lodgings and found Mariota fuming. She was seated in the solar, but threw her sewing down in disgust on the bench when she saw us enter the room.

"Had I known it would be like this, Muirteach, I swear I would not have come."

"What is it? Mariota, what has happened?"

"There are schools here lecturing on medicine, the town is full of them, but I cannot attend, as a woman. It is so frustrating."

"Did you ask?"

"I visited one, on School Street. I went this morning, after you left. The master barely acknowledged me. He said only men could attend the lectures. They are closed to women."

"I am so sorry, *mo chridhe.*"

"I showed him the letter of introduction from my father, but he paid it no attention. It seems they've not heard of the Beatons here, my father's reputation counts for naught. As do I. While these great louts of students spend all their time in the taverns, and care nothing for their books! It is so unfair! *Och,* I wish I was a man!"

"For myself, I am very glad that you are not." I put my arms around her and pressed my cheek against her hair, inhaling her sweet scent. Mariota relaxed against me for a moment and I felt her breathing quiet a bit. But she could not leave it yet.

"Muirteach, it is maddening, just. To be here and not be able to listen—and what a chance it would be to learn."

"*Mo chridhe,* you might find, were you able to attend, that you know more than the masters. You are a fine healer, with experience. And you've had your father to teach you."

She moved away, irritated. "That's just it, Muirteach. How will I even know? I won't have the chance to find out. It is just so unfair!"

I agreed with her that it was, but it seemed I could say nothing to mollify her.

"It's all well for you to sympathize, Muirteach, but you've never had to forgo something due to the mischance of being born a woman."

"No, I was not born a woman," I agreed. But nothing I said improved her mood, and after a time I retreated, with the excuse that I needed to help Donald with his Latin, leaving Mariota to her sewing.

Donald had left us to our discussion and was in his chamber, strumming at his lute. He glanced up as I entered. "Do you think they've found Jonetta?" he asked.

"I am sure we would have heard something, had she been found." I was worried for the lass myself, a nagging fear that nibbled at me like a mouse gnawing at a crust when it thought no one watched. There had been far too many times in my past experience where someone going missing led to a bad end. "Perhaps she just ran off with someone she met at the tavern. She is a comely girl. But Grymbaud and his men are searching for her. They'll find her soon enough," I reassured Donald, although my words did not reassure me.

The next morning Mariota remained in a foul mood, and I thought to improve it by asking her about the strange parchments we had found. Donald went again to the morning lecture, and while he was gone I began to examine the parchments again. The second sheet seemed to have writing on it, not so many drawings, but try as I might I could not make out the faint ink of the words. I called Mariota to examine it. Her brow furrowed as she studied the sheet.

"It's no language I've ever seen, Muirteach. It is not Greek, nor Latin."

"Aye, and for sure it is not the Gaelic. Could it be French?"

"I'm not thinking it is. Perhaps it is Hebrew. Or Arabic." Mariota shrugged her shoulders. She was wrapped in her plaid, as the day was rainy and damp and the morning was chill. "I wonder if the bookseller knows anything of it? I've been wanting to return to his shop. It might be interesting to see if he had other sheets of it. Perhaps we should go visit him, Muirteach. Donald will be busy at the school for some time."

Hoping to improve her mood, I agreed. We took one of the parchments with us and made our way into the town through the drizzle, to the stationer's shop. It was still early, and Master Bookman was just opening the shutters in front of the store, pushing up the wooden awning and setting a few of his wares out on the wooden shelf that faced the street. He greeted us, his stocky face smiling at his first customers of the day.

"And what could I be showing you today? A romance for the lady, perhaps? I have something quite new, *The Book of the Duchess*. A man named Chaucer has just written it. A sad story, the poor lady died so young. Or she might enjoy *Sir Gawain and the Green Knight*, if she enjoys tales of chivalry."

"What of your medical texts?" Mariota demanded.

"What does a lady such as yourself need with medical texts?" Adam Bookman retorted.

"Her father is a physician," I interjected. "She has some interest in the topic as well."

"And she can read?" asked the bookseller, as if Mariota was not there.

"Of course," Mariota bristled as she answered. "Latin, Greek, Gaelic and some French."

"And I will look at *Sir Gawain and the Green Knight*," I added, hoping to calm the situation, and my wife.

Master Bookman shrugged his shoulders and gave me a complacent smile. "Oh, very well, in that case." He handed me the copy of *Sir Gawain*. "We do have some medical texts. I have a rare copy of the *Tacuinum Sanitatis* that might be of interest. And another treatise on urine. Also several of Galen's, and Ptolemy: *On Complexions*, and the *Quadripartitum*. There may be several here, just let me go and fetch them from the back room."

We stood in the street, huddled under the shop awning to stay out of the drizzle, and examined the books. As a raindrop dripped down my neck, I looked up and saw Master Clarkson approaching the bookstall. I greeted him, but he seemed somewhat preoccupied and stood impatiently, folding his arms and tapping his fingers against his forearm as he waited for the bookseller to reappear.

"Master Bookman, you and I must speak," he said, his lean face impatient.

"Oh yes, Master Clarkson. I am at your service," Adam Bookman said, as he deposited several books in front of us. "Just give me leave a few moments, good folk, and examine these books while I speak with this gentleman."

Master Clarkson and the bookseller withdrew to the back of the shop, but I could hear snatches of their conversation while Mariota pored over the medical texts. Clarkson seemed to be wanting to redeem a pledge but the bookseller was reluctant, saying that Clarkson owed him money still. I wondered a little at their talk, but it was none of my business, for all that. Mariota meanwhile seemed entranced by the medical texts. At length I opened *Sir Gawain and the Green Knight* and lost myself in the story, struggling some with the unfamiliar English.

The door of the shop slammed open and Master Clarkson left abruptly, walking down the High Street as quickly as he had come.

"He did not seem to be in good humor," Mariota observed. "He is the master of the college?"

Just then the bookseller reappeared. "Excuse me, just a matter of business that needed attending to. Did any of these texts seem as though they would interest your father?"

Mariota ignored the implication and picked out two books, the treatise on the examination of urine and another text by Galen on the complexions and what they revealed of a patient's humors. At the last moment I added *Sir Gawain* to the pile. The tale had captured my fancy, and I justified the purchase thinking that reading it would improve my English. We had the funds to pay for the volumes, as his lordship had made sure we were well supplied with money for the time we were in Oxford.

I asked the bookseller about the parchment and if he had

others from the same source.

"Those were just some old parchments that were sold by one of the schools. I do not think I have any others, someone just brought in a few sheets to sell."

We thanked him, took our purchases and left. Mariota wanted to walk up School Street. The narrow street was crowded with houses and halls and jammed with students jostling each other as they left the lecture halls or waited outside other buildings until the last moment before going in. There was a babble of voices as many of them attempted to remember the lessons they had just heard.

We paused before one of the halls. "There," said Mariota, "that is where many of the medical lectures are given. It is said that Master Rudolfo, from Salerno, is a very fine lecturer. I would love to hear him," she said, and looked so wistful that my heart hurt sharply to see the expression on her face.

"There's nothing for it, white love," I said, "you know women cannot attend the lectures."

Mariota nodded, and we continued down High Street, although she did make one more stop at the cloth merchant's as we passed by his stall, picking out some blue wool of stout weave.

"A new kirtle?" I asked.

"Something of the sort," Mariota replied.

We turned onto School Street and Mariota said she would go on to the widow's through Smithgate. I decided I should go check on Donald and entered the hall. The lecture room was simple, wood benches around the edges and a lectern at the front where the master spoke. Julian Delacey was lecturing on grammar, from *De partibus orationis ars minor*. Delacey was somewhat short, with a ruddy complexion, and to me he seemed a pompous fool. I took a seat at the back and waited for the lecture to end. It was not a stimulating topic. Delacey asked the questions and the students, most of whom looked to be about the same age as Donald, chanted their answers back.

"How many attributes has a noun?"

"Six."

"What are they?"

"Quality, comparison, gender, number, form, case."

I saw Anthony and Crispin, who were seated a ways down the bench from Donald, writing something on their wax tablets and smirking. Master Delacey apparently did not notice. Then they passed the tablets down the row toward Donald. He glanced at the tablets, his face reddened, and he slammed them shut. Delacey did notice this and he fixed Donald with a glare, his hazel eyes bulging somewhat from his face. "You will show me your tablet, young man."

"But—" Donald started to argue, then shut his mouth, walked up to the podium and handed the tablet to Delacey. The master opened the tablets, and his face also reddened. The boys sitting on the benches began a rumble of excited whispering, and I saw Crispin nudge Anthony, both of their smirks wider now.

"So this is what you think of the art of grammar."

Donald said, "I am sorry, sir."

"I will speak with the Master. He will decide your punishment."

I groaned. Whatever had been on that tablet, it did not seem it was an explanation of the attributes of a noun.

"The lecture is ended," Delacey announced and exited the room, carrying the tablets and leading Donald by the ear, followed by an excited crowd of students and myself.

Master Clarkson was at the lecture hall in a private office. Delacey went in with Donald and closed the door behind them. In short order, all three returned.

"This young student has not attended well," said Master

Clarkson in stentorian tones. "He has made a mockery of the art of grammar."

"Let me see," I asked, "as I am responsible for his behavior here."

Master Clarkson thrust the tablets at me. There was a crude picture of a woman with very large bare breasts, and someone had jotted down the attributes of a noun with arrows such as "size—large, gender—female, form—round, comparison—softer."

"Are you sure these are his tablets?" I asked. "I thought I saw someone pass them his way."

"He does not deny that they are his," the Master retorted. "And he must be punished. He will be thrashed in front of the other students. I will be lenient on account of his new arrival here and his parentage."

It did not sound lenient to me. But Donald imperceptibly shook his head at me and I did not intervene.

The students were assembled and Master Clarkson vigorously thrashed Donald's backside ten times with a blackthorn stick. My own body shuddered as I listened to the blows, almost as if I myself was being beaten, but Donald bore it like a man and did not cry out.

After it was over, Donald walked stiffly away, his hands fisted, but the other first-year students followed him, exclaiming and talking. The look he gave Anthony and Crispin spoke volumes. I saw him say something to Anthony but I did not catch the words. I could guess, however, and hoped Donald would have the good sense not to fight with him right away.

"I'm leaving," said Donald hotly to me in Gaelic when I caught up with him. "I'll not be staying this afternoon for the stupid disputations."

Given the situation, I felt it best not to argue. "Why don't we go to The Green Man and have some ale? Or go back to our lodgings? No doubt Mariota can fix something that will make your back feel somewhat better."

"I hate them. They are great louts. I will get them for this," Donald swore as we left the lecture hall and walked to an alehouse. We ordered some ale and two meat pastries.

"It didn't hurt," Donald insisted, although I did not for one second believe him. I had heard the sound of the stick. "But they'll pay for this, just see if they don't. Master Clarkson too. And that Delacey. They'll all pay."

"Your father would have been proud of you."

"I could not tattle on them, like a babe," Donald retorted. "But I'll have it out of them later." Just then our ale arrived and we drank awhile in silence.

The door of the tavern opened. "Oh no," Donald groaned, and I silently echoed his sentiments. Anthony and Crispin entered the tavern and sauntered up to us.

"I'm sorry—" Anthony started to say, but Donald did not let him finish. He punched him and Anthony struck back, knocking Donald to the ground. Then Crispin entered the fray. Within an instant the three boys were at each other, pummeling and rolling in the grimy rushes on the floor, while the tavern keeper shouted he would loose the dogs on them if they did not stop, and I strove to pull them apart. There was a pitcher of ale on the trestle table and I grabbed it, threw it in their faces, and managed to grab Crispin by the back of his robe and push Anthony away with my other hand.

"Is it fools you all are?" I yelled. "Do you all want to be expelled? For that is no doubt what will happen if you do not stop this now."

There was blood running from Anthony's nose, while Crispin's eye looked red and puffy. Secretly, I was glad to see that Donald had acquitted himself well, although I tried to sound stern. The three boys glared at each other, then started to grin.

"Now," I said, "all three of you will sit down and share some ale and put this behind you. Then we will go and see if my wife has some magic ointment that will put you all together. And stop all this."

After two mazers of ale, the boys were chattering as though they had been friends for years. After three mazers, we left the alehouse and made our way back to the Widow Tanner's.

The good widow was speechless when she saw the students approach, and turned away darkly with statements that she should have known better than to rent to students, but I tried to reassure her while Mariota doctored the boys with a salve of arnica and calendula flowers. Then Donald got out his lute and before too long all three of the lads were singing songs in Latin, something about Dame Fortune and squandering one's time in taverns. I hoped it would not prove prophetic, in regard to Donald's academic career.

# CHAPTER 4

The next morning I went with Donald to the morning lectures. When we returned, Mariota was not at the widow's. "She went out," Widow Tanner informed me. "She said she had to run an errand. She probably went to the market for something, perhaps more cloth."

"Perhaps." I thought little of it, and after dinner Donald and I returned to the schools and listened to the senior students at their disputations. Phillip Woode was participating this afternoon, his dispute to be judged by Master Clarkson. We had heard no more about Jonetta, but the undersheriff had not bothered Woode again. I had noticed nothing unusual about his behavior, and, since his conversation with Master Clarkson of a few days past, he seemed to spend the majority of his time at the college, concentrating on his studies. He seemed a nice enough man, and I hoped things would settle down.

The disputation took place in one of the lecture rooms. The topic to be debated was universals, more specifically, how one could know for certain that all right triangles inherently share the same qualities. The topic held little interest for me, and I imagined it held even less fascination for Donald and the major-ity of bejants gathered to listen in the hall. However, a few of the students listened intently as the master posed the question and the senior students responded.

As he began his response, I realized that Phillip's self-assessment was correct. He was a poor debater, indeed. He stuttered and paused, seeming to forget his Latin. It was difficult to listen to him, and I felt embarrassed for the man. I felt sure he was not as stupid as he sounded, but I was glad it was not my place to judge the disputation. The logic was so convoluted it made little sense to me.

I tried to attend to what was being said.

"Do genera and species exist as substances in and of themselves," Phillip's opponent was saying, "with form and material substance, or are they mere concepts?"

"As a substance," Phillip replied, "they might be either material or immaterial."

"And which do you reason them to be? Are they intrinsically present in sensible objects, or do they exist apart from them?"

"I, I cannot say," Phillip muttered, flushing red.

Not surprisingly, the master judged the other student the winner of the *disputatio* and the session drew to a close. The students exited the room, the younger ones jostling and elbowing each other as they rushed outside to play some kickball in the back yard. Donald went along with Anthony and Crispin, the bad blood of the day before apparently forgotten.

Phillip stood by himself in the corridor. "Come," I said, "let me buy you some ale. No doubt you're thirsty after all that talking."

He made a wry face. "No doubt I'd prefer to drink to the point where I could forget I made such a fool of myself. I fear I will be returning home before much longer. Well, I guess I've no greater ambition than to try and teach letters to disobedient eight-year-olds at the parish school. But for now, my ambition is to get very, very drunk. Lead the way, and I will follow."

Donald, Anthony and Crispin were in the midst of a heated game and paid little attention as I told them we were leaving. As Phillip and I left the hall, we passed Brother Eusebius, walking quickly in the other direction toward the road that led to the north beyond. He seemed preoccupied and did not greet us as we passed him and entered the town gates. A crowd of students was leaving the lecture halls on School Street; it seemed some lectures were just dismissing. "I know I could be a fine physician," Phillip bemoaned as he bumped into a fair-haired youth wearing a blue tunic. "But I fear I will never get the chance, unless I can pass these disputations."

"My wife comes from a family of physicians," I offered. "She is quite knowledgeable. You could study with her some, perhaps. I can ask her." I thought it might distract Mariota to have a student of her own.

We reached The Green Man and entered the tavern. Mistress Jakeson saw us and walked the other way, into the kitchens. In short order her husband came out and spoke to us, bringing us some wine.

"Have you had any word?" Phillip asked Master Jakeson.

"Nothing," the tavern keeper replied. "It's as if she's been spirited away."

I shuddered and took a gulp of wine to drive the unpleasant sensation away. The last time I had dealt with a vanished person, back the previous fall on Colonsay, it had not ended well. I prayed this would have a happier resolution, but feared, with each day that passed, that grew less likely.

We finished our wine, and then drank some more. Eventually, we thought to head back toward Balliol, before the gates were shut entirely. I left Phillip banging at the gates of Balliol Hall. It seemed the gatekeeper had locked them early. I hastened back to the widow's. I thought of Mariota and wondered if she would be angry.

But when I arrived back at our lodgings, Mariota seemed in the best of moods. She was poring over a text by candlelight, humming a little tune. Donald had returned a bit earlier and, miracle of all miracles, seemed to be actually studying as well.

At least he was leafing through a book and making a few marks on his tablets. He slammed the book closed when he saw me, though.

"And where were you?" he interrogated me.

"Phillip Woode and I went to an ale-house. Who won the ball game?"

Donald shrugged his shoulders. "I did, of course."

"Of course." I turned to Mariota. "What are you reading?"

"This treatise on urine. It's fascinating. Muirteach, were you knowing that the smell of the urine of someone with the honey disease is sweet?"

There were times I wondered why I had married a physician. "No, *mo chridhe,* I was not knowing that."

"Well, it is true. And that someone whose humors are choleric will give off great quantities of urine. While the phlegmatic types tend to retain it."

"Is that so? It is late, white love. Come to bed."

"I will in a bit, I just want to read a little more."

Donald retreated to his room and fairly soon after that I heard some snoring. And it was not long after that, that I was snoring myself while Mariota read by candlelight.

The next morning, early, I awoke to a pounding at the door. I heard the sound of excited voices, and then Widow Tanner knocked at our chamber. I opened the door and saw her, clad only in her shift with a mantle thrown over it, her gray hair straggling down over her shoulders. Behind her I was surprised to see Anthony and Crispin, now seeming to be the best of friends with Donald.

"You must come quickly," the widow said.

"What is it? What has happened?" I asked, throwing on my tunic and *brat,* as my heart began to pound more quickly and the last vestiges of sleep left me.

"It is Master Clarkson. He's dead. Murdered in his chamber last night."

"His head was bashed in," Anthony added with gruesome detail. "There'll be no lectures or disputations today. And Donald was telling us yesterday how you solved murders for his father. Master Delacey sent for you. Come, we must make haste."

The sun was just rising when we got to the old Balliol Hall. Inside, scholars milled around, the young boys talking excitedly while senior students spoke in lower murmurs. I passed by Phillip Woode, speaking with Brother Eusebius, and made my way up two flights of narrow stairs to Master Clarkson's chamber.

Before I reached the doorway I smelled the coppery scent of fresh blood. I forced myself to step over the threshold and reluctantly looked around. The chamber was not large and I did not have to search for long. Master Clarkson lay sprawled on the floor, face down, presumably as he had fallen. The murderer had bashed the back of Clarkson's head to a pulp.

I felt my stomach roil and prayed I would not vomit then and there. I took a few breaths to steady myself while I observed. Masters Delacey and Berwyk stood in the room, staring at the corpse in silence. A large and heavy pewter candlestick, the base of which was covered in blood and brains, lay on the wooden floor. Some blood seeped down from the corpse's head and pooled beneath it. My stomach heaved again.

"We haven't moved him," Master Delacey stated.

"Shouldn't you send for Grymbaud? Or the coroner?" I asked.

"No, no, not until we know more. It is a matter for the hall at this point," Master Delacey responded hastily. I looked away from the gruesome body and watched the two men. Delacey's complexion was not so red now, his face ashen as he surveyed the corpse. I wondered what Delacey intended to do with the body, but Master Berwyk interrupted.

"Julian, it is foul murder. We must send for the coroner. And the chancellor of the university."

Reluctantly, Delacey agreed and a messenger was sent to rouse the men, leaving Master Berwyk and myself with the unpleasant duty of guarding the corpse. I swallowed bile and tried to control my responses while I faced Master Berwyk.

I had not met Master Berwyk before. He had a quiet and calm manner in spite of the dismay he must surely have been feeling to see his colleague lying there dead.

"It is a shocking and foul thing—unthinkable," he murmured to me. "I scarce know what to say."

I did not know what to say either. After a few more words we fell into an uncomfortable silence while I wondered if Berwyk had murdered Clarkson. Berwyk's nose looked as though it had once been broken, despite his seemingly gentle demeanor, and he was tall and strong.

It was not too long before Chancellor deWylton and the town coroner, Thomas Houkyn, arrived accompanied by Grymbaud. The officials looked at the body and, most perceptively, agreed it was murder. Houkyn left to assemble a jury and the chancellor conferred with Masters Delacey and Berwyk outside the chamber, but Grymbaud remained behind and spoke with me a moment. "Muirteach, these university men won't look kindly on outsiders investigating here. The man was killed, and by one of their own, I'd warrant."

"He is most certainly dead," I observed.

"Aye, and the college gates locked up, so no one could enter nor yet leave. It's a bad business, and those university men will close ranks tighter than a choirboy's bum when it comes to the coroner or myself investigating. I'm but the undersheriff, for all that the High Sheriff is seldom here. He spends time with the rich and mighty in London town, and leaves the rough work to me."

I said nothing, and Grymbaud continued. "And to add to that, we've still seen no sign of that girl, Jonetta. I've no doubt she's run away with some tinker, but her father still insists that cannot be. The end of it all is that I need an extra man, someone neutral, with no close ties to the town or the university. Will you look into things here for me? I'll speak with the chancellor and make it right with him. You've some connection with the university so he'll likely approve it. This nasty case falls under his jurisdiction; town justice counts for nothing with these scholars." I think the man would have spat on the floor, except he remembered where he was and the dead body that lay a few feet distant. "The inquest will be called for tomorrow, I'd think."

"What of the coroner? Won't I be poaching on his jurisdiction?" I protested. I did not want this charge. I did not know the ways of this land, their laws or customs. It was not my affair.

"I'll speak with him as well. Houkyn and deWylton are like two tomcats fighting, there's been bad blood between them for years. Houkyn will know he won't get too far investigating things at the college. He's a practical man; he'll agree to it." Sensing my hesitation, Grymbaud continued. "I need your help. It was a foul slaying, and the bastards are like to go free of it. Look there."

I followed his gaze, to the bloodied corpse of Master Clarkson still lying ignominiously on the floor. Clarkson had seemed a good enough man, and yet he lay murdered. So I in turn agreed, despite my misgivings, and Grymbaud left after speaking with the masters and the chancellor.

Master Delacey strode over to where I was standing, followed by Master Berwyk and Chancellor deWylton. "So, he's made you his lackey."

"You sent for me first," I said mildly. "I've some experience in these matters."

"Well enough, you can have the mess and welcome to it," Delacey muttered brusquely, and stalked away. My hands clenched as I watched him leave the room.

Chancellor de Wylton, a lean man with a saturnine complexion and a growth of unshaven beard on his chin, spoke, breaking the somewhat unpleasant silence left in Delacey's wake. "Grymbaud says you've solved mysteries before."

"Aye, I have," I replied. "For my lord back in the Isles in the north."

"Perhaps that is to the good. You'll see the situation with fresh eyes and not have too many preconceptions of the scholars here. Yes, it will be well for you to look into this."

Good for everyone but myself, I thought, but did not voice that. And it had been a grievous murder. It would be good to bring the killer to justice.

"Who found the master?" I asked.

"Ivo, the gardener and gatekeeper, came in to light the fire, as he does everyday. It was he that found him," Master Berwyk replied. "Then he raised the cry."

I had seen Ivo out in the back garden, the day before as I waited for Donald.

"Send for him, let me speak with him," I said, "and send for my wife. She is at our lodgings, at the Widow Tanner's. Leave everything in the chamber as it is for now."

"But we must lay out the body," said Brother Eusebius, who had appeared in the doorway while we were speaking. "It is unseemly."

"Let my wife examine it first. She is a physician, in our country. There may be signs that will point us to the killer."

"But women are not allowed in the lodgings," Eusebius protested, "and women cannot be physicians. The whole idea is preposterous."

"Her father is a noted healer," I retorted. "And she herself has some skill. Now, are you wanting me to help you solve this murder, or not?" There is nothing so dithering as academics.

"Perhaps, in this case, an exception can be made," Chancellor deWylton suggested.

Berwyk nodded. "Crispin, run back to Widow Tanner's and get the mistress. Bid her make all haste."

While I waited for Mariota to arrive, I looked around the room. A pile of disarranged parchments lay on a wooden table, along with several books. A horn inkwell and a quantity of quills sat on the table as well. A few more books were piled up on the floor. Not surprising, for a studious master.

A chest, unlocked, stood against one wall. I opened it and saw a few tunics, *braies,* and two changes of linen; again, nothing unexpected. A pitcher and bowl for washing stood on another small table, and the narrow bed stood under a wooden crucifix on the wall.

I stepped around the body to examine the books. Aristotle's *Priora Analytica, Posteriora Analytica,* and *Sophistica Elenchi,* along with Aquinas's *Summa theologica.* The parchments all seemed to be parts of some writing Clarkson had been working on; at least all were in the same hand, and seemed to deal with theological questions.

The door to the chamber opened and Phillip Woode stuck his head in. "Sir, we've fetched Ivo to see you."

I looked at the bloody corpse. "Perhaps we could use another room. Is there anything suitable?"

"I think the small room downstairs that they use for disputations would be free. Come this way."

Donald, who had followed me to the college, still loitered outside the chamber door, craning his neck to see inside. I motioned to the lad. "Donald, you stay in front of this door. Let no one in until Mariota arrives. Then send for me."

Donald nodded, and I followed Phillip and Ivo down one flight of stairs to a smaller room off the main hall. There was a table inside, along with two stools and a bench. "This will suffice."

"I will send for some ale," Phillip volunteered, and he left us to our business.

Old Ivo was tall but broad-shouldered, somewhat stooped over, with long graying hair that hung down around his cheeks. His clouded green eyes looked troubled.

"It is a wicked thing," he said without waiting to be asked. I agreed that indeed it was.

"How long have you served here?"

He blinked, as if surprised by my question. "A good long time, since I was but a lad. And my wife too, rest her soul, we served here together. She cooked for the scholars, before the plague took her, the second plague, that were some thirteen years ago."

"Where do you bide?"

"I have a small cottage at the end of the backlands. I sleep there, and my daughter as well."

"You have a daughter?"

"Aye, my little Avice. Although near a grown girl she is now. She works here. In the kitchens," he volunteered.

"And it is your custom to light the fires for the masters."

Ivo nodded. "Aye. For Master Clarkson, and Masters Delacey and Berwyk. They all four have braziers in their rooms. Brother Eusebius, though, he does not often use his. He seems not to feel the cold."

"So you went in to light Clarkson's brazier this morning?"

Ivo nodded again. "I carried some coals from the kitchens. I knocked on the door like I do every morn, but there weren't no answer. So I knocked again, louder."

"And when was this?"

"Early, well before Prime. It was still dark, but the moon was setting."

"And you saw no one leaving the grounds? And heard nothing unusual last night?"

Ivo shook his head no. "I locked the gate up tight last night, after dark, just as the moon were rising. No one could have gotten in."

"So what happened? When you knocked?"

"I pushed the door open; I was thinking that the master might have fallen asleep at his desk. He sometimes stays up late, working. The door weren't locked, it were easy to open."

"And then—"

Ivo shrugged his broad shoulders. "He were lying there on the floor. It were clear he was dead. There were the blood, and he weren't breathing."

"So what did you do?"

"I went and fetched Master Delacey. That's all." He shook his head again. "Such wickedness, here . . ."

Just then Phillip knocked on the door with the news that Mariota had arrived, and it seemed I had learnt what I could from Ivo. I dismissed him and went to see Mariota. She stood, breathless, in front of Master Clarkson's chamber.

"I came as quickly as I could," she said. "What is it you are wanting?"

"Just for you to have a look at the body, *mo chridhe*, and see what you can tell us about it. I must warn you, though, it is an unlovely sight."

"I've seen the dead before, Muirteach, as you well know."

Indeed I did. One of the first times I had met my wife, she had been examining my father's corpse. I motioned to Donald to open the door. He had not left his post, standing in front of the door like a gallowglass, and assured me no one had entered in the time I'd been speaking with the servant. Finally, he stepped aside and I pushed the door open.

We entered the room again, Donald crowding in behind us. I heard him gasp a little as he took in the scene. Mariota did not quail at the sight but bent to examine the body. It was cold, already stiffening, and I did not really need my wife to tell me what had caused his death. The heavy candlestick still lay on the floor, covered with congealed blood and other matter. It looked as though one strong blow had been struck, felling the master, and then another smashing the skull in to complete the deed.

"He was facing toward his table when he was attacked," Mariota said. "And then he fell forward."

"And the murderer struck again, to make sure he was dead," I continued, trying to match my wife's objectivity, and perhaps failing a bit in that if the queasiness that had returned to plague me was any sign of things. "How long ago do you think he was killed?"

"Perhaps five or six hours ago. The body is already stiff. Before Matins, I'm thinking."

"Whoever did it might well have gotten some blood on his tunic."

"Perhaps not," Mariota responded. "His skull is bashed in, but there were not great gouts of blood flying when he was struck." She sighed.

Donald watched with wide eyes. He picked up the candlestick. "It's heavy. A good enough weapon."

"And close to hand. Perhaps the killer did not come intending murder," I said.

Donald put the candlestick down again. He looked quite pale. I judged that the presence of death subdued him somewhat.

"Why don't you find Anthony and Crispin," I suggested. I

reached into my purse. "Here's some coin—take yourselves into town and buy them a meat pie or something."

Donald swallowed and looked torn.

"No doubt they'd want to hear of what you've seen. And perhaps they know something useful. You can ask them of it for me."

Donald looked grateful at the excuse, took the coins and left to find the other lads.

"That was kindly done, Muirteach," Mariota told me, and then she returned her attention to the corpse. "The killer must have been a tall man," she said. "For Clarkson is not a short man, yet this blow came down on him."

We rolled the body over, but there were no additional marks on it. Just the open eyes of Master Clarkson, staring with surprise. I remembered the fiction that the eyes of a dead man would show his killer, but Master Clarkson's eyes showed us nothing.

Mariota picked up Clarkson's hands and examined them. "There is no blood on his fingers, just ink. I do not think he fought back. He was struck from behind, unknowing." She sighed. "Well, there is nothing else to be learned here." She closed the eyes of the corpse. "They can call for the women who will do the laying out." She made the sign of the cross and shivered. "It could have been almost anyone. But they would have had to have strength, and height."

"Old Ivo swears he locked the gate last night. It must have been someone from the college."

"One of the scholars?"

"Perhaps."

Mariota shivered again, despite the sun, which had climbed higher in the sky and now began to find its way into the room through the narrow window, illuminating the corpse and the bloody floor all too well.

"I will talk with Phillip Woode. Perhaps he knows something of Master Clarkson's habits, or who might wish him ill." I did not add that I had heard Phillip Woode argue with Master Clarkson twice in as many days. I liked the man and was loath to think him a murderer.

"Perhaps you could speak with Avice, Old Ivo's daughter," I asked Mariota. "Ivo said she helps in the kitchens here. Perhaps she remembers when her father left, or she may have heard something in the night."

"Aye," said Mariota. "I'll see to it." And she left me with the corpse of Master Clarkson.

I've seen my share of the dead, but I never really get used to it. The cold vacancy, where just a short time ago there was alert life and warm awareness. Master Clarkson had clearly been caught unawares by his killer.

Just then the door opened again, and Masters Delacey and Berwyk entered. They walked past the corpse and started to pick up the books on the table and floor.

"Where are you taking those?" I inquired.

"They are the property of the college," Master Delacey said somewhat pompously. "We must ensure they are not stolen or misplaced."

"Before the body is even laid out?"

"We've sent for the good wife who'll tend to the corpse. She's coming soon."

"And I will be wishing to speak with everyone who stays here, in the hall. Can you provide me with their names?"

"There are, or were, Master Clarkson, ourselves, Brother Eusebius, and two senior students, Phillip Woode and Fellow Swithin. But Swithin was called home two weeks ago. His father is ill and not expected to live, and we do not know when he will return. That is all who live in the hall, and we lock the doors at curfew."

"Old Ivo swears no one entered the grounds last night, so the killer must be here still."

"In the college!" Master Berwyk remonstrated. "I refuse to believe it."

"The man is dead," I pointed out, feeling a tide of annoyance rising in my chest, "and clearly not by natural causes. He did not die of a fit; someone bashed his head in. Someone is guilty of foul murder. When did you last see the master?"

"I saw him at the evening meal," Master Delacey responded, "then he left. He usually studies in the evening, in his chamber. He does not like to be disturbed."

"Do either of you have any idea why someone would wish to kill Master Clarkson? Did he have enemies?"

For learned men they were most obtuse. Neither Master Delacey nor Master Berwyk could think of any enemies, or anyone at all who would wish Master Clarkson any ill, while I myself could think of several, including, judging from the speed with which they had appropriated his books, Masters Delacey and Berwyk themselves. But I contented myself with asking for leave to interview the fellows, one by one, in the small room used for disputations. And the masters, having no other recourse and wanting to involve the coroner and civil authorities as little as possible, agreed.

# CHAPTER 5

Phillip Woode entered the room and I gestured for him to seat himself on the bench facing me.

"I will be speaking with all the scholars," I said, somewhat unnecessarily. "It is likely the killer came from the hall. Are you knowing any enemies that Master Clarkson had?"

Phillip gave a little laugh. "Besides myself, you mean? For surely I did not like the man. He was threatening to expel me, and then I would have no choice but to go back to my home and try to teach little brats their letters. But I did not kill the man."

"You did not speak to him last night, after we returned from the ale-house?"

I thought Phillip hesitated a moment, but he replied firmly, "No. I banged on the gates, when you left me, and it took Ivo an age to open them. He complained about me being late, past curfew, and threatened to tell Master Clarkson. But I beseeched him not to, and finally gave him a silver penny, and Ivo relented. He said he would not tell."

"And then what did you do?"

"I staggered up to my pallet and fell asleep. And heard nothing until the commotion early this morn."

"And you know of no other enemies who might have wished to harm him?"

Phillip thought a moment. "Master Berwyk was complaining the other day that Clarkson had borrowed a copy of his *Isagoge,* by Porphyry, and had not returned it. That is a text of logic," Phillip added, seeing my confusion.

"That book was not in his room this morning."

"Perhaps Clarkson already had returned it. It was some days ago that I heard Master Berwyk complaining about that."

Master Berwyk had certainly not mentioned anything of the sort to me. But somehow I doubted he had gotten his book back, so eager had he been to carry off the books in Clarkson's chamber.

"Anyone else?"

"Well, when Clarkson was elected master, some months ago, the expectation was that Master Delacey would win the election. But he did not."

"Did Master Delacey want the position?"

Phillip shrugged. "It is an honor. But there are many duties involved. Perhaps he did not mind so very much. Master Delacey is intent on studying the canon law." He stood to go. "If you will excuse me, there is a lecture I must attend."

I let him go and wondered whom to speak with next. There was a knock on the door and a young lass entered, carrying an earthenware pitcher. I guessed her age to be about thirteen, or a bit more, barely out of her childhood. She had a thin face, with long brown hair that fell about it, although she had made efforts to restrain her locks with a tie behind. Her eyes were wide, and she glanced nervously behind her as she shut the door.

"You must be Avice," I said. "Here, sit down."

"Aye, sir, my father was saying you wanted to speak with me. And I brought you some ale," she said, putting the pitcher and a mazer down on the table between us.

I poured some ale and took a long swallow. My throat was dry from talking, and the ale was sweet.

"It be a terrible thing, about Master Clarkson."

"Did you know him well?"

Avice dropped her eyes and stared at her hands on the table. "Oh no, sir, I barely knew him at all. I stay in the kitchens and rarely even speak to the scholars."

"But I imagine you notice things. Did Master Clarkson have enemies? Did you hear any arguments between him and the others?"

Avice raised her eyes. "My father was saying the other day he heard Master Clarkson saying something about heresy. That he'd tolerate none of that here."

"Did your father hear who he was speaking with?" Ivo had not told me of that.

Avice looked confused. "I can't rightly say. Was it Master Berwyk? Surely heresy is a wicked thing."

"As is murder."

Avice suddenly began to cry. "I didn't kill him, sir. It weren't me."

A flood of awkwardness overcame me. So now I had reduced a child to tears. I took a deep breath and tried to gentle my voice. "No one said that you did. Here, stop your tears, sweeting. I didn't mean to fright you. Stop crying." My words had no effect, and the girl sobbed more than ever. "Here, have a little ale."

I didn't know what I had said to start the lass crying like that, and I desperately wished she would stop. I poured some more ale into the mazer and handed it to her. Avice sniffed a little and wiped her eyes and her nose with the back of her hand, stopping most of her tears. She took a gulp of ale, then another, then looked up at me. She had somewhat protuberant front teeth, although she was pretty enough with light brown hair and blue eyes. But of a sudden I thought of a cornered rabbit.

"Last night, did you hear anything unusual?"

"Oh no, sir."

"Did your father leave your dwelling at any time? Did anyone seek entrance to the college late, after the gate was locked?"

"Very soon after, there was a hammering, and Da got up to see to it. It was that Master Woode, that's what he said when he returned. He was not pleased about it, neither."

That accorded with what I remembered. When I left Phillip at the gate, it had been locked.

"Sir, please can I go?" Avice's voice interrupted my thoughts. "I've duties to attend to in the kitchen."

I gave her leave to go, and went to find Master Delacey. I climbed the wooden stairs to the third floor and found him in the chamber he shared with Ralph Berwyk. Julian Delacey was seated at his desk when I entered, speaking to Master Berwyk. Neither man looked pleased to see me.

I asked to speak privately with Delacey and he grudgingly agreed to see me in the downstairs room in a few minutes, making it plain he wished me gone. So, obligingly, I left and descended the stairs to the ground floor.

I walked outside, enjoying the fresh September breeze after the close inner air of the murder room. I breathed deeply, feeling my lungs expand and, for a second, aware of the ceaseless beating of my own heart. How could it be, I mused, that the sky was so blue, the day so lovely, and inside the tenement a man lay murdered? And why had he been slain?

I could have wondered how I had wound up in the thick of yet another murder to investigate but that would catch no evildoers. I had agreed to help find who committed this heinous crime. What I had to do was find the murderer. And I thought I would not have to look very far.

In the far back of the yard was a small cottage. I guessed that was the place where Avice lived with her father. As I watched, I saw Avice walk back toward the hut, crying bitterly. It seemed she had taken the death of Clarkson much to heart, and I wondered at that.

Certainly Anthony and Crispin seemed less disturbed, as I saw several of the younger students kicking a ball around in the back, seemingly happy to be free of lectures for the day. Although perhaps they should not have been there, they seemed loath to leave the college grounds and get back to their own lodgings. One gave the ball a hard kick and it landed in front of me, nearly hitting me. I wished I could have played, but the limp I have makes it hard, so I threw the ball back at them and went back inside to speak with Master Delacey.

Julian Delacey was a short man, stocky, with reddish hair and a belligerent manner. He seemed personally affronted that someone had been murdered at his college, thus disrupting his scheduled lectures and disputations. Phillip Woode had said Delacey was studying canon law, hoping for a position with the church at some point, although he had yet to take holy orders. From the little I knew of lawyers, I thought perhaps he would make a good one, for he seemed argumentative enough.

"Now," he said, sitting down across from me, "what was it you needed to speak with me about? There is much to be done here today, and I can spare little time."

"Your chamber is near to Master Clarkson's, is it not?"

"Yes." Delacey nodded. "And what if it is?"

"Did you hear anything untoward last night? Any sounds of a struggle?"

"I heard nothing. I would have told you before this if I had." Delacey's jaw thrust forward in an unlikeable fashion as he spoke and once again I felt my hands tighten as I listened to him speak.

"What were you doing last night?" I asked.

"Studying. I have obtained a text of Johannes Andrea and I was deeply absorbed in it. I heard nothing."

"No one entered the master's room?"

Delacey shook his head no. "Not that I heard. But I was deep in study."

"And what of Berwyk? Where was he? Do you know?"

"He often goes out. He has a woman in the town. But he was back before Ivo locked the gate, and asleep soon thereafter. I heard him snoring as I read."

"You heard nothing else?"

"Just that Phillip Woode, coming in late, from some ale-house or another." I decided not to mention I had been at the same ale-house, and let that go while Delacey continued. "The man's a drunk. And suspected of far worse. There was that matter of the missing tavern maid. He should have been expelled before this. Has she been found?"

I replied I thought not, and asked him quickly, before he could continue, "When did you last see Master Clarkson?"

"Before the evening service, in the chapel here. He said at supper that he would not attend, that he was much involved in a matter of deep study."

"And when you returned, his door was closed?"

Delacey nodded. "Yes, although after I heard Phillip Woode return, I thought I heard footsteps down the hall, to Clarkson's room. But, as I said before, I was not really attending." He rose. "You have nothing more for me, then? I must go. There is a lecture I must attend, death or no death, in the town. Learning does not wait on idlers. *Tempus fugit.*" With that he stalked out of the room.

Master Berwyk was tall, with brown eyes and hair and a nose that looked as though it had been broken in a fight at some point. Although strong, he seemed a thoughtful type, and it did not surprise me to learn that his subject was the three philosophies.

He folded his tall frame up on a bench, sitting a little hunched over at a table, by virtue of his height, and looked directly at me with troubled deep brown eyes. "So you have dealt with murder before this."

"Aye," I told him. "Donald's father is a great lord in Scotland, and sent me here with his son, as the boy was in some difficulty in the north. But I have helped his father find the guilty parties in some killings, in his lands."

"I wondered, somewhat, at your being involved," mused Berwyk.

"Grymbaud said Houkyn and the chancellor do not get on well. This seemed best to all concerned."

Berwyk nodded with a faint smile and I continued. "When did you last see Master Clarkson?"

"Yesterday, before the evening service in the chapel. After Woode's pathetic disputation in the afternoon. I cannot understand it," he went on, "the man is not stupid, not by any means. But he does not dispute well."

"I understand Master Clarkson had a book of yours that you wanted back."

"Yes, my Porphyry. A very valuable text. It was not in his room, when Delacey and I removed the books. Have you found it?"

"No."

"Strange."

I agreed that it was. "Could it have been stolen? Perhaps someone took the book and Master Clarkson came upon him unawares, and was killed for it."

"It is a valuable text," Berwyk agreed. "And hard to come by. But it would mainly be of interest to masters of philosophy, such as myself. And I certainly did not kill the man to get my own book back."

"Had you any reason to dislike Master Clarkson?"

Berwyk shook his head and was either sincere or a better actor than most academics. "Not I. He mentored me when I first came to Balliol. He was strict and sometimes critical, but he had the best interests of the scholars at heart."

"You went to town last night?"

Berwyk nodded. "I have an elderly aunt who lives in town. Mistress Bohun. Through her I met a widow, a woman named Torvilda Bonefey, who lives near Southgate. I keep company with her. I lodged with her when I first came to town and it turned into more over the years. I saw her last night. You can ask her. She'll vouch for me, right enough. Or ask my aunt."

That accorded with Delacey's words.

"Have you heard any talk of heresy in the college?"

Master Berwyk's brown eyes looked puzzled. "Heresy? No. Wycliff used to be master here some years ago. The man is somewhat controversial, but no heretic."

"No, I am speaking of someone now here at the college."

"Wycliffe is now at Lutterworth, he left Oxford after he received his doctorate. And as I just said, he's no heretic. I've heard nothing of heresy here. Why?"

"It was something the lass said. Apparently her father overheard Clarkson saying something to someone."

"Well, I know nothing of it."

I thanked Ralph Berwyk and gave him leave to go.

By now it was mid-day, and the main meal of the day was being served to the fellows and masters in the New Hall. I left the college and walked back to our lodgings, hoping to speak with Mariota, but instead as I entered our rooms I saw Donald, Anthony and Crispin, smirking about something near Donald's desk. It irritated me that these boys were mirthful when a man had just been murdered and perhaps I spoke harshly, but the upshot of it all was that Anthony and Crispin left to try and get their luncheon, and Donald went with them, stalking away. I felt it was good riddance and went into the chamber I shared with Mariota.

She was not there, and I wondered at that. I had looked forward to telling her of my interviews with the masters of the college. Perhaps she would have some insight that I had missed. But I was tired, my eyes gritty and sore. I lay down upon our bed and fell asleep, as the chamber was stuffy and the day warm.

When I awoke, Mariota had returned. She was putting some clothes away in a chest as I opened my eyes.

"Where were you, *mo chridhe*?" I murmured sleepily.

"*Och*, I was just in the town."

"Shopping?"

"Not exactly."

I sat up on the bed. "Mariota, be careful. There's been a murder, and that missing tavern girl—"

She laughed. "It's a town, Muirteach. There are people every which way one turns. I'll be safe enough."

She sat down next to me, and we didn't speak for a while. Then I told her about the morning and my interviews with the other masters.

"I left after the good wife came to lay him out, poor soul," said Mariota.

"And went into town."

"Yes, Muirteach, I went into town. That is not a crime, is it?" For some reason, Mariota seemed very annoyed, and I found myself at a loss to respond.

"Just be careful, *mo chridhe*. Be careful."

After dinner I returned to the college. The coroner had called the inquest for later that afternoon, but before that I wished to speak with another of the inhabitants of the hall. I had not yet spoken to Brother Eusebius and I found him in his room, writing on some parchment. He came with me willingly enough and we went down the stairs to the small wood-paneled chamber I was beginning to know so well.

"How well did you know Master Clarkson?" I asked him.

"I have been a fellow here for five years," Eusebius said. "And he was here when I was made a fellow."

"Did you get along?"

"Well enough. He had his scholarly interests, theology, while mine are more in the area of natural philosophy."

"But he had no enemies?"

"Master Clarkson was a man of strong opinions. He felt he knew what was right."

"And this caused him to have enemies? Who?"

Brother Eusebius didn't answer immediately. "He was an upright defender of the faith, and against heresy."

This accorded with what I had heard before. "But who here is a heretic?"

Brother Eusebius shrugged his shoulders. "I do not know. Surely the Lord made us creatures of reason for His own ends. The natural sciences reflect the harmony of the Lord's creation."

"But Master Clarkson did not believe this?" I asked.

"I did not say that," Eusebius answered.

"Did he accuse you of heresy?"

"Of course not. I simply try to divine the meanings of the Creator, to elucidate them, to puzzle out the secrets of Our Lord's meanings, as reflected within the natural world. That does not make me a heretic."

"Do you know of any enemies he might have had?"

Eusebius thought. "I certainly was not his enemy. Nor were any others here, we all quest for knowledge. Although there was an issue over some missing books of Master Berwyk's. I believe Master Clarkson had pledged them to the bookseller, and Master Berwyk claimed the books were his."

"So Master Clarkson stole the books? And pledged them at

the bookseller's?"

Eusebius shook his head. "No, he did not steal them. Most books belong to the college. Although generally, if one of us is assigned a book, we can keep it as long as we wish, until our death, even."

"But Berwyk felt the book was his?'

"Indeed. And I believe he was quite annoyed when Master Clarkson could not return the book."

That accorded with what Berwyk had told me, although he had not known of the bookseller. I could well believe that a motive for murder. Books were precious and costly. But the murder had not yielded the book back, so perhaps it made little sense after all. However I remembered the conversation I had overheard between Clarkson and the bookman a few days ago.

"Well, I must go," Eusebius said. "I have a lecture to prepare for tomorrow. Although we held no lectures today, due to this unfortunate happenstance, the students will be at the hall on School Street on the morrow."

"On what subject do you lecture?"

"Aristotle, for the first-year students. I must take over Clarkson's lectures for the time."

I was on the verge of mentioning again that my wife was a physician, but something stopped me. I bade Eusebius a good day, and he left to prepare for his lecture.

In a short time, the coroner arrived and the jury was summoned. The twelve men, all members of the "Northern hundred" as the area of Oxford north of the city walls was known, shuffled into the small room downstairs after having viewed the body. Most of them were merchants or other inhabitants of the suburbs, and they looked suitably impressed at being in the halls of the learned college. They heard the evidence. Houkyn described how the body had been found, in a pool of blood in its chamber. It did not take long for the jury to return a verdict of "willful murder by persons unknown." Which, of course, was what we had known all along.

# CHAPTER 6

After that was over, although the afternoon was far advanced, I first stopped at the Widow Tanner's and then crossed into the town at Smithgate and paid a visit to the bookman. The sky had clouded over and looked as though rain might begin to drizzle down at any moment. Fortunately, it held off for the short time it took to walk to the shop off High Street where I found the stall still open. Master Bookman greeted me and asked after Donald, for apparently he remembered our somewhat well-filled purses of a few days before. He did not mention Mariota, but showed me some rare medical books.

"I am looking for a certain text today, the *Isagoge,* by Porphyry."

Master Bookman went back and rummaged around the piles of his merchandise before returning with the text. "I can let you see it, as I do have one copy, but the book was pawned. I cannot sell it to you at this time."

"Who pawned it?"

"Master Clarkson, the one who was just murdered at that college. A bad business, by the sound of it, and I do not think he'll be redeeming his pledge, unless it were on the Judgment Day." The bookman flashed a grim smile, although I failed to share in the humor. After an awkward moment he continued. "But others in the college may wish to take over his pledge."

"Aye," I said, "I imagine that is true. Were you aware the book was stolen?"

Master Bookman stuttered. "Certainly not. Master Clarkson heads his college, or did, God rest his soul. Surely he wouldn't steal."

"I will let Master Berwyk know where the book is. It is he who owned it, or said that he did. Perhaps he will want to redeem it." I paused. "There is something else I am needing to ask you," I said. I pulled the palimpsest from my bag. "We bought these old parchments from you, and found this on one. Do you have any idea as to whose it might be? Where did you get the parchments you sold us?"

The bookman examined the parchment. "It is very curious. Sometimes the parchments are not cleaned well and the text remains visible. If they are scrubbed with pumice that happens less often, but just scrubbing them with milk and oat bran does not do nearly so well." He looked more closely at the words. "It is strange. Perhaps it is some kind of medical text?"

"Perhaps. Who gave you the parchments to sell?"

"They were old ones found in a back building—I think it was Master Clarkson himself who brought them in. At the same time he pledged the *Isagoge.*"

That was stranger yet.

"Do you have any idea what language these might be written in?"

Master Bookman pored over the parchment again. "Truthfully, I've no idea. It is a curious thing, is it not? Well, you are welcome to stay and examine my books, although I will be closing up very soon. Unless, of course, you have pressing business elsewhere." I thought he sounded hopeful.

I spent some time searching through some other books and parchments but found no other sheets that matched the strange one we had found. Finally, I abandoned the quest and left the shop.

Frustrated, I thought of The Green Man. Some wine would

taste fine on this dreary evening. I walked down the High Street to the ale-house, where I found Master Jakeson. There was no sign of his daughter and I judged she had not yet been found. I hoped again she had run off with someone who was treating her kindly.

I was surprised to see Eusebius in the tavern. I sat down next to him, although he did not look too happy to see me. "I thought you were preparing a lecture."

"It is done. I had need of refreshment."

"As do I. Here," I offered, "let me pay for your claret."

Master Jakeson refilled Eusebius's mazer and brought some wine for me.

"Do you come here often?" I asked.

"Often enough," said Eusebius.

"It is a sad thing, about his missing daughter."

Eusebius said nothing for a moment and sipped at his drink. "Aye," he finally said. "Jonetta."

"Yes, that's her name. Did you know her?"

"Beautiful," Eusebius mused, and I judged this had not been his first glass of claret. "She's beautiful."

"Aye, she's a bonny lass. You've no idea what happened to her?"

Eusebius seemed to come to himself. "Of course not." He drained the mazer. "What would I be knowing about her? She's just a tavern maid."

"But a lovely one."

"Indeed she is," he assented, put down his drink, and frowned. "I thought, one night recently, she seemed overly familiar with a chapman, a peddler. By his accent he came from the north."

"That's of interest. What did he look like? Perhaps she ran off with him. The undersheriff would wish to know."

"Perhaps. The man was tall, dark-haired. I think he had

brown eyes and his jerkin was russet. You'll inform the authorities?"

I nodded.

"Well, God keep the lass safe, wherever she may be." He rose. "I'm back to the college. Master Clarkson is laid out in the chapel. I must go and keep vigil."

"I'll join you," I said. We left the tavern and walked up High Street and out the town gates. I went with Eusebius to the small chapel in the college, where the cold bulk of Master Clarkson's corpse lay before the altar, covered with a pall. The burial would take place the next day. I seated myself in the back and observed the masters at their prayers. Berwyk, Delacey and the others. Phillip Woode. Even the younger students had attended. Who among these people had committed murder?

As some prayers drew to a close, I left the chapel and the college and made my way back to our lodgings. It was a dark night, with little moon, and I was glad to see some candlelight glowing from the window of our room. Mariota must have lit it for me, I thought, with a glow of happiness.

When I entered the room Mariota was bent over her text again, oblivious to the candle that had nearly melted down to a puddle. She looked up when she heard the door. "*Och*, Muirteach, it is you. How late is it?"

"Late enough to burn up your candle, *mo chridhe*. Where is Donald?"

"He was playing that accursed lute in his room with Anthony and Crispin, but they left some time ago. They had brought some wine from a tavern. I imagine he's asleep the now."

I peeked into Donald's chamber. The lad was stretched out on his pallet, face down, buried in his pillow, snoring. I came back to our chamber and smiled at my wife. "Droning worse than the pipes. I don't think he'll wake until the morning."

"Did you find out anything else?"

"Master Berwyk accused Clarkson of stealing a book of his, and Clarkson pawned it at the bookman's."

"But it is Berwyk's book?"

"He claims it is. Oh, and I ran into Brother Eusebius in the town. He says he remembers seeing Jonetta with a chapman some nights ago. Perhaps she ran off."

"I hope so, and I hope he treats her kindly," said my wife, mirroring my earlier thoughts.

I sat down next to Mariota on the bench and rubbed her shoulders, inhaling her elderflower scent. "What are you studying now? Can you not put out the candle and come to bed? It's late."

"Aye," she sighed and rubbed at her eyes. "I had hoped to study more tonight."

"There's no rush, is there, *mo chridhe*? Come to bed."

For a moment I thought Mariota looked as though she was going to say something, but she did not speak. She turned and raised her lips to mine, and she smelled of elderflowers, her breath tasting of sweet cloves and cinnamon. I pinched out the candle between my fingers, oblivious to the brief pain from the hot wick.

The next morning Mariota and I rose early and went to attend on Master Clarkson's funeral mass. The masters of the college looked fatigued, as all had kept vigil for their departed colleague. I thought I saw Master Berwyk nod off at one point and all looked relieved when the mass was over and the mortal remains of Master Clarkson interred in the vault below the chapel.

As Mariota and I left the service, she left me to return to the Widow Tanner's. I saw another figure heading up the street, toward the wastelands north of the town. There were some old buildings there, past the Benedictines' college, left empty for several years since the days of the plague. The widow had said the town council wanted them torn down, but the heirs, who lived in London, had not agreed, and the buildings were falling down where they stood. Beggars and such like squatted in the structures, I'd been told.

I headed for the college, to speak with Master Berwyk. I thought perhaps news of his *Isagoge* might prove illuminating. There was to be meal, after the mass, and most lectures had again been cancelled. I hoped the younger students would not take it upon themselves to murder their teachers for the sake of cancelled lectures.

I met Master Berwyk as he was leaving the hall. His brown eyes looked sad and troubled. "It is a wicked thing," he said, "and a sad reminder of our own mortality. We never know when our end will come."

"Indeed," I said, and added, "I spoke with the bookman yesterday. He has your *Isagoge*. Master Clarkson pledged it for a loan."

"But it was not his to pledge!"

"Whether it was or not, it is there. And I doubt the bookman will release it until he gets his money."

"That book never belonged to the college. I bought it with my own money, money my poor father, God rest his soul, had given to me. If the man wasn't dead already, I swear I'd kill him." He stopped and laughed. "There, now I am the wicked one, am I not? God forgive me, the man is barely settled in his grave."

"Why would Master Clarkson do such a thing?"

"He seemed to think little of others—it was always the college."

"But what would he have needed the money for?"

Berwyk shrugged.

"I heard he was speaking with someone about heresy at the

college. Do you know anything of that?"

Berwyk shrugged again, impatiently this time. We'd spoken of heresy the day before. "I'd heard nothing of that, as I've told you. And Wycliffe is long gone, as I told you yesterday. He's no Lollard, although some here might be. Well, I am off to the bookman's to see if I can redeem my book. Or at least to see what he wants for it. Perhaps I can persuade him to let me redeem it little by little. I must have my book back."

"I'll go with you," I offered.

The streets of town were full, as crowds of students headed toward High Street from School Street. Most walked in groups, boisterous and loud, as they headed for ale-houses. I noticed one youth walking alone, wearing a hood and a blue tunic, who seemed to glance at me and then walk quickly to the other side of the street, as though wanting to avoid me. There was something familiar about the lad.

We saw him again as we neared the bookseller's stall. The boy seemed about to approach, but then he saw us and began walking quickly away.

"I will leave you," I excused myself to Master Berwyk. "I must attend to something."

Leaving him, I walked rapidly after the boy, who darted into an alley off of High Street. I ran after and caught up with him, grabbing him by the arm.

"Let me go, sir," protested the youth.

"Indeed I shall not."

"I was doing naught to you. Let me go."

"I think not." I kept my hold on the lad's arm and turned him around to face me. "Mariota, what are you doing here?"

The hood fell back, and I looked into the lovely blue eyes of my wife.

# CHAPTER 7

"It's nothing to you, Muirteach. I was attending the lectures," Mariota said, quickly pulling the hood back over her head and tucking her hair back inside. "Medical lectures."

"But *mo chridhe*—"

"What, Muirteach," my wife hissed in a low voice, and I could tell from the edge in it that she was annoyed. I myself had to restrain the urge to throttle my spouse. "Am I to just sit and sew with our landlady all the day? I shall go mad. And to be so close to all this knowledge and not be able to hear some of it—what else would you have me do?"

"But what if they find out?"

"No one will find out," she pointed out, "unless you tell them. I enrolled as William, from Uist. It's the back of beyond. No one will think to question it. And I just attend the lectures and go back to the widow's. I won't be idling in the ale-houses, unlike most of my peers."

"Does she know of this?"

Mariota nodded, her chin thrust forward defiantly. "Aye. I had to tell her, as I have to leave in men's garb. She helped me. If any one inquires, she will tell them that a William lodges there. And now, sir," she continued in a louder voice, as two men started down the alley toward us, "I must be on my way. Good day to you."

I walked with her. "I am not letting you walk alone through these streets. It isn't safe."

"It certainly won't be safe if you expose me. Muirteach, let me be." And with that she walked rapidly to High Street and left me standing, dumbfounded, in the alley.

I stalked home, furious. Scarlet anger coursed through my veins. As I walked, dodging the filth in the streets and the occasional chamber pot emptied from upper stories, I cursed my wife, my charge and my overlord who had insisted we come on this foolish journey. As I crossed through the Northgate and passed Old Balliol Hall, I cursed all academics foolish enough to get themselves murdered, and every student in the town for good measure.

My mood did not improve when I entered our lodgings and heard Donald plunking away at his damned lute. He should have been studying. It was all I could do not to barge into his chamber and break the hideous instrument over the lad's head. I briefly considered what a nice fire the wooden instrument would make. Where had he gotten it? I remembered the shop and mulled the possibility of taking the lute and breaking it over the shopkeeper's crown instead.

"William" had not yet arrived home and I went to find Widow Tanner. I charged into the kitchen and found my landlady seated at a table in the kitchen shelling beans.

"Where's 'William'?" I demanded.

Widow Tanner's face blanched paler than the white beans she was shelling. "William?"

"My wife, damn it. Where is she? What were you thinking of to aid her in this harebrained scheme?"

Widow Tanner stood upright. "And is it so wrong for her to want to study?"

"Can't you see it is not safe? The town is full of murderers. Not to mention licentious students!"

"She'll be safe enough," the widow protested.

"Do you really think she'll be safe if the masters discover she's not a lad? Or those students?"

"Sir, she was determined. I could not dissuade her. Nor do I think it so very wrong."

"Aye, so you colluded with her. Where is she?"

"She's returned safe enough and went to your chamber to change her garb."

I had not looked in our chamber, incensed as I was. Now, feeling somewhat foolish as well as furious, I left the kitchen and threw the door of our room open. Mariota was just closing the lid of the chest, now dressed in her own long shift and kirtle. She turned to face me, biting her lip. "Muirteach, I know you're angry—"

"And why should I not be?"

"Muirteach, can't you understand? It's the only way I can attend the lectures; that's why I wanted to accompany you! That's why I came on this journey."

"Just to hear lectures? Not to be with me?"

"Well, of course I wanted to be with you," Mariota amended, unconvincingly I thought. "But now that I'm here, how can I just sit and sew with the widow? I want to learn, Muirteach. Surely you can see that and not hold it against me?"

"And surely you can see that there's a murderer running loose in town and a missing woman who has yet to be found! Think about what you're doing, *amadain*!"

Calling my wife a fool did little to improve the tenor of our conversation. Mariota turned away from me, her back stiff, took her medical text and went over to the table. She sat down and began to read.

"Mariota, you must see reason about this. It isn't safe!"

My wife did not answer and continued looking at her book. Through the wall I could hear the discordant sounds of Donald's lute playing and I realized he had probably heard every word.

I tried another tack and lowered my voice. "*Mo chridhe,* it's not that I'm angry with you." This last statement may not have been entirely true.

"No?"

"Of course not. But you must see it isn't safe."

"But Muirteach, you are not being logical. I'm dressed as a lad, not a lass. So therefore, I should be quite safe from kidnappers of women."

"Curse logic! Suppose you are found out."

"I won't be discovered."

"But what if you are?"

"It is not against the law to dress in men's garb."

"But I am very well sure that to lie about your identity and falsely enroll in the university may well be against the law—or certainly against the statutes of the university!"

"Well, we shall see. But I am not intending to be discovered."

"Mariota, I forbid it!"

"You cannot stop me, Muirteach. Do not even think of trying to."

I judged it foolish to continue our conversation. With great effort, I shut my mouth tight and stalked out of the house, ignoring the anxious looks of Widow Tanner. I had it in mind to go into town and get very drunk at Master Jakeson's tavern, but that made me think of the still-missing Jonetta and as I walked, I decided I did not wish to visit there. So I walked the short distance to Old Balliol Hall, thinking perhaps Master Berwyk had returned from the bookseller's with news of his *Isagoge.* I entered the hall and went to the room Master Berwyk shared with Master Delacey and knocked.

The door opened and Master Delacey stuck a truculent face out.

"I'm seeking Master Berwyk. Is he within?"

"No. He's not returned from town. He's probably with that whore of his, Torvilda."

"And where does she lodge?"

"I've no idea. Pennyfarthing Street, I think I've heard him say. Near St. Ebbe's. Now, if you'll excuse me, I've studies to attend to."

His tone irked me but I was in none too patient a mood after my conversation with my wife. "Well, when he returns, tell him I need to speak with him."

Delacey perked his ears like a hound scenting prey. "Oh? And why would that be?"

"That is my affair, not yours." With that I left him and stalked out of the hall. In the backlands I noticed Ivo tending some cabbages in the garden. I walked over to where he labored. The cabbages and leeks looked green and healthy and I surmised the scholars would be enjoying a great deal of them in the days to come.

"Ivo."

The old man stood up and stretched his back. "Aye?"

"I wanted to ask you something. About the night Master Clarkson was murdered."

"Aye?" The old man brushed the dirt from his hands. "I've already told you what I know."

"You said you had locked the gates. But I was with Master Woode and when we returned to the college the gate was already locked."

"Aye, it were. I heard him banging on it and roused myself up and let him in, then locked it up again, tight enough. No one else came in."

"So it must have been someone from the college. Unless someone came in earlier and hid themselves. But then how did they leave?"

"Well, they weren't getting out by the gate. That were well locked up."

I looked at him. "You've worked here a long while."

"All my life," Ivo returned, "since I were a lad. But I told you that afore."

"So you know the masters well."

Ivo shrugged and scratched absent-mindedly through his tunic at a spot on his arm. "I'm but a servant."

"Yes, but still you know the place."

"Happen that I do."

"Do you have any idea who might have done this thing? Do you know of anyone with a grudge against Master Clarkson?"

"He were a hard man. Strict-like. But them students need a strict hand. Young lads and such they are, always rowdy and carousing, not attending to their studies. They'd play ball back here and trample the cabbages with not a care for the garden, nor for them that works it."

I nodded. "But are you thinking any of the scholars killed the master?"

Ivo shook his head. "I've no way of knowing that. I know he had words with that Phillip Woode. I heard them, so I did."

I had heard them too. "Have you ever noticed Phillip Woode to have a bad temper? A violent disposition?"

Ivo shook his head again. "No, I never did. He's a friend to many of the younger lads and likes his ale, but I've never known him to fight. He be a kind man, at least I've never seen him in a temper—except for the words I heard with the master."

"And others? Who else might have a temper?"

Ivo stretched his back again and reached for his hoe. "That Master Delacey. He did fight and argue in years past. But not so much now as in former times. He's on his dignity, he is now. Thinks he's better than the others and wanted to be master of the college himself. But the other scholars voted for Clarkson."

"Well, he studies the law, I believe."

"So he does."

"Your daughter mentioned you'd overheard Master Clarkson speaking to someone of heresy. When was that?"

"I were outside the hall, and I heard Clarkson's voice through the window. He spoke loud enough, when he was out of humor. He just said something about not tolerating heresy here."

"Did you hear who he was speaking with?"

"No, sir, just Master Clarkson. His voice carried when he were angered."

That I knew; I'd heard him myself.

"Now, sir, I'd best get back to these greens. I know nothing to help you."

Although Ivo had dismissed me, I did not leave but stood watching him hoe around his cabbages. "Those are fine plants."

"Aye, they did well this year, they did."

"Your little daughter. Avice is her name?"

"Aye?"

"She's a fine girl. It must have been hard, raising her here. With all the young lads around, I mean."

"She's a good girl, my poppet. But it were hard, especially after my wife was took. She's lacked a mother these past years. Still, she's a good girl. I've no complaint of her."

"The lads don't bother her?"

"She's still but a child and of modest temperament. No, they leave her well alone for the most part."

"It's happy I am to hear that. She's a sweet lass."

"Aye, so she is," Ivo replied.

I left the old man bent over his greens and quit the college, thinking to find Torvilda's lodging on Pennyfarthing Street. The sun was still somewhat high in the sky, and I reasoned I had some time before dusk. If Master Berwyk was not there, I might at least learn more about him from his woman. So for the second time that day I crossed through Northgate and entered the town proper.

Pennyfarthing Street was down the High Street, in a poorer section of town. The streets were narrower, the houses less well built, few of stone, most of wattle and daub or wood. Some of them looked to be collapsing one against the other as though they gained support only from their proximity to each other. Torvilda's house, when I found it, was a bit nicer than some, a two-story dwelling made of wood with slate shingles on the roof. A tabby cat came running up to the door as I knocked and waited expectantly, rubbing back and forth against my legs.

At length the door opened, and the cat ran inside. A young woman picked it up, then turned to face me. She wore a green dress with a brown over-tunic, her hair modestly concealed by a linen wimple.

"Are you the Widow Torvilda?"

The woman let the cat go, then nodded and looked at me through narrowed eyes. "Who are you?"

"I am Muirteach MacPhee."

"A student, are you? I've no rooms to let at present."

"No, I am not a student. I'm looking for Master Berwyk. I'm told he can often be found here."

"Who told you that?"

"He did himself. Is he here? I'd like to speak with him."

I heard Master Berwyk's voice from inside the house. "Torvilda, sweet, who is it?"

The woman shut the door and through the wood I caught the murmur of voices. In a moment it opened again and I saw Master Berwyk and the woman standing together. Master Berwyk looked relaxed, but the woman still had a guarded look to her eyes, which I noticed were a lovely shade of green.

"Muirteach, it is good to see you," Master Berwyk greeted me. "Torvilda, this is Muirteach. He is from the north, from

Scotland, and has been helping the authorities with the sad killing of Master Clarkson. Muirteach, this is Mistress Torvilda
Bonefey. You must excuse her welcome; it is seldom people seek
me out here. How did you find the place?"

"Master Delacey said I might find you here, and told me
Mistress Bonefey's lodgings were on Pennyfarthing Street. For
the rest of it, I asked directions. But how did it go with the
bookseller? Were you able to redeem your *Isagoge*?"

"Perhaps in time it may be possible. But come inside, and we
can speak in more comfort than here on the stoop."

I was ushered inside to a main room, simply furnished but
boasting a fireplace. The same tabby cat was ensconced in a low
willow basket by the fire. I heard soft mewing sounds and a
loud purr and realized the cat nursed kittens.

Mistress Bonefey bade me be seated, left the room, and
returned shortly with a jug of ale and two leather mugs. Then
she disappeared again, leaving us to our business.

"And so what happened at the bookseller's?" I asked again,
after taking a long sip of my ale.

"Master Bookman was at first not too forthcoming, but I
examined the text and it is indeed my book. I showed him some
notations I had made on it, and he finally began to believe me.
But he refuses to let me take ownership without repaying the
pledge."

"And is it a large amount of money?"

"Large enough." Master Berwyk grimaced and drank some
more ale. "I'm hoping he will hold it for me until I can come
up with the sum. I will sell what I can, and perhaps I can do
more tutoring, take on another student or two to come up with
the money. I paid him some today—a shilling, all I had, but he
wants seven to redeem the pledge."

Seven shillings was a goodly sum. "But he will hold it for you
until you can gain the funds?"

"I believe he will. And I'm glad of that at least. I would hate to lose that book."

"When did you lend the book to Clarkson?"

"It was some few weeks ago. And then when I pressed him to get it back, the man lied. He claimed to be not through reading it and asked to keep it a bit longer. It was not until you told me, after his death, that I discovered he had pledged it." Berwyk shook his head in disbelief.

"So you did not go to his room to ask him for it that night, and discover it was gone, and hit the man in anger?"

"No. I knew nothing of its being absent until we looked through his texts that next day, Master Delacey and myself. Although I was angry enough, when I learned of it. But by that time the man was dead."

"So you were not angry with him before?"

"Indeed I was angry," Master Berwyk responded. "Angry he had not returned my book to me. But I did not know he had pledged it until after his death, and it was not I that killed the man."

"As you say," I returned.

"You must believe me, Muirteach."

"Who can vouch for you that night?"

"You can ask Torvilda, as I said. And perhaps her lodgers may attest to it, should you not believe Torvilda's words."

"I shall do so," I replied. "Who are the lodgers?"

"She has two. They are young students from the West Country. Their names are Justin Penwarred and Vortigen Pen-wryth. They saw me here that evening and will vouch for me should you not believe Torvilda."

"Where might I find them?"

"Here. Or should you choose to seek them out, they attend the extraordinary lectures on School Street. Justin wears a green hood and Vortigen a brown one. They are often together and frequent an ale-house at the end of Catte Street. The Red Cockerel, it is called. You'll find them there now, I'd expect. Lectures are ended for the day now and they've yet to return here."

I nodded and said I would seek them out. Torvilda might lie to protect her lover but the lads might not if I could find them before they were warned.

"What of that lad you saw earlier?" asked Master Berwyk. "Was that Donald, your charge?"

"No," I replied shortly. "I mistook the lad for someone, that was all."

Master Berwyk nodded and although he seemed curious I did not enlighten him. I had no idea how to handle that problem. Mariota and I had never seriously been at odds but this situation did not seem as though it would easily be reconciled. Perhaps, I thought desperately, a kitten might charm Mariota out of her black mood, although I doubted it. She could try out remedies on it, if nothing else.

"So your tabby has kittens?" I asked, changing the subject abruptly.

"Torvilda's cat. She has six of them and is a proud mother."

We rose and looked at the litter, nursing happily. They were still young, squirming as they jostled for position at their mother's teats. Most were striped brown and black, like the mother.

"What will Mistress Bonefey do with the kittens?"

Master Berwyk shrugged. "It's her affair. She might sell them. The mother's a fine mouser."

"I might take one. Would you ask her for me?"

"Indeed."

"And I should speak to Mistress Bonefey as well, before I leave."

"For certain. You might mention the kitten to her yourself."

Master Berwyk called to Torvilda, who came in and stood by the hearth, wringing her apron in her hands from nervousness. But she answered my questions readily enough, confirming that Master Berwyk had been with her two evenings ago, when Master Clarkson had been killed. Although truthfully I had not thought she would say otherwise.

I finished my ale and took my leave. The sun was lower in the sky and I walked briskly up High Street, despite my bad leg, which was beginning to ache. I turned east toward Catte Street, hoping to find young Justin and Vortigen in the ale-house. All the taverns were busy at this time of the day, crowded with students. I found The Red Cockerel, a dilapidated ale-house at the corner of the street. Although in poor repair, it was a large building and seemed to do a good business. I entered and ordered a beaker of ale while my eyes adjusted to the dim light and I scanned the room for Justin and Vortigen.

A babble of voices speaking in what I took to be Cornish led me to a table by the sidewall, under a high, unshuttered window. Light filtered in and through a haze of dust-motes I saw a number of young students, boys really, not much older than Donald. They were speaking busily in a language that had no relation to English or Latin, but they appeared to be playing some kind of drinking game. As I watched, the boys chanted "Vortigen, Vortigen," while a boy in a brown hood raised the leather mug to his lips and drained it as the voices continued. The lad threw the mug back down on the table and then looked up at me as I approached.

"Such prowess deserves another tankard," I said in Latin, for Cornish was far beyond me. "Might I buy you and your friends another round of drinks?"

"And why would you do that?" another lad demanded, somewhat suspiciously.

"I have my reasons." All of the boys glared at me. "Chief

among them is that I am seeking Justin Penwarred and Vortigen Penwryth. Might they be among your party?"

"Why are you searching for them?" a tall lad in a threadbare green hood asked. I felt quite sure he was Justin.

"I am seeking information." A tavern maid came by and I ordered a round of more ale for the boys.

"And who are you?"

"My name is Muirteach MacPhee. I am from Scotland, but am helping the coroner and Undersheriff Grymbaud with certain matters. There has been a murder; a master at Balliol Hall was found slain."

The ale arrived, and the boys stopped glaring and began drinking. The atmosphere became a bit less hostile.

"We had heard of that," replied the lad in the green. "But what has that to do with us?"

"You are Master Justin, are you not?"

"Indeed. But what can you want with me?"

"It is a simple matter. You lodge with Mistress Bonefey, do you not? On Pennyfarthing Street?"

"Yes, myself as well as Vortigen here."

"And you know Master Berwyk, who visits Mistress Bonefey from time to time?"

"He is her lover," Vortigen snickered and made a suggestive gesture. I longed to give the boy a smack, but figured that would not help me on my errand.

"But he seems a kind man," Justin put in. "He helped me with some points of grammar."

"So you do study?"

"Sometimes."

"Well, was Master Berwyk there at your landlady's two nights back?"

"Indeed he was. We got back just at dusk—the Vespers bells were ringing at Saint Frideswyde's—and he and Mistress

Bonefey were there in the solar."

"How late did he stay?"

"He helped me with my grammar, and that was quite late— Mistress Bonefey had lit the candles. I think he stayed the night, for he was there in the morning when we left for the early lecture before Prime."

"Well enough," I said. "Thank you. And you might ask Master Berwyk if you have need of a tutor. It is possible he would take you on, as he has need of funds."

I left the lads finishing their ale and trudged slowly back up the High Street to the Northgate, dreading the thought of seeing my wife.

I had not quite reached Northgate when a voice hailed me. Turning, I saw the stout form of the undersheriff walking quickly up through the crowds of High Street toward me. "Muirteach!"

I greeted him as he drew closer.

"It is a lucky chance, running into you like this," he said.

I was not feeling quite so fortunate, as I had little to tell the man, but I nodded pleasantly.

"What have you learned so far?" the undersheriff inquired.

"I am sure Master Clarkson was murdered by one of the fellows," I replied, "unless a stranger scaled the walls and departed the same way. The gatekeeper swears the last person he let in was Phillip Woode, and I was with that man earlier in the evening. He had argued with Master Clarkson a time or two, but I doubt that Woode has murder in him."

Grymbaud shook his head and did not seem convinced. I continued.

"Master Berwyk also has a motive; Master Clarkson had borrowed a book of his, an expensive text, and then Clarkson pledged it to the bookseller to get funds for the college. But there are folk who avow that Berwyk was with his mistress that night, although Delacey lied to me about that. He claims Berwyk spent the night in their chamber at the college. Master Delacey had wanted to be elected the master of the college as well, and lost the election to Clarkson, so there could be jealousy on that score. But nothing clearly points to the guilty party as of yet."

"Hmmm," the undersheriff muttered, and picked at a mole on his chin. He had shaved within the last few days but showed a fair growth of dark stubble on his jaw for all of that. "Phillip Woode again. He seems to be involved in all these matters—for did he not have an interest in that tavern wench? The girl that's gone missing?"

"Aye, Jonetta."

"Yes, Jonetta."

Then I thought of what Brother Eusebius had said, of seeing Jonetta with a chapman, and told the constable. He frowned slightly as he heard my news. "Did he say what the peddler looked like?"

I tried to remember Eusebius's exact words. "Tall, well favored, dark haired, with a northern accent. Wearing a russet jerkin. It was several nights ago that he saw them, a night or two before the lass went missing."

"There are several chapmen around the town who might meet that description. It could be Walter of York, although I don't believe I've seen him in town for a bit. The man could be a good ways from town by now, with the girl as well." He shook his head. "Well, I'll have my men seek them out. I don't think Master Jakeson will be overjoyed to hear this news."

"Well, having a daughter run off with a peddler may be scandal, but at least the lass is still living."

"Let us pray that she is," Grymbaud returned darkly, and turned to go. "Keep at it, Muirteach," he encouraged me. "Those academics are a nest of vipers. Arrogant and prideful, they are." Grymbaud spat in the gutter, then continued. "Any of them might have done the deed, and have no scruples about lying to you. They hold their intellectual accomplishments far above the laws of God. And those young ones, always carousing and wenching—and claiming to be immune to the rules of the burgh, holding that they are in clerical orders." He snorted and spat again. "Fine clerks they are, indeed."

I wondered somewhat at these bitter words, but did not question Grymbaud further. No doubt he had had trouble often enough in the past keeping the peace between the townsfolk and the students. Instead, I took my leave and slowly continued my trek toward the Widow Tanner's. My leg hurt me the whole way.

# CHAPTER 8

When I arrived at the Widow Tanner's I found that Donald was not there, and neither was my wife. The shadows were lengthening and Widow Tanner nervously said that Donald had gone out in the afternoon with Crispin and Mariota had left shortly after. I was happy to hear she had dressed in her own garb.

"She said something about going into town, to the shops. They are just closing now, so doubtless she will return shortly. Come, the soup is ready. Come and eat now. You look done in, sir."

"She had better return quickly," I observed darkly, and then sat down to supper. Mariota could eat when she returned. I was not waiting on her. And if truth were told, I did feel somewhat better after I had eaten the bean soup, sausages and cabbage the widow had prepared. The soup smelled tantalizingly of some sort of herbs. The ache in my leg receded somewhat and my mood improved along with it. I was just beginning my second bowlful when the door opened and Mariota entered. She hesitated on the threshold when she saw me, then lifted her chin defiantly, walked into the room and took a seat at the table.

"And where have you been?" I asked, not liking the tone in my own voice but speaking anyway.

"I went into town, Muirteach. To the shops. I needed wax tablets. But something happened on the way back that you should know about."

"And what is that?"

"Well, on the way back I saw that little maid from the college. Whose father is the gatekeeper."

"Avice?"

"Yes, that is her name. She was leaving the grocer's stall, carrying a basket full of plums. She could scarce lift it. She is a tiny maid."

Widow Tanner brought Mariota a trencher and Mariota helped herself to some soup and took a spoonful. "This is delicious. Tarragon?"

"Aye," returned the widow. "And a bit of leeks and parsley, and rue." The widow prudently left us alone at the table and Mariota continued.

"Well, she recognized me from the college, the day the master was murdered, and we got to talking. I helped her carry her basket. She's but a child still."

"Yes?" I wondered where all this was leading, and still felt angry with my wife, who showed no sign of deferring to my wishes.

"Muirteach, I think she is with child herself."

"What?"

"As we walked we got to talking. The poor lass has no mother, she died some years ago."

"Aye, Ivo told me as much. Of plague."

"But Avice complained to me of feeling queasy, and then when she heard I was a healer she told me more. She must have felt she could confide in a stranger, as I know no one to gossip with. She's not had her courses in some three months. Muirteach, the girl is pregnant."

"And by who, I wonder?" I mused, thinking of the bitter tears I had seen Avice crying on the day Clarkson was murdered. But she had protested she had not known the man well. "Could it have been Master Clarkson?"

"She did not say. She took it hard enough when I suggested she might be with child. I had to stay with her some time before she calmed down. That is why I am so late."

"And does her father know of it?"

"She has not told him, but she fears perhaps he does. She's just beginning to show and he might have noticed. She says he's been questioning her lately, suspicious of where she's been."

"He told me his daughter was a good girl."

"And so she is. The poor thing knows next to nothing—she is so young. Someone took cruel advantage of the lass, and now she'll pay the price. While the lout will no doubt deny it all."

"Well, I'll speak with her again tomorrow. Although doubtless it was one of the lads there, and no bearing on Clarkson's murder at all."

Just then we heard a noise from the front of the house, and a crash, and Donald's voice, swearing. I groaned. Mariota looked at me and grinned. For a brief instant, we were in harmony. Then she frowned a little bit and the moment vanished.

"I'll go see what it is," she offered. "Although doubtless it is the ale he's had to drink that's making all that racket."

I nodded shortly and left her to it, closed my eyes while I leaned back against the wall, and thought longingly for a moment of my home in Islay and the few happy months we had spent there, before the Lord of the Isles had sent us on this accursed trip. I missed my dog. At least he adored me without reservation.

In a few moments Mariota returned with Donald, who seemed flushed and agitated. He stumbled a little as he crossed the room to the benches by the trestle table.

"And how have you been keeping yourself?" I asked him sarcastically in Gaelic. "Hard at your studies, were you?"

Donald's chin thrust forward a fraction, despite his drunken state. "I was with Anthony and Crispin. Surely it's not wrong for me to have friends."

"Well, let us hope they are able to remain as students here. For to do that, some study is required."

"*Och,* Muirteach, let the lad be," Mariota interjected. "Let's not quarrel more this evening."

Donald meanwhile had taken one look at the bowl of bean soup the Widow Tanner set before him and turned somewhat pale. "I am not hungry," he muttered. He got up and rushed from the room and I guessed he was going to be sick in the privacy of his own chamber. I found I was not sorry about it.

Widow Tanner returned to the room and looked momentarily confused at Donald's disappearance.

"He said he was not feeling well," I said to her. "He's retired to his chamber."

"He's drunk," our landlady retorted bluntly. "Do you think I've never rented to students before?" She picked up his bowl and returned to the kitchen, leaving Mariota and myself in awkward silence.

"I meant what I just said," Mariota ventured as the silence grew longer. "Let us not quarrel any more tonight."

"And have you come to your senses?" I asked her belligerently.

"About the lectures?"

I nodded.

"Muirteach, I must go—can't you understand that? *Och,* it is hopeless," she said after a moment when I obstinately remained silent. With that, my wife got up and left me alone at the widow's fine table. I glared at the tapestry hanging on the wall—a fine rendition of Penelope weaving as she waited for Odysseus to return. It was a shame all women were not so biddable. I thought of going back into town to a tavern, but it was late and I was exhausted. So after a few moments I left the table and my now cold bowl of soup and joined my wife in our chamber.

I heard the drone of Donald's snoring through the wall separating our rooms. Mariota had already stripped to her shift and was lying in bed, her back turned to me and her eyes shut tight. She'd left a candle burning on the small table, for it was now quite dark. I wondered if she was truly asleep, but did not try to rouse her. Instead, I also removed my outer garments and washed my face in the basin of water that stood next to the candle. I put out the light and joined my wife in bed, turned my face to the opposite wall and lay there stiffly, but found I did not sleep.

I awoke the next morning to find the spot in bed next to me empty. The day was just breaking and there was enough light in the room for me to see that Mariota was already up and dressed, in her boy's garb of blue hooded tunic and hose. She turned and spoke to me when she saw my open eyes. "Muirteach, I'm off. I'll be back after the lectures today."

"*Mo chridhe*, wait," I murmured, but she was already gone.

The sleepiness of a moment before lost to me, I rose, dressed and made my way to Balliol, where I went looking for Avice. I found her near the kitchen outbuilding behind the halls, scrubbing at a large cauldron. It seemed the cook used the lass as a bit of a drudge. Avice's eyes were red, and she gave me a frightened glance.

"Hello, Avice. I was wanting to speak with you."

"I've work to do," she responded, bending her head industriously to her scrubbing.

"It won't take long. But it is important."

She raised her head and put the rag down for a moment. "But I must clean this. Cook is needing it, to prepare the meal." She picked up the rag again and continued rubbing at the kettle.

"Avice, my wife told me she spoke with you yesterday."

Avice did not reply but I could see tears trickling down her

108

cheek while she scrubbed. I felt like a fool, but continued anyway. "She told me that you are with child."

Avice nodded, crying harder now.

"Does anyone know?"

"My da, he guessed it," she said in a whisper.

"When?"

She looked at me a moment. "I'm not sure, exact-like. But he accused me a week or so ago. He said I must be with child, that my belly was swollen. I did not think it possible. At least I hoped not."

"Had you lain with a man?"

Avice bent her head back to her kettle and did not answer.

"You must tell me. Who were you with? Was it one of the students?"

The lass shook her head no.

"Well, then, who was it?"

"He made me do it," she finally whispered.

"Who did?"

"He said he'd have us turned out if I did not. That my da would lose his place here, and I as well. That we'd be beggars at the gate."

I did not like the sound of this but I had to keep questioning her. "Who was this, Avice? You must tell me."

Finally, the lass turned to me. "It was Master Clarkson, him that was killed."

There was a fine motive for murder, if ever I'd heard one. For if a daughter of mine had been so shamefully used, I would have torn the man limb from limb.

"When did it start?"

"A few months ago, after he was elected master and moved into that room. He would call me to bring coal or wood to build up the fire, and then he would bar the door. At first he would just touch me. He said I was growing into a fine big girl.

And then . . ." The girl could not finish, but still kept scrubbing at the cauldron. I feared she would fill it with her tears.

"And then what?"

"Master Clarkson said he wouldn't hurt me, but it did hurt, what he did. At least the first time."

It was as if now that the girl had started to speak, she could not stop. I listened while Avice continued.

"But he said I must be quiet and not cry out, and he would give me a silver penny. Then the other times it did not hurt so much, but still I did not like it. He had rotten teeth and his breath stank. But after a time I got more used to it. I did not want us to lose our place. And the master gave me a penny every time. I saved the pennies."

"And your father knew of this?"

"Not at first. But when he accused me last week, I told him."

"So he knew it was Clarkson?"

Avice nodded mutely. "I told him what the master had said. That he'd make beggars of us if I told anyone, and I begged my da to say nothing. I don't want to be a beggar."

"No, you won't be a beggar."

"No," Avice agreed, "I won't. For I've saved my pennies."

I said nothing for a time, wishing the world a different place. What future would there be for a lass got with child whose father was a murderer? No matter how justifiable the act might have been. Still, certain things had to be done.

"Where is your da this morning?" I asked as Avice finally finished cleaning the cauldron.

"Out in the garden."

I went to speak with Ivo first, before I summoned the coroner and Grymbaud. For it did seem as though the killer of Master Clarkson had been found. And as I walked to the vegetable garden in the backland I found I wished that I had been the one to murder Master Clarkson.

I found the old man bent double over his cabbage plants.

"Ivo," I said gently, "I've just been speaking with your daughter.

"Aye."

"Ivo, I know the lass is with child. And I know who the father is. And who his murderer must be."

Ivo looked up at me and I could see his face pale behind the grime of the garden that covered it. "I wish it were me. When I saw my child, with the belly of her beginning to swell—she's but a child, and a good girl. I went to his room that night, after the gates were locked, to speak to him. To tell him it weren't right, what he had done to my lass. I wish I had killed him, may the saints forgive me. But the man was already dead."

"You found him dead?"

"Aye."

"But you said nothing, raised no alarm?"

The old man shook his head obstinately. "No. It was a better end than he deserved. I kicked his body, to make sure he did not live. Then I left him there. And went to the chapel and said a prayer of thanksgiving that he'd bother my lass no more. Then the next morning, when I came to light the fires, I raised the hue and cry."

"You know I will have to tell this to Undersheriff Grymbaud. And it is likely he'll arrest you for murder. You could hang. You'd best tell the truth. Did you kill him?"

"I've already told you I did not. But no man what has a daughter would blame me if I had."

With a heavy heart I left Balliol and walked into town to Oxford Castle to find the undersheriff. The castle looked as though it had seen finer days, but the stone walls still stood, and it looked strong enough. Grymbaud was sitting at a table in his small office, drinking some morning ale and speaking with his deputies. He offered me some ale but I declined. I had not the heart for it.

I told him what I had discovered.

"That is a sad story," said Grymbaud, "but I'm thinking this old man is our murderer."

"Will he hang?" I asked.

"Perhaps. But I doubt a jury of townsfolk would convict him. There's no love lost between the town and the colleges. Ivo's a poor servant and in view of what you've told me of his daughter, the killing might be justifiable."

I sighed with relief, but Grymbaud's next words did not reassure.

"Still, no one likes servants who murder their masters, however provoked. And as it involves a college master, it could go to the chancellor's court—that is the university court. Although Ivo is but a servant, not a clerk. Perhaps the county sheriff will have jurisdiction. But when the students and clergy of the colleges get wind of this, they'll be like to hang him. And then we'll have more riot and bloodshed on our hands. I'd best bring him in to gaol. To the castle gaol, as it is murder. Town offenses are sent to the Boccardo," he explained to me. "If nothing else, the arrest will keep the old man safe until the assizes. I'll see to it." The undersheriff turned to give orders to one of his men, who downed the last of his ale and headed out the door. "Are you coming?" Grymbaud asked me as he stood up and reached for his sword.

I had to, although my soul felt as heavy as lead. I accompanied the undersheriff and his man to the college, where we found Ivo still working among his cabbages. He did not struggle as two burly deputies restrained his hands, still dirty from the garden. His stooped figure looked pathetic, old and tired, held between the guards, but Ivo showed stolid dignity as he repeated to Grymbaud that it was not he who had killed Clarkson. Meanwhile, a crowd of angry students milled around, and as we left the grounds of Balliol and headed through the Northgate back to the castle the crowd grew in size, their noise and shouts rumbling like thunder. A few rocks were hurled but the undersheriff and his men ignored them, elbowing their way through the crowd until, at the last, we reached the castle gate and pushed our way through to it. Grymbaud set guards at the gate, for the crowd was loud, agitated and angry. He gave orders for Ivo to be taken to a cell below and the old man was hustled away by two more guards.

"He'll not be mistreated?" I asked. "He insists he did not do it."

"A confession would be a good thing," Grymbaud returned laconically. "Still, he's but an old man, and sore provoked. No, he'll not be mistreated. But if you don't think him the murderer, you'd best find who killed that cursed pervert. And fast. For I've no wish for bloody riots in the town, nor for the chancellors of that damned university to be breathing hot on my neck for the old man's hanging. And they will do that, never doubt it."

# CHAPTER 9

I had to wait awhile in the castle before the crowd dispersed. The undersheriff offered me a cup of ale, which I drank without thinking, trying to ease the discomfort I felt with what had just passed. Ivo had reason enough to kill Clarkson, and had access to the master's room. He might well have killed the man. I would have, if the lass had been my daughter. But somehow I felt he was innocent.

The wrongness of it irritated like a blister from a shoe that cramped too tightly. Ivo, although tall, was bent and stiff with age, and I wondered if the old man possessed the strength to slay Clarkson. Although anger could have given his blow added power, and Clarkson had been caught unawares, from behind. The thought of Ivo's old stooped body in fetters in a dungeon made me profoundly uncomfortable, and yet I did not see what else I could have done.

I finished my ale and got up to leave the castle. The students and rest of the crowd had disappeared. As I left and made my way through the remaining stragglers I wondered about Mariota and hoped she had had the wit to return to the widow's after the lecture and miss the melee.

So if Ivo was not the guilty party, who was? Phillip Woode? Berwyk? Delacey? I made my way back to Balliol and was thankful to see Mariota, dressed appropriately in women's garb, approaching the college gate from Canditch.

"I am glad to see you, wife," I said, hoping I sounded appropriately severe. "That was a near riot—do you see now why you must not go abroad in that way?"

"I was fine, Muirteach, naught happened to me. I had just returned after the lecture and heard what happened. The poor lass! So they've arrested her father—Muirteach, do you really think he did it? What happened?"

I told her of my conversation with Avice and her father and of Grymbaud's arrest of the old man.

"*Och*, the poor lass. She'll wind up on the street, a beggar, as she feared. Or probably worse. I wonder if the widow needs a serving maid—for I do not see how she can remain at the college once the story comes out."

We entered the college gate, open and untended now that Ivo was gone. We asked for Avice at the kitchens but were told she had vanished. Things were deceptively quiet, as most of the fellows had gone to the afternoon lectures in town. In the back garden, by their hut, Mariota found Avice sobbing into the grimy straw pallet that served as her mattress. Not surprisingly, we discovered that Delacey had turned her out, saying the college could not harbor a whore and the daughter of the murderer of the master of the college.

"But I am sure he would not have done it. That night he just got up to answer the gate," she sobbed. "His back was paining him awful that night. He could not have slain Master Clarkson. But they will hang him and I will have no place to go."

"You have no other relations?" Mariota inquired.

"No. Da came from Brackley as a boy, but we never went there. And then we heard they were all dead, when the plague came through. It was always just me, and Ma when she were alive, and Da. They'll hang him," she repeated. "Why did you have to tell?" Avice looked at me accusingly. "Oh, what will become of me now?"

"Your father will be safer in the gaol than out here, with

bands of students accusing him of killing the master. Those youths are angry—they might well slay him before he comes to trial. And he has not been found guilty as yet. Perhaps the jury will acquit him."

"But when will that be? And what's to become of me," Avice sobbed again. "Where am I to go?"

I thought of Mistress Bonefey. Perhaps if Widow Tanner would not take the girl, Mistress Bonefey might be prevailed to.

"You can come with us," said Mariota. "Gather your things together. We will find a place for you."

As we left the college and walked down Canditch toward Widow Tanner's, someone threw a clod of mud, which caught the lass square on the cheek. I turned but saw no one.

When we arrived at the widow's, Mariota took Avice to explain the situation to our landlady. I wondered how successful my wife would be, but she and Widow Tanner seemed on fine terms, so I hoped something could be done for the lass. Meanwhile, I went to our rooms and saw the door to Donald's chamber open. A murmur of voices came from inside. I poked my head in and saw Anthony and Crispin, as well as Donald, sitting on the bed drinking from a flask of wine. When they saw me, they burst into excited questions all at once.

"Is it true the old gardener killed Master Clarkson?"

"I heard they'll hang him tomorrow!"

"And that Avice was the master's whore?"

"They said they found a bloodied knife in his cottage—that he had stabbed the master with it."

"No, Crispin, that cannot be true," Donald interjected, "for I myself saw the body. There were no stab wounds on it."

I tried to quiet them down and told them what had happened, that Ivo had been taken to gaol in the castle and was awaiting trial. "And Avice has lost her position. She's here now, in hopes the Widow Tanner needs a serving maid."

At this Crispin looked suggestively at Anthony and my arms ached with the desire to give them both a clout. "No, none of that," I added. "The poor lass may well have lost her father. Master Clarkson abused the girl, and she is but a child. She was not his willing whore. And if I hear a one of you speaking of her with disrespect, I'll knock your brains out. Do not think I will not do it."

I must have made some impression on the boys, for apart from a scowl on Donald's face and some raised eyebrows that I chose to ignore, they settled down.

"So you have solved the murder," crowed Donald after a minute. "I knew you would. Wasn't I telling you both about the murders Muirteach has solved for my father in the Isles?"

"I am not altogether convinced that Ivo murdered Master Clarkson," I admitted to them. "Although he certainly had cause."

"Well then, who?" asked Donald, and I had to admit I did not know.

I left the boys and encountered Mariota in the hall outside our chamber. "Widow Tanner has agreed to take the lass, for a time," Mariota told me, much to my relief. "At least until her father's case is tried."

"And she knows of her condition?"

"Aye, Muirteach. The woman has a kind heart. And no children of her own. So perhaps the lass will fare well here."

I hoped so. Despite all the happenings of the morning, it was yet but mid-day and Widow Tanner called us all for dinner. Anthony, Crispin and Donald emerged from Donald's room and our landlady gave permission for the boys to stay and eat. It was not long before all three were spooning stew onto their trenchers and eating with abandon. I thought perhaps Anthony and Crispin stayed to get a glance at Avice, but she remained hidden in the kitchens. *So now she is a seductress, a woman of mystery,* I thought to myself cynically, remembering the girl's scared rabbity face.

"Did you attend lectures this morning?" I asked Donald.

"Yes, until we heard the uproar in the streets."

"And whose lecture?"

"Brother Eusebius," contributed Crispin, in between mouthfuls of bread and stew.

"I am tired of grammar," Anthony declared, reaching for another piece of bread. "And he makes it dull."

"I cannot imagine anyone making it of interest," Donald said. "It is dull as dry bones."

Not for the first time I wondered at the Lord of the Isles' ambition to have a scholar for a son. The man wasted his money and my time here.

"And what of Jonetta?" asked Donald. "Have they found aught of her? Perhaps Ivo killed her too."

Crispin snorted.

"It is thought she ran away with a chapman," I said. "Actually, it was Brother Eusebius himself who saw them together, a few nights before she went missing. Doubtless she is enjoying the wandering life with her chapman even now."

"And breaking her mother's and father's hearts as well," Mariota put in tartly. "I wonder who wrote that strange manuscript you found?" she asked after a moment, to change the subject. "Have you uncovered any more of that mysterious writing?"

"A few more pages," Donald admitted. "But there are no more pictures of those women."

"I know," Crispin added, disappointed. "I have soaked many of the parchments, and looked thoroughly, but there are no more women."

"There are some that look like zodiac wheels, and some of plants," said Anthony.

"Perhaps you could recognize them, Mariota," Donald added as he finished the last of his stew. "If it is an herbal indeed. After all, you are a Beaton. Her father," he explained to the other boys, "is a famous physician."

"Aye, perhaps we could learn enough from that to translate some of the words. For it's in no language that I recognize. Go and get them, Donald."

Widow Tanner had come in to clear the table and Donald returned from his chamber a few minutes later with a pile of parchments. We spread them out on the table and puzzled over the sheets for a time, but none of us could make any sense of the strange script or the faint illustrations.

"The plants are like none I recognize," Mariota admitted, confounded. "See, this one could be mandrake, but the leaves are not right. Still, I suppose it could be an herbal."

"Do you think it is in cipher?" I asked.

"But why?"

"Perhaps it is an alchemical manual," Anthony suggested. His voice cracked a bit with youthful excitement. "Perhaps it is the receipt for the Philosopher's Stone that can change things to gold."

"If we could decipher it we would be rich!" Crispin added.

"And no doubt they'd want to keep such information secret and write it in cipher," Mariota said. "But these pictures do not seem alchemical in nature. It is puzzling. Muirteach, perhaps you can decipher it."

"There are strange characters here, neither Latin nor any other language I recognize."

"Master Berwyk spoke in a disputation once of Friar Bacon," Anthony put in suddenly. "They called him Doctor Mirabilis— the wonderful doctor. He worked here in Oxford long ago and wrote of ciphers in one of his texts."

I was amazed that Anthony remembered anything he had

heard, but Master Berwyk was popular with the students and an interesting speaker.

"Show it to him, or the other masters at the college," Mariota suggested. "You are friendly with Master Berwyk, are you not, Muirteach? Doesn't he study natural philosophy?" How Mariota had discovered that, I did not know. "It would be very interesting to hear what he might say about it."

"It might be interesting but I've other matters to attend to," I replied, frustrated. "Leave it to the lads. You can ask him, boys, if you wish. Show him the parchments and see what he says of them."

I had plenty of other more serious matters to deal with, a murderer to unmask, and no leisure time to be following a wild goose chase, no matter how intriguing. I left the boys and Mariota still puzzling over the parchments and paced the streets, wondering how Ivo was being treated in his prison cell.

The next morning I rose early. Donald still snored in his chamber but Mariota was already dressed as "William." I had it in mind to speak further with Phillip Woode and so, as the sun brightened, I walked along Canditch with "William" until I reached Balliol Hall. I said a silent prayer for my wife's safety as she continued walking to Northgate, even as I cursed her stubbornness. Then I entered the college and set out to find Phillip Woode.

I found him still abed and deduced he had been at the drink the night before. He was unshaven and his chamber in disarray, with several books piled up untidily on a desk. There were no signs of Phillip's roommate, although the room held two beds and two desks, and I judged that he was still absent from Oxford. I shook Phillip Woode on the shoulder but he only snored more loudly. I went to the narrow window and threw open the wooden shutter, letting in the morning sunlight and crisp air.

"Wake up," I said, shaking him again. "I need to speak with you."

Phillip stirred and opened one eye. "Muirteach, what is it you want?"

"I need to talk with you."

"Now? I was late to bed."

"Now."

Phillip sat up and reached for his shirt, which was piled in a heap at the foot of the bed. "What is all this about?" he asked, his voice muffled by the garment.

"You know they've arrested Ivo for Clarkson's murder."

Phillip's head popped through the neck of his shirt, his hair rumpled. "Aye, I had heard of that. Of course. There was talk of nothing else here yesterday."

"Well, the night Clarkson was murdered, did you hear anything? What direction did Ivo come from when he unlocked the gate?"

"How am I to know," Phillip returned as he pulled on his *braies*. "The gate was closed. You can't see through."

"Do you remember anything?"

"I was drunk, Muirteach. You know that, you yourself left me at the gate." He stood up and poured some water into a basin and washed his face.

"Well, how long did it take for Ivo to open up?"

"It seems it took a good long time." Phillip made a face. "Faugh! My mouth tastes like an old drain." He rinsed his mouth and spat into the bowl, then reached for his hose that lay on the floor.

"It seemed a long time," he repeated. "But his cottage is far in the back lot, so that would only be expected." Phillip finished pulling on his hose and tying the points.

"But you heard no noise or such to tell you which direction he came from?"

"I might have heard a door slam. The door to the hall, perhaps. But I can't really be sure." Phillip turned to face me. "What is this all about, Muirteach?"

"I was just thinking perhaps you might have heard something that would clear the old man."

"But the authorities have him in custody." Phillip paused and stared at me a moment. "You don't think he did it, do you?"

"He denies it."

Phillip pulled his tunic over his shirt. "He's always struck me as a harmless old man. He's worked here for years, and seems to care for nothing but his cabbages. You're right, it is hard to imagine him striking the master and murdering him. What would be the reason? His daughter? I heard something about that last night, and I also heard that fool Delacey had dismissed the poor girl. There were wild stories flying around. The tavern keeper at the King's Lion was surly, and glared at all the students in the place as if we were about to ravish his daughters there on the table."

I told him more about Avice.

"That explains the tavern keeper's attitude. The townsfolk hate us, but depend on our business. It doesn't take much to start trouble." Phillip pulled his academic hood and cloak on over his *cotehardie,* deep in thought. "Ivo might well have killed Clarkson. I would, if it were my sister used in such a way. Ivo dotes on that girl. She's still but a child."

That was the same way I had felt, so I could not fault Phillip for that.

"But you did not like the man anyway. I myself heard you arguing."

"Yes, my life is easier now that the man is dead," Phillip mused. He could almost have been speaking to himself. "I think

I might have a better chance with Master Berwyk. He might well approve me, should he become the next Master of the college. Then I could enroll in the medical lectures."

"So you had reason to kill Clarkson."

"Is that why you woke me up this morning? To accuse me of murder? Muirteach, I did not kill the master. I went right to my room, as I told you, and to sleep. I saw no one and heard nothing, and know nothing more about it."

"But you have no proof. No one saw you come in."

"Just Ivo, when he opened the gate, and he did not follow me to the hall. He went back toward his cottage. And according to the stories, Ivo said he found Clarkson dead earlier that evening."

"So you cannot clear the old man, and neither can he clear you."

"That is true, Muirteach. But you must believe me. I did not kill Clarkson, and if Ivo did not, as you seem to believe, then who did?"

I had no answer for that. "What about Jonetta?" I asked.

Phillip sighed. "That again. Weren't you satisfied with the answers I gave the undersheriff? I fancied her and she ran away with a chapman. At least that's what I've heard. I know naught of her whereabouts, and I wish that I did. Now, you'll excuse me. I have a lecture to attend on School Street." Phillip brushed past me and left the room.

# CHAPTER 10

It seemed to me later that morning as I munched on a meat pastry I'd purchased from a street seller that everyone had reason to kill Master Clarkson. Phillip Woode had argued with him, Master Berwyk wanted his book back, Delacey was jealous and had wanted to be Master of Balliol himself, while Ivo had the best reason of all.

Although Master Berwyk seemed to be in the clear, since he had stayed that night with Mistress Bonefey. However, if Clarkson had indeed been dead earlier in the evening, as Ivo insisted, perhaps Berwyk had killed him earlier, just after the evening meal, and then gone to Torvilda's. And if Berwyk had spent the night at Mistress Bonefey's, then Delacey also had no one to vouch for his movements that night. Mariota thought the man had been dead for several hours before he was found.

The normal bustle of Oxford town seemed to have an edge that day. The pie man was sullen and glowered at me as he sold me my pastry. There seemed to be an undercurrent and as a group of students walked by, on their way to School Street, I overheard a voice whisper behind me, "There's them that mistreat young girls."

"Aye," replied another voice. "It makes me sick to see it, those young clerks walking around, thinking they're above the law. Minor orders, faugh." I heard the sound of spitting.

I turned, curious to see who was speaking, but the owners of the voices had melted away into the crowd. Just then I saw Un-

124

dersheriff Grymbaud approach, and I guessed that was why they had left.

"Muirteach," Grymbaud greeted me.

"How is your prisoner?" I asked.

"He's well enough. Safer perhaps in his cell than he would be at that college. What's become of his daughter?"

I told the sheriff that Widow Tanner had taken in Avice.

"That's good," the undersheriff grunted.

"When will the assize be held?"

"I'm thinking we'll wait and call it after things have settled down a bit here in the town. The High Sheriff will not be back from London for some time; he leaves most things to me. There are no Royal Assizes, so it is up to the Justice to call the assize when he wishes. We work well together; he will listen to me." The undersheriff surveyed the townsfolk milling about the market. "I don't like the feel of this crowd. It's always the case, when something goes wrong at a college. Or in the town. It's like living with cats and dogs, at each other's throats. Even when things are calm it's an uneasy peace."

I thought things did not seem so calm today, and worried for my stubborn wife. And that made me think of Jakeson's daughter. "What of Jonetta?" I asked. "Have you found them, or heard anything?"

"I've sent messages to the other large towns, to be on the watch for a chapman and a woman traveling with him. So far we've heard nothing." He sighed heavily. "If these girls but knew the heartache they caused their parents, but they think of nothing but themselves."

"Aye," I agreed, in perfect sympathy with Grymbaud's sentiments. "There's no stopping a woman once she's set on something."

"Young people today think only of their own pleasure and show no respect for their elders. How is your pastry?" he asked, changing the subject abruptly.

"Not bad," I replied.

"It makes me hungry. I'm on edge, I vow. It's all this business with Clarkson. I'm hoping we'll be spared a riot."

I watched while Grymbaud bought a large pastry from the pie man. "It's good," he said, as he took a bite. I smelled a savory aroma of onion and meat and watched as Grymbaud licked a crumb from one of his fingers. "He swore it was rabbit," the undersheriff said. "I hope so."

I hoped so too, having by now finished my own pie, and decided to return to our lodgings, hoping that Mariota had returned safely from the lectures. Then I thought better of that and started walking toward School Street. Perhaps I could intercept her there and ensure she got home safely. I did not like the tenor of this crowd.

School Street was crowded with young men just out from their lectures. I failed to see Mariota but heard voices I thought I recognized and saw Donald, Anthony and Crispin ducking into a tavern. Apparently they had seen me and were hoping to slip away. I followed them in and saw them just sitting down at a rough wooden table.

"Best to return to your lodgings," I told the boys as I joined them. "The townsfolk are still upset with Ivo's arrest, and things could get ugly."

"I'm not afraid of a few town folk," Crispin declared defiantly as the landlord glowered at him.

"Come, let's have some ale. Muirteach, aren't you thirsty?" Donald wheedled.

"No, I am not, and neither are you. We're leaving now." I left a generous coin on the table and hustled the three boys out of the tavern and back toward Smithgate.

"We asked Master Berwyk about those parchments," Anthony

finally said as the three boys sullenly walked up the street with me.

"And what did he say?"

Anthony shrugged his bony shoulders. "He knew nothing of them. But he kept one and said he would show it to the other masters."

"Aye," Donald put in suddenly. "He kept one of the sheets with the plants and one with the writing."

"He did not keep the one with the women on it," said Crispin. "We didn't show him that one."

I grunted something by way of reply and decided to leave Crispin's fixation alone. I also did not intervene when the boys stopped at a vintner's and purchased a jug of wine, but I was glad to leave the walls of the town and enter the slightly less crowded suburbs, and even gladder to see the walls of the widow's house as we approached. Let the lads drink themselves silly in the safety of Widow Tanner's house; at least they'd not be in the midst of a riot. For I felt a storm was gathering, and I did not like the feeling.

The weather did not help, either. The day was unseasonably hot for so close to Michaelmas, the air sticky, and dark clouds hovered ominously in the sky. We passed Brother Eusebius walking toward Old Balliol Hall, coming the opposite direction from us down Canditch. He seemed intent on something and barely acknowledged us until I greeted him when we nearly collided with each other.

"Oh, excuse me," he said. "I was pondering something—a tenet of natural philosophy." He glanced at the boys' jug. "And so you boys are off to study?"

"Indeed they are," I assured him. "It does not seem a good day to be in town. The mood of the townsfolk is ugly. It is all this arrest of Ivo, and his daughter. And then the missing tavern girl, that makes it worse."

"Ah yes, how was she called?"

"Jonetta," Donald said. "Did Master Berwyk show you that strange parchment we found?"

Eusebius looked curious. "What parchment was that, young sir?"

"Master Berwyk has it," Donald replied. "It has some strange drawings and words on it we could not decipher. It is very odd."

"How did you come by it?" asked Eusebius.

"It is just a palimpsest, left on some used parchment we bought from the bookman," I put in.

"Doubtless it is some scribbling or an old text," Eusebius mused. "You said it was undecipherable?"

"We could make no sense of it," I replied. "It is certainly not Latin, and my wife knows Greek, but she could make no sense of the writing either. It was written in none of those languages."

"A mystery," Eusebius said. "Curious. Well, I must be off to my studies. Good day to you, young sirs." He wandered down the road, again lost in thought.

We had reached Anthony and Crispin's lodging house by this time. Their tenement lay halfway down Canditch, close to the Widow Tanner's. The boys went inside to put some gear away and left me alone standing in the middle of the street with Donald.

"Are you going to study?" I asked, eyeing the wine my charge was carrying.

"We can study and drink wine at the same time, well enough."

The other two boys returned and I abandoned them at our landlady's, with strict orders not to go into town. I turned my back on the house, hoping they would not disobey me. Perhaps they'd be drunk enough when they finished the wine that they'd have no desire to return inside the city walls.

Contemplating these happy thoughts, I walked back toward Balliol with the intention of talking to Delacey. Why had he lied about Berwyk's presence at the hall the night Clarkson had been killed? That would be of interest. And I had not yet seen Mariota.

That concern at least was allayed when I spotted "William's" blue hood and tunic on Canditch as my wife made her way back to Widow Tanner's.

"William," I called.

Mariota did not heed me. I crossed the street and planted myself in front of her. "William," I repeated.

"*Och.*" Mariota flushed when she looked up and recognized me. "Hello, Muirteach. You were calling me."

"If you're going to masquerade under this name, you'd best learn to answer to it," I observed. "Is all well?"

"Yes, Muirteach." I thought my wife looked impatient.

"The mood in the town is ugly."

My wife shook her head a little as if to shake off some troublesome fly. "Aye, I noticed. But no one interfered with me. I'm safe enough, Muirteach."

"I'm glad to see you safe outside the city walls, nonetheless."

"And where are you off to?" asked Mariota, changing the subject.

I told her about Delacey's lie.

"That's curious. Why would he lie about that? He must have known that Berwyk wouldn't lie for him. What reason could he have?"

"That is what I intend to find out."

I left my wife walking toward our lodgings and turned into the college, hoping to find Delacey. He was just leaving the gates, walking brusquely into town.

"Master Delacey, I would speak with you."

"I have a lecture to give. In town." Master Delacey did not slow his pace, and much as I hated to return to town, I did not want to lose the opportunity to speak with him. I walked alongside, keeping up with his brisk step, and although my bad leg bothered me somewhat the anger I felt made the ache less noticeable.

"You lied to me," I said to him as we walked. "I would know why."

Delacey finally turned and faced me. His beard was growing out over his florid cheeks. He needed a shave. "Lied to you about what?"

"About Master Berwyk. You said he had returned to the college the night Clarkson was murdered, yet his leman claims he spent the night with her."

"And would not his whore lie for him?"

"I have two other witnesses who also claim he was there all the night. So it is you who are lying. Why?"

Delacey did not deny it. "That is my own concern." His stubble-covered chin thrust forward ominously as he continued walking.

"No, sir, it is my concern. I am investigating Clarkson's murder and must know where you were."

We passed the pie man's stall and for a moment I smelled fresh-baked meat pastries, but we moved quickly on and less palatable smells filled my nostrils.

"I was in my chamber, as I said, studying."

"But you were alone. No one can vouch for you."

Delacey shrugged his broad shoulders as we walked.

"You could have killed Clarkson," I continued.

"What reason would I have to kill the master?"

"You had wanted to be elected Master of the College. Perhaps with Clarkson gone you would be chosen."

Delacey laughed. "What kind of man do you take me for? I study the law, Muirteach. If I had wanted to remove Clarkson I'd have found lawful means to do it."

"Perhaps. But what if you had a sudden opportunity? I can

see you're a man with a temper."

"Aye, I have a temper. It is a grievous fault. I'm trying to restrain it even now." I saw Delacey's fists clench a moment, as if he wanted to throttle me. The sentiment was mutual. Then he took a breath, and his hands relaxed as he continued in a more even tone. "Besides, what would it profit me to kill Clarkson? There's no guarantee I'd be the next Master. The fellows could well elect someone else."

"There's no one who can vouch for you?" I fancied Delacey hesitated a fraction before he answered.

"I saw the other fellows at the evening meal. But no one after the meal, not until Berwyk arrived early the next morning and we found Clarkson's body." He turned his head again to scrutinize me while we walked. "They've already arrested Ivo. It was you yourself who called the authorities. Why are you still pursuing this matter? Don't you believe he did it?"

"I have doubts. He had reason to kill the man, well enough, and the opportunity. But he insists he is innocent."

Delacey laughed harshly. "So would any man with sense."

"I'm not convinced. And I'd not like an innocent man to hang for a murder he did not commit. Especially not if it was I that put him in prison."

We had reached School Street by now and Delacey's lecture hall. "That is fair enough," he answered me. "But I must go. I regret I know nothing to help you."

"And no one can vouch for you?" I asked again, like a stubborn dog gnawing at the same scrap of bone.

Delacey hesitated.

"No one?" I repeated.

"No one," he replied, suddenly decisive. "Make what you want of it, Muirteach."

Delacey abruptly turned toward the lecture hall, leaving me standing on School Street. A younger student dressed in the robes of an undergraduate had been hovering on the street. I saw him approach Master Delacey as he entered the lecture hall. The two spoke briefly, then Delacey passed through the door, leaving the youth outside. I wondered who the boy was. He looked somewhat familiar, perhaps another student I'd seen about the town or the colleges. Perhaps Delacey tutored him. While I wondered, the lad disappeared into the crowd.

Despite the undercurrents in the city, the taverns and ale-houses in the area of the schools seemed well visited. I passed a drunken group of students, dressed in rich finery, walking three abreast down High Street while some shopkeepers glowered disapprovingly. I walked more speedily, hoping to pass the group and put some distance between us. Of a sudden an upper window opened and, with no warning cry, a pot of filth was dumped into the roadway directly in the oncoming students' path, drenching one with a disagreeable mixture of piss and some solid matter.

"Did you see that?" the victim demanded as he attempted to shake the shit from his gown. "That was deliberately done!" He gestured angrily and shouted, "Show yourself, you!"

The shutter above them slammed shut.

"They can't ill-treat you that way," his friend said.

"No, I'll not stand for it," the youth declared, fingering his sword. "They'll answer to me for this."

"They'll answer to us all," his friend added with some swagger.

The shopkeepers lining the street meanwhile had heard the uproar and many had come to stand outside their stalls, hands crossed, glaring at the students, while other clerks had spilled onto the street from the taverns.

"Who lives above?" demanded one of the original three. "For they meant to sully my friend, dumping filth out from above with no warning cry."

" 'Tis no more than such as you deserve. Debauching young maids," a voice muttered from the crowd.

" 'Tis my house and no doubt my good wife emptying out some filth. And it landed right on target," joked a cordwainer, a brawny man.

"Aye, like attracts like," the pie-seller added.

The other merchants laughed with him and the young student purpled with rage. The undersheriff and his men were nowhere to be seen, and I found myself fervently wishing I was anywhere but where I was. I saw one of the merchants reach for his knife and another fondle his cudgel, while the rich student made to draw his sword.

A loose stone clattered on the pavement and for a timeless second the two sides faced each other. Then another stone flew and the moment was broken, the groups flying at each other's throats. Cries went up, "A riot, havoc!" and more students came rushing from the area of the schools while merchants and apprentices spilled out of the shops, armed with staves and knives. I heard housewives slamming shutters closed above stairs as I tried, unsuccessfully, to dodge the blow of a staff.

It wasn't my quarrel. I ran, and took the first turn I came upon, a small alleyway between two shops. Thankfully, the hit had not been a hard one and no one thought to pursue me. I made my way through some back gardens and over toward Northgate. From here, the noise of the melee was somewhat lessened and I caught a glimpse of Grymbaud's men rounding the corner onto High Street toward the fracas. I left the town and academics to their fun and gratefully headed back to the suburbs, hoping the city walls could contain the mayhem.

# CHAPTER 11

I arrived back at the Widow Tanner's as the sun set, casting a red glow over everything. I fancied it looked like blood. I was glad to enter our lodgings and leave the ugly light behind. Rufous, the widow's little dog, yapped at me as I crossed the threshold and I bent to give it a pat. It licked my fingers and as I caressed the warm fur I wished again for my own dog. I wanted only to relax and shut the outer world away for a bit. However, the sound of a discordant lute playing from Donald's chamber made me suspect that would not be my fate. My head throbbed as I climbed the stairs to our rooms.

I entered our chamber. Mariota sat at the desk, reading some medical text. She looked up and saw me. "Muirteach, you look a fright! What has happened?"

"There was a riot in town."

"Your head—*mo chridhe*, let me get a compress. It is bleeding and swelling like a goose egg. Does it ache?" Mariota stepped outside our chamber and called for Avice to bring a basin of water and some cloths.

Perhaps that blow had not been as glancing as I thought. I explained what had happened while Mariota busied herself gathering materials for a compress and Avice watched, wide-eyed. Rufous had followed Avice into our chamber and milled around excitedly until Mariota petted the dog and he settled down.

Avice seemed a bit dazed; perhaps the blood on my head

made her think of her poor father. I realized as I looked at her that I did indeed have a splitting ache in my head. Just then Donald, Crispin and Anthony burst into the room and Rufous began to bark again. I was thankful to see that Donald had left his lute in his chamber.

"We heard you speak of a riot. Through the walls," Donald said. I wondered briefly what else Donald could hear that way, not that Mariota and I had been particularly loving of late. "What happened?" my charge demanded, sounding for a moment like his father.

"There was a riot. Near School Street. Some dame dumped her chamber pot out on a student and I had the misfortune to be caught up in it."

"Are they still fighting?" asked Crispin.

"We should go and see—what if they need help? Do you have a sword, Donald? Go and get it," said Anthony.

"You'll do no such thing," I said. "Grymbaud and his men were coming just as I left. He's no doubt put a stop to it now. You'll all three of you stay here, out of harm's way."

"Aye," said Mariota with some vehemence, as she wound a bandage around my head. "Do you want me to have to nurse the three of you after you've gotten your heads bashed in?"

"If I'd been there, with my sword, I'd have spitted the man who cudgeled you," Donald swore, surprising me with this declaration. "I'd have run the bastard through."

"I'm home safe enough now. But thank you," I offered, saying another private prayer of thanksgiving that my charge had not been caught up in the mess. I was supposed to be watching over him, after all.

I noticed Crispin eyeing Avice in a speculative manner and was glad when Mariota quickly dismissed the lass. Rufous followed her down the stairs.

"That wench is the cause of all this trouble," Crispin declared.

"Indeed not," Mariota retorted. Her voice rose as she spoke. "What kind of a churl are you? What happened to her is not her fault; it's Clarkson who should be blamed for it and he's no doubt paying for it even now, wherever he's gone to. Avice is a mere child. It's the men who are causing these problems in the town. Now out of here, all of you. Muirteach needs to rest and from the way you're speaking I've no wish to be near you."

I did not know if Crispin was chastened by her words or not but at least the boys left our room. After a few moments the sound of Donald's lute and voices raised in a drinking song filtered through the walls. I groaned.

"It is bad, is it not?" Mariota murmured. "They are abysmally out of tune. Here, I'll give you something to help you rest."

I drank the mixture she brought mc, lcancd back against the bolster and closed my eyes with relief. When I opened them a few minutes later Mariota was sitting at her desk again, reading. It had grown dark and she'd lit a candle. I watched her for a long time through half-closed eyes, until the boys stopped singing.

The next morning Anthony and Crispin burst in while we were sitting at the widow's table breaking our fast on small ale and her good bread. Widow Tanner was a fine cook.

"They've cancelled all the lectures!" Crispin announced.

"Because of the riots," Anthony added. "Although Grymbaud's men stopped the fight last afternoon before it amounted to much."

Avice brought the lads some glasses of ale and I thought I saw her smile shyly at Anthony, who flushed. Then she glared at me and scuttled away to the kitchen. I drank more of my ale, wishing it were something stronger.

"A free day," Donald exclaimed. "No boring lectures to attend. Let's go get some wine in town."

"You are not to go into town," I said, wondering if the chancellor had been wise to cancel classes. Students in the taverns would be worse than students in lectures.

Widow Tanner bustled in with some more bread. "What is it they are wanting? Wine? They can get it from the vintner up the road, just past the tannery. Master Gibbes. It's the last house before the Benedictines' College. The boys will not need to go into town and can keep well away from any troubles."

"Thank you. Perhaps I'll go with them. Would you like some claret for the house?"

"No need, sir, but thank you for the thought." With that Widow Tanner returned to the kitchen.

If the lads were buying wine, I thought, I might as well buy some also. Although whisky would have been more to my taste. My wife would not mind me. I was tired of playing nursemaid to a young lordling with no sense, obnoxious companions and an ill-tuned lute, and even more wearied at the thought of poor Ivo in gaol while his daughter looked at me like I was the devil himself for sending her father to prison. It might be a good day to get very drunk.

The sun shone benignly over a blue sky as the three lads and I made our way to Master Gibbes's. The vintner's wife happily sold us a small jug of claret, her first sale of the morning I surmised, and we started back to Widow Tanner's. It seemed the boys intended to spend the day in Donald's chambers again. At least that way it would be easier to keep an eye on them.

Anthony was carrying the jug. Donald felt it beneath his dignity to do so and Crispin, who more and more minded me of a stoat, had managed not to be involved. Suddenly I saw Anthony stumble as he kicked a stone in the road. He recovered himself but then set the jug down.

"What is it?" I asked, stopping. Donald and Crispin were far ahead and seemed not to have noticed Anthony's fall. "Are you all right? Is the jug too heavy for you?"

"No, I'm managing it well enough. It's just this—look."

Anthony picked up something that glimmered. "It was under the stone. It's pretty."

It was a pewter medal on a broken chain, similar to a pilgrim's badge, but with a bail so it could be worn around the neck. The design was a curious one, of the pious pelican feeding her young.

"It is indeed. Well, you are the finder so that means it is yours. What will you do with it?"

"I'm not sure," Anthony muttered and thrust it into his pouch. He picked up the jug and we followed Donald and Crispin back to the widow's.

Later, after the noon meal, we heard noisy uproar from the city walls, and the sound of excited running in Canditch. Then I heard the front door slam. The boys had disappeared before I could stop them. I swore and looked in Donald's room. It was empty, as was the wine jug on the floor, and Donald's sword was gone. I swore again and started out after them. All I needed was for the son of the Lord of the Isles to get himself killed in an Oxford riot.

There was a crowd of students headed into the town and I followed them, looking for the three boys as I rushed along, jostled by others. The crowd grew thicker at the intersection of Northgate and High streets and reached its height at a small chapel on a corner. The chapel, surrounded by townsfolk, seemed to be afire; smoke was drifting out of the thatch on the roof. I saw the undersheriff and some of his men pushing townsfolk back from the door. A chain of men had formed with water buckets, ineffectually trying to put out the fire.

"What's happening?" I asked a student next to me, as we were both elbowed aside by some burly graduate students.

"A fight started. There were some university men that ran inside, but some townsfolk trapped them in there and set fire to the roof."

"Who was in the chapel?" I looked frantically through the crowd for my charge while my heart pounded rapidly.

"Some Balliol men, I heard."

"Are they out?"

"I think so. The undersheriff and his men came and put a stop to it. They're bastards." The student spat. "All these townsfolk are. Stupid fools."

I caught a glimpse of Donald on the other side of the crowd and some of the tightness in my chest began to ease. I headed toward him. The crowd began to disperse, urged on by Grymbaud and his assistants, although more men were pressed into the water chain. Mostly townsfolk, but I saw a few students as well. The smoke decreased, and I saw Anthony's red head in the line.

I spied Phillip Woode, Master Delacey and Brother Eusebius, looking somewhat dazed, outside the chapel as I went over and spoke to Donald. "You are well?"

Donald shrugged. "I was in no danger, Muirteach. You're worse than a nursemaid."

I ignored his last comment. Grymbaud saw me and motioned me toward him.

"Stay here," I told Donald. "I'll return directly."

Donald ignored me and followed me over to the undersheriff.

"I'm glad to see you, Muirteach. This is a bad thing."

"It looks as though the fire is under control. And it seems no one was seriously hurt."

"Aye, I've arrested the cordwainer for arson. We've witnesses that saw him set the roof afire."

"What of the other men involved? Jakeson, and the rest of them?"

"It'll do no good to have half the town arrested. I've let them go for now."

"So all's well."

The undersheriff looked grave and I got the feeling all was not as well as it seemed. "Come inside, Muirteach."

A brawny guard stood at the front of the chapel. He let us pass but kept Donald outside, to my relief. I followed Grymbaud in. The chapel was dark and smelled of a thick smoke that stung my eyes and caught in my throat.

"What is it?" I managed to ask the undersheriff as he walked toward the interior of the chapel. I felt a sinking feeling in my guts as I followed the man.

"Here."

I looked and as my eyes adjusted to the smoky dimness saw a form lying behind the rood screen. I followed the undersheriff closer and recognized the bulk as a body, wearing the dark robes of a college master.

"Who is it?"

Grymbaud rolled the body over. My throat clenched as I saw the white face of Master Berwyk.

"What happened?"

"He looks to have been stabbed. Here, on the backside, is a wound." Even in the dimness, I could see the spreading stickiness of blood on Berwyk's garments.

"Is he alive?"

Grymbaud shrugged, but just then we heard a groan.

"He's alive—barely."

"Let me send for my wife. She's a physician, with experience in wounds and such matters."

Grymbaud had no objection. He agreed it might be better than calling a physician from the college, and even sent an armed guard with the message to the Widow Tanner's to escort Mariota back. While I waited for her I spoke with the undersheriff as we tried to make Berwyk a bit more comfortable. He had lost a great deal of blood and was not conscious. I prayed that Mariota would arrive soon.

"Do you think he was attacked outside, and ran in here for safety? Who was with him?"

From what Grymbaud had been able to learn, Berwyk, along with some other masters, had been walking down High Street when several townsfolk accosted the university men. There was an altercation, and the men had run in here for safety. "So probably he was stabbed outside the church and ran in here for sanctuary."

"Who were the townsfolk involved?"

"We've already arrested the cordwainer for arson, and the mercer seems to have been in it. Also a bookseller. That tavern keeper was present as well, the same one whose daughter ran off."

"Jakeson."

"Aye, he's the one."

"Have they found the knife?"

Grymbaud shook his head no, and I watched his lips tighten.

"What of the other clerks in the church with him? Did they see anything?"

"We've yet to speak with them. There was a great deal of confusion."

"Who were they?"

"That tall blonde master."

"That would be Eusebius."

The undersheriff nodded. "Aye. And Phillip Woode, and one other. The short little arrogant bastard."

"Delacey?"

"Aye, that's the one."

"Well, they must know something of it, then. Why were they in town?"

"It seems they had come to check on something at one of the lecture halls, to see if it was safe. They heard a rumor it had been set afire."

"Were they ambushed, then?"

Grymbaud shook his head, reminding me of a bear. "That does not seem to have been the way of it. They ran into the townsfolk on High Street and words were exchanged. Phillip Woode was accused by the cordwainer of molesting Jakeson's daughter, and that set the whole thing off."

"What a waste. Berwyk's a good man."

"And one of my townsfolk is close to being a murderer."

Just then the door of the chapel creaked open, emitting a ray of light and with it the welcome form of my wife.

"We're back here," I called and took a deep breath. Surely Mariota could save the man.

Mariota examined the wound and bound it tightly to stop the bleeding. "He's lost a great deal of blood and the wound is deep. It will be prone to fester. Is there an infirmary?"

"Best to take him to his college. Unless you could nurse him?" Grymbaud asked Mariota.

"He has a woman," I put in, "that lives on Pennyfarthing Street. She would want to know of this, and she could nurse him. She is called Torvilda." Grymbaud sent a messenger off to fetch Mistress Bonefey while Mariota sponged Berwyk's face and gave him some tincture of poppy as he groaned. Even in the darkness of the chapel I could see how pale he was.

"Fetch a stretcher," Grymbaud ordered after Torvilda arrived. Her face was nearly as white as her lover's, after she saw him, but she readily agreed to nurse him at her house. It wasn't long before she and Mariota departed, along with some of Grymbaud's men to carry the stretcher and see them to Pennyfarthing Street. Which left me with the undersheriff again.

"We must speak to the other fellows he was with," I said. "Perhaps one of them saw who knifed him."

"Yes, and I'll do some interrogation of my own," Grymbaud replied, blinking a little as we emerged into the afternoon light. "In the meantime, let us not say how severely the master was injured. Pray God he pulls through. The last thing we need is another excuse for the clerks to attack the townsfolk."

I agreed wholeheartedly.

The bucket team had dispersed, and Anthony, Crispin and Donald were not to be seen. Things seemed quiet enough in the town now, with the crowds scattered, but I began to see how deceptive this might be.

I tracked the boys down to a tavern where I saw them sitting at a table with Phillip Woode. The tavern keeper glowered at them and the other students that filled the room, but apparently the pennies the students paid outweighed other concerns. I joined Donald and the others and ordered a cider. The smoke of the chapel had left a scratchy roughness in my throat.

The boys pelted me with questions and I answered that Master Berwyk had been slightly injured but was recovering. Then I asked Phillip Woode what had transpired earlier that day. Phillip had a bruise on one cheek but otherwise seemed unharmed.

"We were at the college, looking at some manuscripts, and a messenger came to the door, saying that the Balliol lecture hall on School Street was in flames. So we grabbed our swords and went to see." He stopped speaking and took a drink from his mug of wine, then shrugged. "When we arrived, there was nothing to be seen out of the ordinary. It was odd."

"Who brought the message?"

"A young student, Eusebius said. I did not see the lad myself."

"So you were on School Street," I prompted.

"Yes, and then we walked back, down High Street. We all thought the matter strange. It was there we saw Master Jakeson and the others. The cordwainer was there and that bookseller, the one we visited. I made the mistake of asking Master Jakeson if he'd heard anything of his daughter."

"The last I heard, she'd run off with the chapman."

"That's what he told me. But then things got ugly, and more townsfolk gathered, and he wanted to know what reason I had to ask after Jonetta. It got out of control quickly. I think Delacey threatened them with the courts and more fines, and none of them liked that. Grymbaud's men were nowhere in sight and someone threw a rock. There was fighting, but eventually we ran. We were greatly outnumbered."

"Did you see who knifed Master Berwyk?"

Phillip shook his head. "Let's get some more wine," he said, and signaled the tavern girl, who approached with alacrity. She did not seem to share her father's distrust of students. At least, I assumed the owner was her father, but the lass eavesdropped shamelessly as she took our order for more wine. "No, I did not see," Phillip answered as the girl delivered a new pitcher of her father's cheapest vintage. "It was all confusion for a time."

"When you reached the chapel, did Berwyk complain of his wound?"

"Not a word. But soon after that we smelled the smoke, so he must have had other things to occupy his mind, as we all did. We could have been trapped like rats and burnt to death." He shuddered, drank deeply and set his cup down.

"Apparently the cordwainer's been arrested for arson," I observed.

"He'll face a steep fine, or other punishment. Since the riots twenty years ago, they've been strict about these disturbances," Phillip said. "As they should be."

"Perhaps it was all a ruse to get you into the town. People are upset about Ivo's arrest; they might well decide to take it out on Balliol masters."

Phillip shrugged. "Perhaps."

"Who do you suppose knifed Master Berwyk?"

"Some cursed townsman."

"Did he have any enemies?"

"I don't know. Ask him. You said he was not sorely injured." Phillip looked puzzled. "Berwyk is generally well liked."

"He claimed the bookseller had his copy of the *Isagoge*—the one Clarkson had stolen and pledged. Berwyk claimed Adam Bookman refused to redeem it to him."

"That's no reason for the bookseller to knife him. Rather the opposite. Berwyk told me he was paying the fee to redeem the book. And Bookman wanted a lot for it—what was it Ralph told me, seven shillings? Now Bookman's lost that money."

"But he still has the *Isagoge*. It's a rare text."

"Yes, and valuable."

"Still, no one saw the bookseller near Berwyk."

"It was chaos, there was a great deal of pushing and jostling. Bookman was in the front of the crowd. I suppose he could have knifed Ralph Berwyk."

# CHAPTER 12

We left the tavern soon after that and walked back to Northgate together. We met with no trouble on that trip.

When I arrived home Mariota had sent a message. She would stay the night at Torvilda's to help tend Master Berwyk. He sounded in a bad way and, worried, I set out again in the dusk after eating a hasty supper with Donald. As I left the house, the sound of Donald's lute drifted out through the shuttered window and made the walk through the darkening streets to Torvilda's house less onerous in comparison.

I arrived to find Master Berwyk still unconscious. He seemed to be running a fever and Torvilda was sponging him with something while Mariota mixed a draught over the fire. An older woman sat anxiously in the chamber, fingering her beads and murmuring prayers. I guessed her to be Berwyk's aunt.

The room was lit by a tallow candle, which gave off a somewhat rank odor that mingled with the sharp scent of vinegar from the compresses and wood smoke from Torvilda's hearth. I recognized yarrow and willow bark among the piles of herbs on the table. The tabby cat and her kittens, their eyes now open, still resided in the box by the hearth. There was no sign of the lodgers Justin and Vortigen, although the door to the other room they rented was closed. Mariota looked up and seemed glad to see me, but Torvilda did not take her eyes from her patient.

"How does he?" I asked.

Mariota shook her head. "The wound went into the abdomen. If it does not fester he might recover, but he is choleric, his humors very unbalanced. We must just wait and see."

The cat left its kittens mewling, got out of the box and rubbed itself around Mariota's ankles.

"There, there, Puss," Mariota said to the cat as she put the draught down on the table. She bent and picked up one of the kittens, which immediately began mewing loudly. The cat made a chirping noise and Mariota set the kitten back down in the box, where the mother joined it. The kittens started to nurse again hungrily.

"Thank you for coming, Muirteach," my wife said to me as she picked up the potion and took it to Master Berwyk's bedside. "But it was not necessary."

"Donald was playing that damned lute," I replied. "I thought to escape the noise."

Mariota smiled a half-smile at my jest and then turned to concentrate on getting her patient to swallow some of the medicine. Torvilda turned to my wife and asked how she thought Master Berwyk fared. Mariota responded that he was in God's hands, not the most reassuring answer. At length Torvilda said something to my wife, then burst into tears, caught up her mantle, and left the house.

"She has gone to church to light some candles for him and pray to the Virgin for his safe recovery," Mariota told me. "We've done what we can here and must wait and see."

"Must you stay the night?" I asked.

"She is distraught and needs company. The lads that lodge here are asleep. And I do not mind staying. I must watch him, for he could easily turn worse. Sometimes there is bleeding in the organs. If we can get him to take the willow bark and his wound does not fester he might do well enough. The next few hours should tell."

Although I am not generally a praying man, I was sorely tempted to join Torvilda at the chapel. What had happened to Master Berwyk was a sad thing, and I was not sure that the townsfolk were to blame for it. But instead of going to the church I stayed with my wife while she ministered to her patient. It seemed a short time before Torvilda returned, her face somewhat more composed.

"How does he?" she asked.

"About the same," Mariota replied. "You should sleep. I'll watch."

Torvilda shook her head no and sat down on a stool by the bed. She took out her wooden beads and began to say the Rosary. The candle flickered and smoked and I began to nod off from where I sat in the room's only chair with a back. Eventually I drifted into an unsteady doze.

A noise roused me. The candle had gone out and the chamber was dimly lit from the coals of the fire, but I saw Mariota bending over Master Berwyk. His aunt stood close by. Torvilda slept on a pallet by the bed.

"Is he awake?" I asked, standing up and stiffly walking to the bedside.

Mariota nodded. Master Berwyk's face was flushed and his eyes glassy. His body seemed to give off heat. He groaned and tossed, then groaned again in pain.

"Is he conscious? Perhaps he knows who did this to him."

"Speak softly, Muirteach. The poor lass is exhausted and just fell asleep."

"Master Berwyk, can you hear me?" I spoke close to his ear.

Berwyk stopped groaning a moment and gave an imperceptible nod.

"Who did this to you? One of the townsfolk?"

He shook his head from side to side, whether to answer my question or just out of pain I could not tell.

"Can you speak? Tell us? Who did this?"

"Behind. Couldn't see."

"Were you in the chapel? Or was it on the street?"

Berwyk closed his eyes and swallowed. "Thirsty—"

"Now, Muirteach, you've bothered him enough." Mariota brought a mug to the bedside. "Let him rest. And we must get this fever down," she whispered, reaching again for the basin and cloths that sat on the small table nearby to sponge down the patient. "He's burning hot."

Torvilda startled awake, saw her lover and sat upright. "He's awake?"

"Yes."

"Ralph, it's Torvilda."

"Sweeting."

"You must get well, Ralph."

Master Berwyk smiled a little.

"You must."

"Aye, sweeting." He groaned again as Mariota sponged his body with the vinegar and water.

"Here, let me," Torvilda remonstrated and took the sponge from Mariota.

Mariota left her and approached me with a whisper. "Muirteach, I think you should fetch the priest. I'm not liking the look of this."

I nodded. "Where?"

"Master Berwyk's aunt could go with you. To Saint Ebbe's. She says it is close by."

We lit a lantern and Berwyk's aunt and I walked through the darkness to the nearby church, where we roused the priest from his slumber. He came readily enough, and administered the last rites while Torvilda and the older woman wept by Berwyk's bedside.

I left them and returned to the chair, watching the coals and listening. After awhile all was silent, the priest left and I surmised Berwyk had drifted again into unconsciousness. The cat and kittens purred by the fireside and I too slept for a time.

I awoke to light shining in from the opened shutters. I glanced at the bed and my heart sank. Berwyk lay unnaturally still, dead, while Torvilda and his aunt washed his body. Torvilda's eyes were red and tears streaked down her face as the older woman tried to offer some comfort, although her own cheeks were wet. Mariota, grim-faced, was gathering her supplies together in her pouch. She saw me and shook her head.

"When did he die?"

"Soon after the priest left. He lapsed into unconsciousness and died shortly after."

"So now there are two murderers to find."

Mariota shrugged. She had dark circles around her lovely eyes and I guessed she had not slept. "There's nothing more to do here. Torvilda and Berwyk's aunt are together, they'll not be alone."

"We must inform the college. No doubt he has other family to notify as well. Has his aunt sent a message?"

Mariota nodded, then sighed deeply. "I could not save him."

"He was sore wounded, *mo chridhe*. That was an ugly cut."

"If I'd known more, perhaps I could have done more."

I took her in my arms and held her a moment. Then she pulled away.

"You're exhausted, *mo chridhe*. I doubt anyone could have saved him. Come, you need to rest."

We left the sad house on Pennyfarthing Street and slowly walked up to the college. It was early still, the town just stirring into life. I smelled the smoke of morning fires, and a stronger burned smell still lingered as we passed the chapel where the Balliol masters had been besieged and Ralph Berwyk had been fatally stabbed. The chapel was in ruins, a stinking mass of blackened thatching and fallen timbers where the roof had once stood. Mariota stood silent, exhausted, while I looked at the ruins again.

Who had killed Berwyk? And why? Had the master been a random casualty of a senseless riot, or had his murder been more intentional?

The bookseller immediately came to mind. He had Berwyk's book; it was valuable and they had argued about it.

I kicked idly at a charred timber still lying in the gutter, turning it over. Underneath, in the mud of the street, I saw a knife. I picked it up. It was a small knife, the type most everyone had for eating and cutting meat. Someone had lost it in the street. But underneath the mud and ashes that covered it, I could see blood on the blade.

"Look, Mariota. This knife could be the one used to stab Berwyk."

My wife examined the knife with me.

"Yes," she agreed. "The blade is stained with blood, as though it was thrust deep." She sighed and looked close to tears. "This could well be the weapon that killed the poor man."

We passed through Northgate and I realized we would have to inform the authorities as well as the college of Berwyk's death. But first I wanted to get my wife home.

I left Mariota with Widow Tanner, who fussed over her and helped her to bed. Donald still slept in his chamber. I drank a glass of small ale and then left the house again to seek out the undersheriff.

I found him in his quarters at the castle. He was breaking his fast on some bread and ale but he put the loaf down and stopped eating when he saw me enter the room.

"Berwyk's dead," I said flatly.

"That's not good news. I'll let Houkyn know. He'll call the inquest, for tomorrow morn most likely. Have you told the other fellows?"

"Not yet."

"Did Berwyk say anything before he died?"

"He said he was stabbed from behind. He didn't see who did it."

"Do you think he was knifed on the street or in the chapel?"

I told him of Berwyk's quarrel with the bookseller and showed him the knife I had found. Grymbaud nodded.

"I'll take the man into custody on suspicion of murder. He can join his friend the cordwainer in the cells. Then we'll see if he'll confess."

"How is Ivo?"

Grymbaud shrugged. "He's safe, and well enough. Not lynched by those clerks, at any rate. He asks for his daughter."

"I'll tell her. Can she visit?"

The undersheriff nodded. "But don't send the waif down here alone. What about the other fellows?"

"I thought to tell you first, then the college. It was a bad wound." I left the rest of my thought unsaid, but the sheriff grasped my point quickly enough.

"You mean, a wound too bad to travel far? You think someone in the chapel did it?"

"What reason would they have? It makes no sense."

"None of this damned business makes sense," growled Grymbaud. "It's worse than their damned disputations."

"And then there was that message, summoning the masters into town."

"Yes, that's also odd. It could be that the townsmen lured them in with a false message. That would make a little sense, at least." Grymbaud turned to me. "Try and find out who the messenger was, and who sent him. You don't think any of his fellow scholars knifed him?"

"For what reason? Phillip Woode said he was well liked."

Grymbaud shrugged. "Jealousy?"

"The only one with motive is the bookseller."

Grymbaud nodded. "We'll have him in hand soon enough. And we do have the knife. That was a lucky find, Muirteach, and it should be easy enough to identify the owner. The chancellor has cancelled lectures again today, until things calm down. So you should find all the masters at Balliol—at least what's left of them."

I neared the college and wondered at the quiet. No scholars played ball in the backlands. Of course the day was cloudy and as I marveled at the quiet it began to rain. Perhaps that would help extinguish the madness that had taken over this town.

I entered the college grounds and pushed open the wooden door to the old hall. In the common room I saw Delacey and Phillip Woode sitting at the trestle table, drinking ale.

"Have you news of Ralph?" asked Phillip.

"Aye, and it is not good. The man died. His wound was worse than it first appeared."

Phillip gasped. "I had not realized his wound was serious. You said it was but slight."

"Even slight wounds can fester and cause death," I replied.

"Those bastards," said Delacey, his normally ruddy complexion pale. I did not like the venom I heard in his voice. "They'll pay."

"The undersheriff has already sent men to arrest Adam Bookman," I replied. "He'll pay right enough."

"So that's who knifed him?" Phillip asked.

"They had quarreled."

"Over the *Isagoge*," Delacey interjected. "Well, the book belongs to the college now. No doubt Ralph would want the college to have it."

"The book was valuable," I interposed. "Did Berwyk have family?"

"A mother north of Sheffield. We'll send a letter."

"Tell me," I said, changing the subject, "who was the messenger that came to tell you the hall was burning?"

"I did not see him. We were sitting here, looking at that odd parchment Ralph had. He said those lads had given it to him. Then Eusebius got up and answered the door. He returned with the news that the lecture hall was burning. We all ran off to attend to it."

"And when you arrived it was not aflame."

"No, all was well. I think those townsfolk wanted to lure us into town. They'll pay for this," Delacey repeated.

"Where is Eusebius? I would like to find that messenger."

"He often goes walking. He says he enjoys pondering the wonders of the Creator at those times."

"Where does he walk?"

"Out of town, toward the open fields to the north."

Delacey started to make plans for Ralph's funeral. There were to be no lectures that day, and the following day was a Sunday. The funeral would be held on Monday morning. So that gave two days for things to calm down. I started toward the door, and then turned.

"The parchment you were examining, when the messenger came. Did any of you recognize it?"

"None of us had ever seen anything like it. Berwyk was most curious about it. You've seen it, I take it?"

I told Delacey about finding the palimpsests on the parchment we had bought. Another mysterious thread leading back to Adam Bookman. I resolved to go speak with him. Presumably the authorities had him under guard at the castle now.

As I left the college and turned down along Canditch I saw Brother Eusebius returning. Now, I thought, I might ask him about the messenger. I hailed him and he looked at me with that surprised, abstracted air he had and blinked a little. He had a bundle under one arm, wrapped up in a piece of blue material. "Oh, it is you. The man from the North."

"Indeed, and I've just a quick question for you."

"Of course, if I might be of help."

"Did you enjoy your walk? Where do you go?"

"Out beyond the houses, where there are some open fields. I find I think more clearly there. I ponder the mysteries of our Lord's creation."

"Indeed."

Eusebius smiled. "And your question, sir?"

"Yes, I was wondering about the messenger. Who brought you word that the lecture hall was aflame? You're the only one who saw him. Who was the lad? What did he look like?"

"I was not familiar with the boy. He was slightly built and had fair hair, dressed in the robes of an undergraduate."

"Did he say who sent him?"

"No, but I fear when I heard his news about the fire in the hall I did not wait for him to tell me anything else. I rushed back and got the others, and we ran into town to see."

"And where was the lad then?"

"He had disappeared. No doubt he'd delivered his message and left."

"But there was no fire. So the lad must have connived with some folk, the townsfolk perhaps. You can see why I must find him."

"Indeed," Eusebius agreed, "but, sadly, I know nothing more."

"What clothes was he wearing?"

Eusebius thought a moment. "I believe he wore a blue tunic with a hood. I might have seen him with Delacey once or twice, on School Street."

I nodded, remembering the young undergraduate Delacey

had spoken with a few days before. The description would fit that lad. But then the description would fit many other students equally well. Many undergraduates no doubt were fair-haired and wore blue tunics. Eusebius could have been describing William of Uist. And William of Uist, at least, was not the boy who had delivered the message.

I thanked Eusebius and left him walking up the road toward the Balliol gate while I turned my steps toward Oxford Castle.

The undersheriff was a little surprised to see me again so soon but he had no objections to my interviewing Adam Bookman. I followed the guard down a winding stone staircase into the bowels of the castle, where I found Adam Bookman in a small dark cell with a black eye and bloodied nose. Apparently he had put up a fight, or else the undersheriff's men had been in a poor mood when they apprehended him.

The guard opened the door. In the dim light I could just make out Bookman sitting in the moldy, reeking straw that covered the floor of his cell. There was barely room for him to lie down, and I doubted he could stand upright in the cramped space.

"Adam. Adam Bookman," called the guard. "There's a man here wants to speak with you." I slipped the guard a coin and he retreated down the hallway a bit.

Bookman stood up awkwardly and shuffled to the door. "Who is it, then? Oh, it's you. What do you want with me? You've already got me accused of murder—for it was you, wasn't it, that told them of the book."

"They'd have found out soon enough. Anyone could have told them."

"I didn't murder Berwyk."

"Why should I believe you?"

"Because I'm telling the truth. I met up with that cordwainer and Jakeson and the others. We saw the masters walking down the street and Jakeson had words with Woode about his daughter. Then we fought—but I didn't knife anyone. I swear by Saint Martin. Those masters ran and gained the chapel. Then the cordwainer set fire to the roof."

"So the knife I found was not yours?"

"Indeed not," Bookman said.

"And none of you sent a message to them, that their hall on School Street was aflame?"

Bookman looked confused. "What message? We sent no message." He continued, "You've got the undersheriff's ear. Tell him I'm innocent. I stabbed no one. You've got to believe me."

"Why should I believe you? You've got that damned book. It's very valuable, I hear."

"It's valuable, but I wouldn't have killed for it. Berwyk was going to redeem the volume anyway."

"It was a riot. There was confusion. Who could vouch for you? Who was near you?"

Bookman thought a moment. "The three of us were on the High Street when we met up with them. Jakeson wanted to just let them pass, but then Phillip Woode asked about Jonetta."

"What do you think happened to her?" I asked, changing the topic.

"She was a good lass. I don't think she ran away."

"Then where is she?"

Adam Bookman shrugged his shoulders. "I neither know nor care too much. Not now, when I've been arrested for murder."

"So what happened then? After Phillip spoke?"

"It was the cordwainer who couldn't keep his mouth shut. He accused Phillip of murder. Then he mentioned the old man, and accused all four of the men there of raping young girls and other perverse acts. That set the fuse alight and the brawl began."

"So who was next to you?"

"Jakeson, most of the time."

"Did you enter the chapel?"

"No, it was as I said. They ran ahead and barred the door against us. Until the cordwainer set fire to the roof."

"Do you think someone else could have been in the chapel?" I asked. For if Berwyk had not been stabbed on the street, then he had been stabbed in the chapel. And if no one else had been in the chapel, then he'd been knifed by one of his colleagues.

"How would I know?"

"Do you remember the chase?"

"Well," Bookman furrowed his brow and thought. "The cordwainer started taunting them, then I think it was Woode that struck the first blow. But Jakeson was after him then, yelling that he'd killed his poor daughter. Then they started running, cowards that they are."

"Who ran ahead?"

"Berwyk was last. He landed a blow on Jakeson just as the tavern keeper was about to pound Woode's head against a corner of the house. Then Jakeson let up on Woode and the two of them followed the others to the chapel."

"So, if I'm to believe you, Berwyk was either stabbed by someone already in the chapel or by his good friends Delacey or Eusebius. And no one else came out of the chapel. And the knife was found outside the chapel as well, not inside. What jury will believe this?"

"An honest jury!" Bookman shouted. "One not in the pockets of the damned university!"

"I'll ask. Perhaps some witnesses to the fight can be found."

"I'd be grateful. For whatever you can do."

I turned, leaving the bookseller in his stinking cell. The guard locked the door again and we started toward the stairs. Then I thought of old Ivo. I asked the gaoler and he showed me the old man's cell and let me in. It seemed the old man had fared better than Adam Bookman; at least, I could see no bruises on his face. The straw didn't reek so much and a slit window high in the stone wall let a shaft of daylight in. Ivo didn't look overjoyed to see me. I was the one who had sent him here, after all.

"How are they treating you?" I asked him.

"None so bad. Sir, do you have news of my daughter?"

I told him of Avice's new position and his face lightened a bit. "That's a great weight from my heart, that is. If they hang me it won't matter, just as long as I know she's cared for."

"She seems to get on with the widow," I observed. "And she is safe enough there."

"You found her the place, didn't you?"

"It was more my wife," I admitted.

"Saints bless the both of you. I'm in your debt, indeed I am."

I thought not, since the old man was in prison mainly on my word, and guiltily I bade him goodbye.

# CHAPTER 13

I left the castle and went back into town to speak with Master Jakeson. Bookman had claimed Jakeson was nearby during the melee. So I sought him out at The Green Man. The tavern was close to empty and I found Jakeson wiping the dark wood tables down with a grimy rag. He seemed like a man defeated, all the energy and fight gone from him. It was hard to imagine this man pounding Phillip Woode's head against a wall. He moved slowly, methodically, to his task.

"I wanted to ask you about the disturbance yesterday. You know they've arrested Adam Bookman for the assault on Berwyk. And now Berwyk is dead, it will be murder charges he'll face. Your friend will hang for murder."

Jakeson kept wiping tables. "I'm sorry to hear that. Adam Bookman is a good man. Berwyk was a good man, as well."

"Then why were you fighting with him?"

"It's bad when those students get agitated."

"From what I heard, you townsfolk were the instigators. You're lucky you are all not in gaol."

Jakeson had the grace to flush. I watched the color spread on his grizzled cheeks.

"What happened?" I asked again.

"Those masters came down High Street with that Woode amongst them. And words got started—let loose—it got out of hand. There they were, without a care in the world, and my Jonetta gone—"

"Adam Bookman claims you were close to him as the masters were chased into the chapel. He claims Berwyk struck a blow that hit you, just as you were about to hit Phillip Woode. Then they ran into the chapel for safety."

"Aye, that's close enough to how it happened."

"So where was Bookman? Could he have knifed Berwyk? Or can you vouch that he did not?"

Jakeson put his rag down on the table and straightened up, thinking.

"Let me see it in my mind, like. We met them on High Street. I had just come out of the tavern and was speaking with the cordwainer, passing the time of day, and then Adam Bookman came along. It was then that we saw the masters walking back toward Northgate Street. They were coming from School Street way. And then that young one, he asked me about my Jonetta."

That accorded with what Phillip Woode himself had told me.

"Then the butcher showed up and he started berating them, as to how they'd mistreated that poor girl at the college. Everyone knows about Ivo, in chains now at the castle. Unfair, it is. And my own daughter gone now—who knows where; it was too much, all of it, too much to bear—I'm thinking the butcher said something about Woode, and Jonetta."

"So the words turned to blows," I put in.

"Aye, that they did. My anger got the better of me. But then Berwyk accused Adam Bookman of stealing some book. That's an outright lie. Bookman, he's but an honest merchant. So it got out of hand, and quick enough too, and we chased them to the chapel. I had my sights on Woode and was just about to bash him when Berwyk hit me. The next thing I knew they'd been chased into the chapel and then the cordwainer blocked the door and set the roof afire."

"And where was Bookman?"

"Close to me, but after the blow I took there are a few

minutes I do not remember."

"Did you see him stab Berwyk?"

"No, I did not."

"And did you see Berwyk run into the chapel?"

"They were all running, like rats, until Berwyk hit me. Next I knew, they was all inside, and the butcher called to me that we had trapped them, and to bar the doors tight."

"So you didn't see Berwyk after he hit you?"

Adam Jakeson shrugged his shoulders. "It was a brawl and a chase. I am ashamed and sorry for my part in it, in particular as the man is dead, but I did not see him knifed, nor did I see him enter the chapel."

"But Bookman was close to him. He could have stabbed him."

"He was close, yes. But then as I've told you, Berwyk hit me, and I don't recollect what happened right after that. I can't say yes, and I can't say no."

I held out the knife I had found and showed it to Jakeson. "Do you recognize this knife?"

Jakeson shook his head no. So I was no closer to the truth, and Bookman that much closer to the noose.

I stopped back by Widow Tanner's for the noon meal. As I passed Donald's chamber I heard a rummaging sound and looked in. The room was a mess, bedcovers and clothing strewn about. Donald's accursed lute lay on the bed, a tunic and cotehardie lying across it. There was an empty wine jug on the floor. I saw Donald rise from the other side of the bed, where he had apparently been searching for something under the bedstead.

"Studying hard?" I asked.

"I went to the early lectures," Donald replied, somewhat defensively. "And came back. I was going to clean more of those parchments. They've disappeared."

"I am not surprised you can't find them in all of this," I retorted, although my own dwelling had been none too neat when I had kept house for myself. "Does the widow not clean in here?"

"Aye, she does." Donald again disappeared behind the bed and I saw a shoe come flying up to land on the bed, barely missing the lute. "Muirteach, there was a tall stack of them. I had them under the bed here. They've vanished."

"When did you see them last?"

"A few days ago. That day there were no classes. Anthony and Crispin and I spent some time cleaning a few of them. Then I put them all under the bed. They aren't there. Look for yourself."

I knelt down and peered under the bed. There were certainly no parchments, although I did spy the second shoe and a discarded wine cup.

"That is strange. When did the widow last clean your room?" I asked.

"A day or two ago."

"Perhaps she did something with the parchments," I ventured. "Let us go and ask her."

When we found Widow Tanner she was seeing to the noon meal. She denied having moved the parchments, although she claimed to remember seeing them under the bed. "Although how I could even see them amongst all your lordship's belongings thrown under there, I couldn't say. But they were there, stowed under the bed, right enough."

"And that was two days ago?"

The widow nodded.

"Do you think Anthony or Crispin borrowed them to work on?" I asked.

"Not without asking my permission," Donald returned, every inch the young princeling. "They would not dare."

"Well then, I can't hazard a guess as to where they might be. I'm sure they'll turn up someplace. I'm thinking you misplaced them."

"No, Muirteach, I did not!" Donald protested.

"Best go to the booksellers and purchase a few more sheets, then, if you'll be needing parchment anytime soon."

"But Muirteach, they were stolen."

"I'm doubting that, Donald. You've misplaced them, that is all. Now let us eat and not keep the poor woman waiting. The food will get cold."

I ignored Donald's furious cries of protest and sat down to my dinner. Mariota joined us. Then I left and went back to Oxford Castle, where I told the undersheriff of my conversation with Jakeson.

Houkyn had convened Berwyk's inquest for the next morning. The jury heard the evidence of Grymbaud and myself and then looked at the knife, which Bookman denied was his. They listened to Mariota's description of Berwyk's wound and Mistress Bonefey's red-eyed testimony. Perhaps Torvilda's presence made the jury sympathetic to the slain man, for they quite quickly returned the verdict of murder and indicted Adam Bookman. Then, grumbling about disruptions to the peace and civic responsibilities, the twelve worthy citizens of Oxford returned to their duties.

Mariota accompanied Mistress Bonefey home. I walked with them to Pennyfarthing Street, but Mariota bade me wait for her outside. She said she wanted to speak to Torvilda privately, so I went to a cheap ale-house across the street and drank some sour ale while they spoke.

This day had, surprisingly, been quiet. It might have been the bad weather, or the fact that Grymbaud had increased the number of his men patrolling the city streets, and most university folk had kept to their lodgings. The ale-house was nearly empty and looked sad, dirty and neglected. The greasy grime on the trestle tables was clearly visible in the early afternoon light and the establishment smelled of stale beer and unchanged rushes. I wondered about the mysterious messenger and resolved to ask Delacey about him. I was glad when I finally saw Mariota leave Torvilda's, carrying a basket, and we walked up to Northgate while the rain drizzled down. Mariota said little, and I, saddened by Berywk's death, found I also had nothing to say.

"What's in the basket?" I finally asked to break the silence.

"Torvilda gave me a kitten. She said it was in payment for my services. I told her there was no need, but she insisted. She said it would make her feel better if she could give me something."

"That was kind of her."

"She's a good woman. She deserves better than a slain lover and poverty. Widow Tanner's been complaining of mice. Perhaps she'll be glad of the kitten."

We'd crossed outside the city walls by this time. Mariota continued on home but I stopped by Balliol and learned that Berwyk's funeral would be held on Monday morning, and the university chancellor had decreed lectures would resume tomorrow. I wondered cynically if he hoped to forestall more troubles by keeping students occupied the day a favorite master was buried.

I walked down Canditch to the Widow Tanner's, glad the rain had finally stopped. Outside the kitchen I saw Avice sitting on a stool, shelling beans. The little dog slept at her feet, quiet for once. Anthony stood nearby but when they saw me they both flushed, and Anthony turned and quickly walked into the main house. I did not think the course of this young love would run smoothly, what with the lass already got with child and the lad an impoverished clerk in his first years of study. Still, I wished them both joy of it, as there seemed little enough happiness to be had these days. Then I went inside the house to tell Mariota when Berwyk's funeral mass would be held.

I found Mariota in our chamber, reading a medical text by the light that came through the open shutters. The kitten, a ball of striped fur, was curled up asleep on the wool blanket covering our bed, but my wife looked grim. Mariota did not like to lose patients.

"They say the lectures will resume tomorrow, Muirteach."

"I heard, *mo chridhe*. Berwyk's funeral mass will also be on Monday, after Terce."

"Good. Then I can attend the early medical lectures and return in time for the mass. I would like to be there, as a friend to Mistress Bonefey." Mariota turned toward me, an intent look on her face and her blue eyes wide and hard, demanding. "Muirteach," she said, surprising me with the force of her speech, "swear nothing will happen to you. Ever. I could not bear it if I lost you."

I sat down on our bed for a moment and stroked the kitten before I answered. It stirred a little, but did not wake.

"Nothing will happen to me, *mo chridhe*. The town is quiet enough now. All seems calm. I'm in no danger. But I might say the same to you. I don't think it wise for you to be traipsing around the city dressed as a clerk. Berwyk is dead, the second master slain in just a few days. You are the one taking foolish chances."

"I'm safe enough," my wife repeated stubbornly. "I must learn more. If I'd known more, I could have saved him."

"*Mo chridhe,* no one could have saved him. It was a grievous wound. God chose to take him."

"No, Muirteach, God did not choose to take Master Berwyk. He was killed by man's evil, not God's. And now Torvilda mourns her lover. I could not bear it if I were to lose you."

"I could not bear to lose you, either." I stood and walked

over to the desk, then bent down and kissed Mariota where she sat. The scent of her elderflower perfume filled my nostrils and her hair was like silk, smooth, as I stroked it. I drew her closer to me, and the arguments we'd had the past days faded away. We were here, together.

"Come, love." She responded to my kiss hungrily until at length we broke apart. Then I walked over to the window and closed the shutters. I drew my wife into my arms and we left her studies unfinished for a time. The kitten slept through it all.

The next morning I slept late but woke when the kitten tried to nuzzle and nurse on my ear. The bed beside me was empty, Mariota's tunic and wimple folded neatly on a chair. I guessed she had gone, dressed as "William," to the morning medical lecture. The morning lectures lasted from before Prime until almost Terce.

The kitten kept nuzzling at my ear, purring and tickling me, until finally I moved it away. I saw Mariota had left some milk out for it in a small bowl. I dressed and left it in the chamber, then checked on Donald. For a wonder it appeared he also had gone to the early lecture. Perhaps the few days of enforced vacation had sharpened his appetite for learning. I doubted it.

I left the widow's and walked down Canditch to the Balliol, thinking to seek out Delacey, but he did not appear to be at the old hall. Phillip Woode told me he had a lecture to give in the town, so I walked through the town gates and down High Street until I reached the lecture halls.

I fortuitously found Delacey walking up School Street with the same undergraduate I had seen him speak to a few days earlier. They seemed absorbed in their conversation, and neither of them noticed me until I came quite close.

"Master Delacey," I called out. The lad speaking with Delacey visibly startled. "I would speak with you, and with your friend."

Delacey turned. "Oh yes, what is it, Muirteach?" He seemed much calmer than his young friend.

"Brother Eusebius described the messenger, the lad that brought word of the fire, as looking like your friend here. I thought to inquire if he is the messenger."

The boy looked blank, and Delacey did as well. "No, it was not this lad. This is Richard DeVyse, a student from the south. From Kent, is it not, Richard?"

The lad nodded. "What message are you speaking of?"

I told him.

"Oh no, sir, it was not I. I was studying. I have just begun the Quadrivium and find the astronomy difficult. I am trying to grasp the concepts."

"You seem a studious lad," I observed, mentally comparing Richard's behavior to that of my charge and finding my charge's behavior somewhat lacking. But that was not news. "Can someone vouch for your whereabouts?"

"Yes, I was in my rooming house. My roommate can tell you, for neither of us left that day."

"He is a good boy," Delacey observed with a fondness in his voice that surprised me. "And honest. Richard would not be mixed up in something like that, would you Dickon? His family and mine have been friends a long while. Our lands border each other in Kent."

"And who is your roommate?"

"He is named Borou. He is there now, if you would like to ask him yourself."

I followed Richard and Delacey through a side alley to a student tenement. There in a cramped room on the fourth floor I was introduced to Borou, who vouched that indeed, Richard had been studying on the afternoon in question.

So Eusebius must have been wrong, and Richard was not the messenger. But there were other fair-haired students at the university, and I resolved to find the lad who had delivered the message.

Delacey and I left Richard with his roommate and walked back toward Balliol. "What is your connection with the young lad?" I asked.

I fancied Delacey bristled a little. "As I said, our families are old friends. His father asked me to keep an eye out for the boy and that is what I have done. That is all there is to it."

# CHAPTER 14

I spent the rest of that afternoon searching for the fair-haired student who had delivered the false message about the burning lecture hall, to no avail. Since I had no name and only a vague description, my search proved fruitless. The earth seemed to have swallowed the lad up.

The undersheriff, having apprehended both Ivo and Adam Bookman, seemed intent mainly on restoring quiet to the streets of his town. Townsfolk went about their business, the goodwives of Oxford cleaned their homes, and the students stayed quiet, for the main part, studying or drinking in the taverns. Grymbaud's men patrolled and there were no further incidents. The crisis, I hoped, had passed.

I stopped by The Green Man for a glass of ale later in the afternoon. I found investigating blind alleys to be thirsty work. Master Jakeson was not there, but his wife served me. I hesitated to ask about her daughter, as I knew she'd taken the lass's disappearance to heart. I could see that the woman had lost weight and had deep, dark circles around her eyes. I did not wish to upset her further. So I was somewhat surprised when the goodwife questioned me.

"Sir," she asked, wiping her hands on her apron after she had set down my beaker of ale, "have you heard anything else about my daughter?"

"Not since the friar reported seeing her with the chapman. I am indeed sorry. I know nothing else."

The woman's face fell and she blinked some. But she steadied herself and spoke again. "And what chapman would that be?"

"The friar said he was tall, with dark brown hair and an accent from the North."

"Eh, sir, that's what they said right enough. That's what my goodman told me the friar said. But I don't know what chapman that would be. The description sounds like Walter of York, but we haven't seen him in some time."

"Was this Walter of York friendly with your daughter?"

"She's a beautiful girl and lots of men fancied her. But my Jonetta's a good girl, sir. She'd be friendly with the customers but they couldn't take no liberties. Not with my goodman standing here watching."

"But do you think she fancied him?"

"Not that I ever noticed. She often complained that he smelled of garlic."

That did not sound like a basis for youthful romance to me. "What of this Walter of York? Is he an honest man?"

"He's a peddler, sir, a trader. But I never knew him to cheat. He gave good value, good enough."

Although he smelled of garlic. "And when did he last visit?"

"I last saw him near Midsummer's Eve. So that would be close to three months ago."

"And the undersheriff knows this?"

"Yes, we told him. But he surmised that the chapman came into town secret-like and stole Jonetta away, her being willing. But I can't think that's true, sir. Not my daughter."

"Did Jonetta fancy anyone else? That you knew of?"

Mistress Jakeson chewed on her lower lip a bit while she thought. "There are all those university men that frequent our place. I think she liked that young man from Balliol. The one with the nice brown eyes—Phillip Woode. She spoke to me of how fine it would be to marry an educated man."

I had seen Jonetta with Phillip Woode, that first night we'd been in town. She had not seemed repulsed by his advances. But Phillip swore he knew nothing of the lass's disappearance. And I liked Phillip Woode. Besides, even if he had been involved, where was Jonetta now?

I sipped at my ale while Mistress Jakeson served other customers and wondered about Jonetta and the murders.

Phillip Woode, Delacey, Berwyk, Eusebius. Something I'd heard and forgotten that first day after Clarkson's murder came to mind.

Mistress Jakeson came back and refilled my beaker.

"You must hear quite a lot, working in the tavern," I commented after I thanked her for her good ale.

Mistress Jakeson nodded. "Indeed. Men are talkative after a glass or two of ale."

"Have you heard aught of heresy?"

"Heresy? Such as what?"

"I just wondered."

"There are those who believe we should be able to read God's word in our own tongue. Lollards, they are called. But that, sir, I do not believe to be heresy. That Master Wycliffe, he did often speak of that when he lived here. He said it was no sin."

"Although the church might say so."

Mistress Jakeson made a face. "The church cannot even agree on where the Pope should reside. In Avignon or in Rome."

For a woman, she was well informed.

"That master that was murdered at the college—"

"Master Clarkson?"

"Aye. I heard there had been some talk of heresy there."

"I know naught of that, sir. Although those scholars will talk when they are in their cups."

"Of what?" I drank some more ale and waited.

"I do mind one night—it was those men from Balliol that

were here—Phillip Woode, Berwyk, and the pompous one with the red hair."

"Delacey?"

She nodded. "That'll be his name. And Clarkson and the friar. They argued here one night."

"And when was this?"

"In the summer sometime. I remember as the younger students had mostly been gone, between the terms of study."

"And what was the cause of the quarrel?"

She shrugged. "Who knows? The little I heard made no sense to me. But that Clarkson, him that was murdered, was furious, his face all red. And the little cockerel," here I guessed she meant Delacey, "nearly went for his knife. But it came to naught, luckily."

"Indeed. Well, if you remember anything else, be kind enough to let me know."

"I will, sir," she replied. "I'll see you in here often enough."

And in that fact, at least, she was correct. The ale at The Green Man was good, and I was there often.


Supposedly the murders were solved. Ivo had attacked Clarkson in a fit of rage over his daughter's pregnancy. Adam Bookman had stabbed Ralph Berwyk over the disputed copy of the *Isagoge*. Then why, I asked myself the next day, was I so restless?

It was the Sunday before Berwyk's funeral mass, which was to be held on Monday morning. I paced back and forth in my chamber until I annoyed my wife, who, having returned from mass, was intent upon studying Galen's treatise on urine. She tried to ignore me. Finally, I flung myself down on the bed with a large sigh and Mariota looked up.

"Whatever is it, Muirteach? You're as tense as a rat-catcher's dog. Surely it's not just Donald's music that's unsettling you so?"

Through the wall we heard the sound of the lute. "I'm even thinking he's improved a little of late," my wife added, and waited.

"I just am not comfortable that Bookman stabbed Berwyk. The reason seems flimsy. And nor am I convinced that Ivo killed Clarkson, although he had reason enough."

"I know, *mo chridhe,*" my wife replied thoughtfully. "Ivo seems not to have the strength to kill Clarkson."

"Although he is not frail."

"No, he works hard in his garden. He could have done it, I suppose."

"Yet he swears he did not do so." I paused and listened to the discordant sounds coming through the wall as Donald attempted a more difficult passage. "And Bookman loses by killing Berwyk. Although if the book is unredeemed, he can sell it."

"Still, Berwyk was to pay him for it. It makes no sense."

My wife had echoed my own thoughts. I glanced out the open shutters. The day was fair this close to Michaelmas. The leaves of the trees turned to lovely yellows and golds and red, the sky blue with scudding white clouds. A breeze blew in through the window and from someplace I smelled the tang of apples and cider. I turned from the window and looked at my wife, feeling a surge of affection for the way she seemed to read my mind.

"Come, *mo chridhe.* Why don't you put that text away for a while? Let us go out and walk a bit, out of the town."

My heart leapt a little when I saw my wife close her book.

"It is a bonny day," Mariota agreed, "and my neck is tense from study. It would feel good to stretch my legs and be out in the open. All right then, where shall we go?"

"There is open land to the north, beyond the vintner's. Let's walk back there. It is not so far."

When we told Donald our plans, he, Anthony and Crispin

unaccountably wanted to join us. Somewhat ruefully we agreed. Widow Tanner packed us a few pasties and some cider, and even agreed that Avice could join us as it was a Sunday and the lass at liberty. And so, a short while later, a larger party than I had first envisioned set out walking north, past the walls of the Austin Friary on the right and toward the more open land beyond the houses outside the walls. Apparently other citizens of Oxford town had the same idea, for we passed several other parties enjoying the afternoon.

Among the passersby I was surprised to see Delacey and his young protégée, Richard DeVyse, walking back toward the town. Richard's roommate Borou was not in evidence. We greeted them and Delacey nodded in an almost cordial fashion.

"Fine weather, is it not?" I said.

"Indeed," Delacey responded. "We were just studying and thought to take a short break from the rigors of the *Quadrivium,* it being such a pleasant afternoon. And you as well?"

I did not think that Donald, Anthony and Crispin could have been accused of studying overmuch that morning, but I let that pass and nodded nonchalantly.

"There is a pleasant wood up yonder," Delacey continued in a rare burst of friendliness. "It belongs to the friars, but they do not mind if folk walk there. Such loveliness as Our Lord put in the world belongs to us all."

I nodded again and we bid them good afternoon. Delacey and DeVyse continued back toward town while we walked in the contrary direction. We passed the tannery buildings and the vintner's on the left. Past the vintner's there were fewer buildings, a house that belonged to the Benedictines, then some abandoned houses and sheds, mostly in poor repair. I remembered hearing that the owners had perished in the pestilence some years ago and the current heirs were disputed. On the right we saw some fields and orchards belonging to the Austin

Friars, and beyond that some open lands. Although they may have belonged to the church, I surmised from the townsfolk dotting the landscape that the friars did not mind much if the folk visited them on such a fine day.

We found a grassy spot in a meadow under a beech tree and there we had our little repast. Then, sadly, Donald got out his lute and began picking out a tune. Although I confess the afternoon was so pleasant, even that did not spoil the time. Perhaps his playing had improved, as my wife had said. I lay back, my head pillowed in Mariota's lap, and drifted off to sleep.

I awoke feeling a strange sensation. I opened my eyes, at first seeing only the blue skies and a yellow leaf. Than I realized Mariota had a twig with a few leaves attached and was gently brushing my face with it.

"Leave off, Mariota," I exclaimed, rubbing at my cheek. "That tickles."

"*Och,* Muirteach," she said, laughing, "I wondered how long it would take you to wake."

"An observation of natural philosophy, not doubt," I grunted, sitting up.

"Perhaps," my wife asserted. "But also my legs had gone numb. They are all pins and needles."

"Where are the lads? And Avice?"

"They're off there, gathering a few beechnuts. Don't worry, I can see them."

I glanced in the direction Mariota pointed and saw the four young people in a grove across the meadow. They looked to be having a fine enough time there.

I looked back at my wife. The blue of the sky reflected the color of her eyes, causing them to look an even deeper shade. I kissed her quickly on the lips, and then stood up.

"It will be getting late," Mariota observed as I helped her to her feet. "*Och,* my legs are still tingling," she added, shifting her weight a little gingerly. "There, that is better now," she added, glancing up at the sun, which was lowering in the sky to the west.

The lads and Avice had seen us and came across the meadow, Avice's kerchief full of some beechnuts they had gathered.

"Those may belong to the Augustinians," I observed.

"I see no one," Donald declared with a swagger. I shrugged my shoulders and let the matter drop. We made our way back to the road. The sun was not as strong now and the day was beginning to fade.

We started down the street back toward the suburbs of Oxford, Avice giggling and blushing a little at something Anthony said to her. I raised my eyebrows a little and looked at my wife.

"It looks innocent enough," Mariota murmured to me. "It's good to see the lass smiling. And Anthony seems a nice enough lad."

We were just approaching the vintner's on the right when I felt Donald nudge my side. "Look, Muirteach" he hissed, "isn't that Brother Eusebius?"

I followed his gaze and saw a thin, stooped figure in a worn Franciscan habit walking up the road away from town.

"Brother Eusebius."

The friar stopped and seemed to collect himself a moment, as was his style. He blinked his somewhat protuberant light blue eyes, and then greeted us. "Good day. And so you have been on an outing?"

"Indeed, sir," Donald answered. "It is an amazing day."

"Yes, the elements are in harmony today." Eusebius looked around at the road. There were several other parties of merrymakers returning to the town. He blinked again. "Still, it has grown late, I fear. Later than I thought. The dark is coming.

Perhaps I should accompany you back into the town."

Eusebius's presence cast a bit of a pall on the chatter of the four youngsters and it fell to me to make conversation with the man. But I began to realize talk did not come easily with Eusebius, and my attempts at friendly speech lapsed.

"What of the parchment?" asked Eusebius suddenly.

"Parchment?" I asked, momentarily bewildered.

"Berwyk had a palimpsest. He claimed it to be yours and said you had found it in some old parchments you'd bought from Adam Bookman."

"Oh yes, those. That is a strange affair. They were stolen from our lodgings."

"When was this?" asked Eusebius with concern.

I told him.

"And no one saw anything?"

"The widow had gone out to the market. No one saw a thing."

"Such times we live in," Eusebius murmured. "Some poor student must have taken to thievery, without the funds to buy his own. Still, it's but a few old parchments. They can be no great loss to you."

"But now we will never be able to decipher the manuscript and learn its secrets," Anthony said.

"Perhaps not," Eusebius replied, "and that is a pity."

Crispin had been leering and I heard him whisper to Donald, "Nor will we be able to examine more drawings." I glared at him and thankfully he said no more.

Mariota, who had been silent during this conversation, spoke up. "I hear you are a student of the natural philosophies."

"Yes, I try to follow in the footsteps of the famous *doctor mirabilis,* Roger Bacon, who studied and worked here in Oxford close to a century ago."

"Do you study medicine as well?"

"I attend some lectures. All of the natural sciences are of

interest to me."

"You must forgive my wife her curiosity," I interjected. "She is well regarded as a healer in our own land."

"Indeed?" said Eusebius, staring curiously at Mariota for a moment, almost as if she had sprouted a second head.

By this time we had reached the Widow Tanner's, where we parted company with Eusebius and went inside.

"He is an odd one," Mariota whispered to me as we washed our hands and faces before the evening meal.

"But harmless enough, I think," I replied. "A bit absent-minded, to be sure."

"Did you see the way he looked at me? As if I was some strange creature that had crawled out from under a rock?"

"Well, *mo chridhe,* there are no women doctors in Oxford that I know of. Just a few midwives."

Anthony and Crispin eagerly accepted Widow Tanner's invitation to stay and sup with us. She was a kind woman, to put up with us as her lodgers. I think, despite all Donald's attempts to prove her wrong, she was still proud and impressed to have a young lordling staying in her home. And she seemed to enjoy young people, having no children of her own. Perhaps Avice would do well enough here, even with the baby.

# CHAPTER 15

Berwyk's funeral mass was to be held at Saint Mary Magdalene's and I thought it wise to be there early. The chapel was nearly empty at this hour of the morning, except for Berwyk's bier in front of the altar. Several large candles burning gave off the scent of beeswax. As my eyes adjusted to the dimness, I saw the figures of Torvilda Bonefey and Berwyk's aunt kneeling before the body. I knelt and tried to pray for Berwyk's soul.

The church filled and the mass began. I wondered not to see Mariota there, and felt ill at ease as I scanned the crowd entering for the mass. She had left our lodgings early, to attend her lecture, but had thought to have time to change and be at the funeral. Perhaps, I thought, she had arrived late and was standing with the crowd in the back. I craned my neck to try and see but couldn't glimpse her while the priest droned on and waved the censer over the body. The scent of incense grew stronger, almost masking the odor of Berwyk's decaying corpse. Vortigen and Justin arrived, and I saw Donald, Anthony and Crispin among the mourners. Anthony looked to be crying. I saw him wiping at his cheeks and red eyes with one hand, and I remembered how popular Master Berwyk had been. It was a senseless death.

But what if the deaths of Berwyk and Clarkson were related? What tied them together? Again, I thought of the *Isagoge*. Clarkson had pawned it and Berwyk wanted it back. Which did not look well for Master Bookman.

The mass finally over, the mourners filed by the corpse to pay final respects before the burial. I looked anxiously, my heart beginning to hammer against my ribs as I waited until the church was empty, searching for either Mariota or for William of Uist, but neither of them did I see.

My mouth dry and heart thudding now in earnest, I raced back to Widow Tanner's, searching the streets, today crowded with students, for Mariota's face. I barged into the house and our chamber, ignoring the good widow's startled look. Mariota's blue dress lay neatly folded as she had left it. My wife had not yet returned. And it was clear from the clothes she had left behind that she still wore the clothing of a lad. My stomach lurched and I felt a pressure in my chest.

Donald entered the room without knocking. "Where's Mariota?" he asked.

"I am not sure," I managed to reply, trying to sound casual. "Do you know a student named William of Uist?"

Donald shrugged his shoulders. "I don't think so. Why do you ask?"

"He's slightly built and wears a blue tunic."

"What's all this about?" Donald's eyes took in Mariota's folded dress and her absence. His gray eyes narrowed shrewdly and for an instant I saw his father in the lad. "She's been attending lectures, hasn't she?"

"Aye, and now she's disappeared." I almost felt relief at Donald's guess. Almost. A cold sweat was on my brow, my heart still pounding so loudly I thought Donald must hear it. "She didn't return after this morning's lecture," I continued. "I must look for her."

"I'll help you search," he offered, sounding remarkably mature. "Perhaps she just stopped off at the bookseller's."

"I do not think so. Mariota told me she meant to attend Berwyk's funeral mass. She never arrived."

"What was she wearing?"

I described William's blue tunic and hood to Donald as we headed into town. I tried to take heart as we walked. It made sense to stop by the booksellers' stalls; surely we would find her there, perusing some rare volume. That of Adam Bookman was closed but we scoured the other stalls without finding any trace of my wife, and again I felt that odd pressure in my chest. Then we ventured to School Street and surprised several masters by looking in on their lectures, still without finding Mariota. She had vanished.

"Whose lecture was she attending?" asked Donald.

"Master Rudolfo of Salerno," I answered. "We should ask him if William attended his lecture this morning."

It was not hard to find the lecture hall where Master Rudolfo gave classes, one of the finer halls on the street. As we entered the building a crowd of students filed out of a room to the right, and inside we found Master Rudolfo. He had a swarthy complexion and dark hair that hung down to his shoulders, but a placid and composed face.

"Can I help you?" he asked pleasantly enough.

"We are seeking a young student of yours named William of Uist."

"Oh, yes, the new student. He enrolled last week and seems a promising boy."

"Was he at lecture this morning?"

Rudolfo frowned slightly. "The hall was dark for that early lecture, at least in the beginning." He paused and thought, his eyes moving upward as if seeing a mental picture of the hall. "Yes, he was there, sitting next to Brother Eusebius, for he asked a question, toward the end, about the choleric temperament. Why do you seek him?"

"We are friends of his, and he did not meet us as arranged."

"Yes, I can tell you are from the north," said Rudolfo, looking at my plaid mantle. "Your friend was at the lecture. Perhaps the lad is at his books and has no wish to go to the taverns today. He seems a studious boy."

"Indeed," I murmured, trying to sound as if all was normal. "Who else attends your early lecture? You mentioned Brother Eusebius? From Balliol?"

"Yes, he attends from time to time, although he is more interested in the natural sciences, I believe. It is a small group. Mostly graduate students. Perhaps I should not have let the lad in but his letter of introduction impressed me. I have heard of the Beatons; in fact, I studied with one in Salerno many years ago."

"Fearchar?"

"Yes, that was his name. And so I let his nephew attend my class. As a favor. And he seems a likely student. But I have not seen the boy since this morning. Try his lodging house."

Although it was instructive to me to learn how Mariota had obtained admission to Rudolfo's lectures, that did little to find her now. Since Rudolfo had no more to tell us on the subject, we left him and walked down School Street, then turned onto the High Street.

"If Brother Eusebius was at the lecture, perhaps he saw where William went. He was at Berwyk's funeral, along with the other masters," I said, leading the way back up Northgate Street toward the gate and Balliol.

We found Eusebius just leaving the dining room, intent on conversation with Phillip Woode and Delacey. Briefly I wondered if they were discussing who would next move into the old hall, as there seemed to be numerous vacancies. Clarkson and now Berwyk were gone.

Phillip Woode noticed me first. "Muirteach. Is there any news?"

I was momentarily confused. News of what? Had Mariota been found? Then I grasped Phillip's meaning. So intent had I been on finding Mariota, I'd completely forgotten about Berwyk's killer.

"They've arrested Adam Bookman," I replied, forcing my racing mind to some discipline. "He's under suspicion for the murder. But I've another question. For you, Brother Eusebius. Do you recall a young student from the north at the early medical lecture you attended this morning?"

Eusebius looked vaguely confused.

"Master Rudolfo's lecture. He said you were seated next to the lad this morning."

Eusebius's face cleared. "Oh, that boy. From the north."

"Yes, that's the one. William's his name. Do you recall where the lad went after the lecture ended?"

Eusebius's face regained its expression of perplexity. He shook his head. "I don't recall. I was so enraptured with Master Rudolfo's explanation of the phlegmatic humors, I fear I noticed little else on my way back. Why do you seek the lad?"

"He's a friend of Donald's," I improvised. It would do little good for the masters to know my wife had flouted university rules and enrolled, dressed as a lad and hiding her sex. And I hoped Mariota would soon appear, at which time William of Uist, if I had any voice in the matter, would mysteriously disappear, never to be seen again.

"What of the messenger who arrived, the day you were attacked in town? The day Berwyk was stabbed. Had you seen him before? I'd like to find the lad and speak with him."

"Ah, yes." Eusebius frowned slightly and seemed to be searching his memory. "He was slightly built, wearing the robes of an undergraduate. With fair hair and blue eyes."

"Do you know his name?"

"Indeed no, I'd not seen him before."

"Then how did he know to warn you, here at Balliol?"

Delacey interrupted. "It is common knowledge who owns our lecture hall. Anyone would have known where to find us."

So that proved little, although I could search the town for fair-haired scholars—after I found my wife.

Perhaps Mariota waited at home for me even now. I took some comfort in the thought although it did not entirely calm my racing heart. We bade the masters good day and continued on our way. The afternoon shadows were growing longer, for we had spent a good while searching in town, and as Donald and I walked back down Canditch I told myself we would find Mariota safe, chatting with Widow Tanner in the kitchen when we arrived home.

Phillip Woode, who had followed after us down the street, interrupted my thoughts. "Muirteach!"

"What is it?"

"I've remembered something. About the day Berwyk was knifed."

We stopped a moment while Phillip caught up with us. While we waited I saw Anthony escorting Avice up the street, headed for Oxford Castle. I remembered that Ivo had asked to see his daughter and guessed that Anthony was escorting her, playing knight-errant. Avice was nicely dressed in a green tunic, with the silver medal Anthony had found tied around her neck with a ribbon. We greeted them, and I stood by while Anthony chatted with Donald a moment. I thought I noticed Phillip looking curiously at Avice before she and Anthony disappeared into the crowd headed for the town gates.

"So, what was it you wanted to tell me?" I asked Phillip as we walked toward my lodging.

Phillip shook his head and ignored my question. "That medal Avice was wearing. Do you know where she got it?"

"I think that's the one Anthony found in the street. He must have given it to her."

"Strange. Jonetta had a very similar one. I'd have sworn they were the same necklace. An unusual medal, a pilgrim's badge, with a pelican on it."

Thinking back, I remembered that Jonetta had indeed worn a similar necklace. "That is strange. I was with Anthony when he found it. It was lying in the street, near the vintner's by the tannery. Perhaps it fell from her neck as they left the town."

"But that road is not a major road heading from the town," Phillip objected. "I'd have expected Jonetta and her chapman to take the North Road. There's not much back there, not after you pass the Augustinians. Just some abandoned buildings from the time of the pestilence and open fields."

"Perhaps she met him there, as it was little traveled."

"Perhaps," said Phillip, but he sounded unconvinced.

"Or perhaps it is not the same necklace at all."

"It was unusual," Phillip protested. "I am certain it was the same pendant."

"Well, perhaps when Avice returns we can borrow the pendant from her and show it to Master Jakeson. Surely he or his wife will recognize it, if it was their daughter's. Now, what was it you wished to tell me?"

"Oh. The day we were attacked in town, Berwyk was the last to seek shelter in the chapel."

"Yes."

"And I saw Bookman, close on his heels as we slammed the door shut."

"So he could well have knifed Berwyk before he entered the chapel."

"Indeed, he must have."

"Yet he swears he did not do it," I mused, although the *Isagoge* tied the two deaths together.

Who else had been in the chapel? Phillip Woode, Eusebius

and Delacey. Had one of them knifed Berwyk? But for what reason? Berwyk was popular with the younger students. Had one of the other masters—Delacey, perhaps—been jealous? Or even Woode? I looked at him suspiciously, but Phillip only frowned a little back at me, his brown eyes concerned. He did not look like a guilty man.

"I am sure it was Jonetta's necklace," he insisted.

"Why are you so certain?" I asked him.

"Because it was I who gave it to her."

# Chapter 16

"You?"

"Aye. I journeyed once to Canterbury and purchased it there. At the shrine of Saint Thomas the Martyr. A little enough thing, paltry really, but pretty I thought. And I could afford it for her. If I could have," Phillip continued, "I'd have bought her gold and jewels."

"How well did you know Jonetta?" I demanded.

"I know—knew—the lass well. I'd have married her, if she'd have waited for me. Instead of fleeing town with that chapman. Although I've never seen the man with her. You'd think I'd have noticed him, there at the tavern."

"Did Jonetta encourage your attentions?"

"Indeed, I thought she did. That is why it surprised me so when she ran off."

"Aye," I said. "It surprised her parents as well."

Phillip turned to me, his face intent. I felt pressure and winced a little as he grabbed my arm, his fingers digging into my flesh in his excitement. "Muirteach, what if Jonetta didn't leave with the chapman after all? What if something else happened to her?"

"Such as what?"

"She could have been slain. Or abducted."

"It's true there's been no sign of either Jonetta or the chapman. Grymbaud says that in the towns where he's inquired, no one's seen them. And the arrival of a chapman is an event in a small village. It is odd," I said slowly.

"What of the outbuildings? Out there, behind the vintner's? Past the Benedictines? Were they searched?"

"We can ask the undersheriff."

"Muirteach, what if her body is lying there, undiscovered and unshriven? We must go and speak with Grymbaud this very night."

"There's something I must see to at my lodgings first, Phillip." It was true that perhaps not every building in the town had been searched door to door after Jonetta's disappearance. But I had problems of my own. "It's growing dark now. I'll speak to Grymbaud tomorrow. Tomorrow we can search the backlands. His men can help with that."

"Indeed, Muirteach. Tomorrow, then. That will have to do." Phillip turned away, disgusted, I thought, at my lack of response as we neared Widow Tanner's.

I entered the front door, my heart pounding like a drum. I saw no sign of Mariota. I began to feel nauseated and my mouth went dry again. *"Mo chridhe,"* I called, but got no answer.

The widow emerged from a back room and looked anxiously at me. She held a wet rag.

"Widow Tanner, have you seen my wife?"

"Eh, no, sir, not since this morning."

"She hasn't returned at all?'

"No, sir," the widow repeated. "I thought her to be with you."

The anxiety I felt exploded into molten rage. "You colluded with her, woman, and now she's disappeared," I shouted. "She never came back this morning. She never showed at Berwyk's funeral mass. She was to meet me there, you foolish old gossip. And there's a murderer loose in the streets of the town."

Widow Tanner's face went pale. Though that did not stop my tirade. "We've searched the town and found not a trace of her."

"Oh, sir, surely she's safe."

"Safe where? Do you see her? Is she here safe?"

Widow Tanner replied with some spirit. "Sir, I know your wife, somewhat. She would not take risks."

"Aye, I know," I ranted. "No risk more than dressing as a man and sneaking into university lectures, as headstrong as any undergraduate. I know she would not take risks. And that is why I am so worried."

Widow Tanner twisted the rag in her hands.

"She would not take risks," I repeated, catching my breath and speaking in a somewhat quieter tone. "So something must have happened."

"Where have you searched?"

"Donald and I searched all the lecture halls this morning. The booksellers. The taverns."

"What of the other lodging halls?'

"Not door to door," I admitted.

"Well, you might look there. Perhaps she was taken ill and carried to one." The widow stopped and thought. "You cannot cover the entire city, just you and Donald. You need more men. You must tell the undersheriff. He is a good man. His men will help you search."

"Yes." It seemed Mariota's scheme would now come into the open. What that would mean I did not know, but I knew I needed help to find her in this city now. I turned on my heels and left the widow's house, setting out for Oxford Castle to find Undersheriff Grymbaud.

It was full dark now, but Donald and I saw Avice and Anthony just leaving the castle gates. "Were you able to see your father, lass?" I asked.

"Aye." Avice ducked her rabbity face down and seemed unwilling to say more.

"Old Ivo was right glad to see her," Anthony put in. "He said he would rest easy tonight, knowing she was safe."

"Good enough then," I said, thinking all the while that I too would rest much easier if I knew Mariota was safe. "Anthony, you'll see the lass home safe to Widow Tanner's?"

Anthony stood a little straighter, proudly nodded assent, and they went on their way. Donald and I passed through the gates and into Oxford Castle. We found the undersheriff conferring with some townsfolk, who exited with serious expressions on their faces as we entered his office.

"Oh, Muirteach." Grymbaud's face lightened a little as he saw me. "Any news, then?"

"No, and I've a problem of my own." I told the undersheriff of my missing wife and his expression hardened as he listened.

"She was dressed as a boy?"

"Aye, going by the name of William of Uist."

"Women." Grymbaud spat on the floor. "They cause all type of problems, when they don't keep to the place God ordained for them."

"My wife is somewhat headstrong," I admitted angrily, "but she is a good healer. It does not surprise me she wanted to attend the lectures."

"Well, would that her disappearance were the university's problem then, and not mine," the undersheriff groused. "But although she posed as a clerk, she is not one. No, no, Muirteach, do not leave. It falls to me. She is a good woman, and was of great help with that Berwyk affair. I'll send some men to help you search. We can begin to check the lodging tenements now. I'll send for torches. Best, perhaps, to start near School Street and fan out from there."

Grymbaud gave his orders and it was not too long before some ten of his men assembled. We set out into the darkness, toward School Street. The moon had not yet risen and the side streets were quiet and dark, our torches flickering over our faces and briefly illuminating those of the few people we passed. As we neared High Street we could see the taverns were busy, although the streets were almost as dark.

Grymbaud sent men to check the taverns, splitting our party into several smaller ones in order to search more quickly. Donald accompanied another party, but Grymbaud and I entered The Green Man. The tavern smelled of ale, wine and smoke from the hearth and bustled with the clamor of thirsty citizens. Master Jakeson approached and we told him of our search. He responded sympathetically, but asked us not to tell his wife, who was busy in the kitchens. He feared the news of yet another missing woman would upset her. Some students were dicing at a back table, but no one there looked familiar and I saw no sign of my wife. It was the same in all the other taverns we tried.

The lecture halls on School Street were locked up for the night, but there were student tenements on that narrow street as well, and we began the slow task of going door to door, rousing students from their evening pastimes. A few we actually found studying, but we did not find William of Uist.

The night grew later and even the taverns began to empty out. We shone our torches in the faces of the revelers straggling back to their rooms, but still found nothing. The torches burned lower and finally Grymbaud took me aside. "We've found nothing, Muirteach. It's late. The torches have burned out. We must stop for the night."

A dark shadow of what I hoped was a cat crossed the alley, on some nocturnal mission of its own. I heard the skittering of what sounded like rats in the gutter and listened for a moment before I replied.

"Come, Muirteach, the men are exhausted. We can start again in the morning, after a little rest."

Donald stumbled over and gave a huge yawn.

"You all can go home," I declared stubbornly, ignoring my

own gritty eyes and weariness, intent only on my consuming need to find my wife. "I must keep searching for her."

"I'll stay with you," Donald volunteered. "Perhaps we'll find something. And it won't be too long until students start heading for the morning lectures. They start early."

"Perhaps we could see who attends Rudolfo's lectures and ask among them. Someone there might have information."

"That's wise, Muirteach," Grymbaud put in. "But I think you'll make more sense of the search if you were to sleep for an hour or two now. That one," and he glanced at Donald, "looks like he needs sleep, even if you do not."

Donald yawned again. "I am happy to stay with you and keep searching," he insisted.

Finally, I gave in and went with Donald back to Widow Tanner's. The kitten was curled up on the bed, but it moved aside a bit when I came in. I thought sleep would not come but my eyes closed as soon as my head hit the bedding, and I unwillingly collapsed into a few hours of disordered slumber.

I awoke with the feeling I had forgotten something. My dream faded, a worrisome dream in which I ransacked piles of parchment, looking for something important I had lost. My heart pounded with anxiety as I searched the towering piles of parchment, all written in some indecipherable text.

I slowly came back to myself and realized it had been only the imaginings of sleep. The kitten still slept, and the moon shone in through the cracks in the wooden shutters. Then I realized where I was, and that Mariota was not there, and my heart began racing again in panic. Mariota had been missing for nearly a day now.

I tried to force my breath to come more slowly and to think rationally. We were to search again today, to ask the students in Master Rudolfo's class if they had seen anything of William of

Uist. And it was time we were on our way. The morning lectures started early.

I roused Donald and after a quick drink of small ale from the widow's pantry we took a lantern and made our way through the quiet streets of early morning into the town toward School Street. A sliver of moon was just setting in the west, while to the east the sky began to lighten, but Oxford was beginning to stir. I smelled smoke as cooking fires were kindled and heard the bang of shutters and doors as townsfolk opened their upper windows, merchants readied themselves for the business of the day, and sleepy students made their way to class.

We made our way to the hall where Master Rudolfo gave his lectures. I did not see Brother Eusebius this morning, but many other students were jostling each other as they went inside and took their seats on the wooden benches. I spoke to Master Rudolfo and he gave me permission to address the students. There were some hushed murmurs among the clerks as I told them of the missing "William of Uist" and asked anyone with information on the lad to send word to myself or to Donald. One of the students, a tall, brown-haired lad, stood quietly and left his place on the benches to speak with us.

I felt that funny tightness in my chest again as I waited for the boy to begin. He introduced himself as James Heresward, from Suffolk. He was a gentle-spoken lad, with a grave countenance, and lodged at some tenements on Canditch. "I believe I saw the lad you seek after the lectures, walking toward Smithgate. I was walking that way, heading home to break my fast," he said. "I tried to speak with the boy, but he is very shy. He passed me and kept walking." James shrugged his shoulders. "That is all I know. I'm sorry not to be of more help."

"Did you see anyone else?" I asked, rubbing my gritty eyes.

"The streets are crowded at that time of the morning," James returned. "There were many folk about but when I left him, the lad was still walking alone, down Canditch."

"And you'd swear to this?" I demanded.

"Of course. Why do you doubt my word?" he responded with some annoyance.

I thanked him and apologized for my churlishness. Then we left.

"So," Donald commented as we walked along crowded High Street, "we know Mariota nearly reached home yesterday. But what could have happened to her? How could she have disappeared so near to our lodgings?"

"I can think of many things that might have happened to her," I said darkly, "and none of them are good." I waited impatiently while Donald stopped at a newly opened baker's stall for a fresh bun. The normally appetizing scent of fresh bread did nothing for me. I had no desire for food; the thought of it made my stomach turn. Finally, Donald paid for his purchase and we continued toward Widow Tanner's. We had just passed Northgate and were starting down Canditch when I saw Phillip Woode hurrying down the street.

"Muirteach," he called, then quieted as he came closer "Good God, man, what is wrong? You look terrible."

"It's my wife," I told him. "She's disappeared."

"God, no. Like Jonetta."

"No, not like Jonetta!" I practically screamed at him. "Jonetta ran off with a chapman. My wife was last seen here, not thirty yards from our lodgings, in bright morning light. And yet she's vanished."

"As Jonetta did. Don't you recall we were to search for her today? With the undersheriff's men?"

I had forgotten our conversation of the day before. But the backlands were as good a place to search as any. I walked with Phillip back to Grymbaud's headquarters in the castle. He and his men had just finished breaking their fast on small ale and bread. The undersheriff did not look overjoyed to see Phillip Woode but he listened to Phillip's story and, after hearing of the silver pendant Anthony had found and Phillip's assertion that it was the one he had given to Jonetta, agreed to send additional men, led by his man Ralf, to search the outskirts with us.

# CHAPTER 17

The search was thorough. The noxious vats at the Widow's tannery were probed and the vintner's wine casks thumped. A few kegs were tapped and sampled, Master Gibbes's protests notwithstanding, and all the outbuildings searched. We searched the Benedictines' college and then we moved across the street to the Austin Friars. Ralf and his men knocked on the wooden door in the stone wall that surrounded the establishment.

"We're seeking information on the whereabouts of two young women, lately missing," Ralf said.

"Two young women?" the Hospitaller echoed, a thin elderly man with concerned brown eyes. "I'd heard one girl from the town had disappeared. Now you say there's another?"

"Aye," Ralf responded grimly. "The second woman disappeared but yesterday."

"She's fair," I interjected, "with light hair and blue eyes. She was dressed as a lad, wearing a blue tunic with a hood."

"Dressed as a lad?" the Hospitaller repeated. I fumed at his slowness. "We had heard of the first disappearance and the troubles in the town. The slayings. But now you say another woman has vanished. This is a bad business."

"Indeed," Grymbaud's assistant said, "and a medal belonging to the first girl, Master Jakeson's daughter, was found on the road outside."

The Hospitaller's eyes widened.

"And so we are searching all the area here. Have you seen or heard aught suspicious?"

"No." The friar shook his head. "We keep the door barred and see little of the outside world, as a rule. Although, of course, some of our friars are active in the university. They come and go into the town, so of course we knew of the trouble. But there are no women within these walls, you can be sure of that."

I had spent time in an Augustinian priory as a young boy. That sect is not as cloistered as some others, and I could well imagine some of the canons teaching in the universities.

"Still, we must search," Ralf insisted, obdurate.

The Hospitaller shrugged. "Come inside. I will call the Prior."

The prior was concerned and although he protested we would find nothing he let us search without further demur.

We found nothing untoward in the place. No hidden women, no trace of anything, except an austere friars' dormitory and a few rooms not so austere. At the end of the dormitory was a fine library. We thanked the Austin Friars and left them to their devotions and their studies.

Outside there were few other buildings to search. The abandoned homes on the other side of the road, past the college of the Benedictines, were quickly looked over. Some had once been fine houses, several-storied, but all had fallen into grievous disrepair. Most were locked up tight, but Ralf ordered the shutters pried open so we could peer in. It was clear that the dwellings were empty and long untenanted. There were some outbuildings, also closed and locked. We pounded on the doors and peered through cracks in the wattle but saw nothing.

"These buildings are long undisturbed," said Ralf. "There's no sign of anyone having been here in a long while. No tracks."

I wiped some of the dust from my face and peered in through another shuttered window.

"It's that damned pestilence. It's hard to see the ruins this town has come to," Ralf swore.

"The same could be said for many places," Phillip Woode observed.

"Aye." The sheriff's man kicked at a brick that had fallen forlornly into the yard. "Well, there's nothing to be found here."

"But she must be here," I insisted. "People do not just vanish. What of the woods behind us?"

Ralf nodded. "We'll search the woods." He stopped. "There are two lymers at the castle, scenting hounds. Perhaps we could have the use of them for a time." He gave orders for one of the men to go to the castle and return with the hounds, and sent me to get some of Mariota's garments from our lodgings with orders to meet them on Canditch.

I went back to our rooms and found Mariota's dress, still lying folded neatly where she had left it the morning before. The sight of it caused a tight lump in my throat and brought tears to my eyes, like a maid. I could not control myself as I picked it up to take back to the men. Mariota must be found. Surely I would sense it if she—I could not even frame the thought. No, we would find her, safe, and together we would laugh about this someday.

The kitten was not in our chamber. I stopped in the kitchen to inform the widow how the search progressed and spied it lapping at some milk from a pottery dish on the floor.

"They think to use the lymers to find her," I explained shortly to Widow Tanner, who was kneading some bread on the worn wooden table while Avice chopped leeks nearby. Rufous prowled underfoot, whined, wanting scraps I supposed.

"Aye." Widow Tanner nodded, her face looking pinched and much older today. "Godspeed. Avice and I are away to the church after these chores to pray to Our Lady for your success."

Perhaps Our Lady was otherwise occupied this day, for when I returned with Mariota's blue dress under my arm, there was still no sign of my wife.

"At least they've found no bodies," Phillip Woode informed me. That comment did little to ease the pit in my gut and the tightness in my chest and throat.

By now the dogs had arrived from Oxford Castle, two gigantic, slavering beasts that tugged against the chains that held them. One was brindled brown and black and the other a lighter color, gray with brown spots here and there. I handed my wife's dress to their keeper and the dogs sniffed at it eagerly, pulling at their leashes.

"Now," said the handler, "let us see if they pick up her scent."

I was suddenly minded of Somerled, the dog I had left back at home in Islay, as I watched the hound sniffing at the garment.

This activity received curious stares from the good folk of Oxford, about their business that morning. Apparently the fierceness of the dogs and the presence of the authorities kept the citizenry of the town at bay as most scuttled by us with an anxious glance at the beasts.

The hounds seemed confused on the street. Canditch Street was a much-used thoroughfare, after all. But after a time they seemed to catch the trail of something. The brown lymer paused, as if wanting to turn into the widow's house, but then picked up the scent again, his nose close to the ground, and followed the trail up the road, past the tannery and the vintner Gibbes's property, past the area we'd searched already that morning, and on up the road. The gray dog followed.

My heart began beating faster, with dread or anticipation. Perhaps we would find Mariota safe at last.

The first hound, all business, put his nose to the earth and moved on steadily, seeming to attend to his task, while the other beast bayed excitedly and started to dart toward the left of the road, but gave up after a bit and was pulled back by his keeper.

Both dogs barked excitedly, then put their noses back to the ground, tugging at their chains and pulling their keeper up the street. We got more stares from passersby, but there were not so many people on this road leading away from the town.

We passed the Austin Friars' on the right and the hounds continued up the road, passing some orchards, and finally pulled into the meadow and stopped, panting, underneath the very tree where my wife and I had sat just two days earlier, enjoying our afternoon in the green.

"This has naught to do with my wife's disappearance," I told Ralf. I explained about our holiday on Sunday.

"My dogs picked up no other scent," their keeper insisted. "So if she came this way with you two days ago, it don't seem likely she's been here since. I'm sorry, sir."

The lymers milled around the spot under the tree where Mariota had sat cradling my head in her lap. The keeper began to rein in his beasts and lead them away from the woods and back down the street leading to town. Disheartened, we straggled along behind, Donald following more quickly, as his youthful stomach growled with hunger and he was eager to break his fast. Phillip Woode and I lagged; I hoped to find some clue we'd missed, but I saw nothing.

One of the hounds ahead, the big brindled one that I fancied was the most intelligent, began whining and pulling to the right. Curious, the handler gave it some lead. The dog nosed around the side of the road, then stopped as if confused. Phillip and I caught up with the man and the two hounds.

"There be nothing here," the handler muttered.

"True." We had checked the buildings behind and found nothing of import. An abandoned house, a derelict kitchen shed and other outbuildings. Nothing else. "She's not here."

The keeper led the dogs away and we turned to go.

"Wait, Muirteach." Phillip surveyed the dirt in the road near where the hound had been sniffing. "Wait," he repeated, with more urgency. "I've found something."

I walked over to stand next to Phillip. In his hand, still besmirched with mud, lay a gold ring.

# CHAPTER 18

"Let me see that." I grabbed the ring out of Phillip's hand. The small gold circle had engraved inside it the Gaelic words *"Mo Chridhe."* I realized it was the same ring I had given Mariota on Colonsay at Yuletide a year ago, when we became hand-fasted, and I fought down the desire to be sick.

"That is Mariota's ring."

"You don't think she lost it on Sunday, as you walked back from your outing?" asked Phillip.

"She did not mention it." I strained to think. "No, now I am thinking she had it on all the evening. I remember . . ." A sudden image came to me of Mariota sitting at the table next to me that night. The light of the widow's candles glinted on the ring, which was on Mariota's hand as she ate. The picture brought a sudden sharp pang, as though a dagger had been twisted oddly in my gut, and the croaked tightness in my throat was such that I could not speak as I looked at the slim circlet of gold in my palm. "I remember her wearing it," I finished lamely, avoiding Phillip's gaze.

"So she passed this way. The hounds were right," Phillip murmured.

"But where is she? And why did the dogs lose the scent?"

"Perhaps she was not here. Perhaps the ring was stolen from her and then dropped."

That did nothing to answer the question of Mariota's whereabouts or to improve my state of mind. I secured the ring safely in my scrip and we looked around. To the right was one of the abandoned homes, a somewhat large building with a stone ground story and a timber and plaster story above it. It looked to be a large old-fashioned hall, with a cross-wing on one end. Behind it were some outbuildings, a kitchen shed and some other sheds. The property bordered the Benedictines' wall on the side closest to the town. On the other side was another abandoned house.

"Who does this property belong to?" I asked.

"I do not know," Phillip replied. "But the bailiff should know."

"Let us look around again." The property, dilapidated and in need of attention, could have done with rethatching and replastering; the roof sagged and in places the plaster had fallen off, revealing aged wattle beneath. A shutter on an upstairs window hung askew and flapped forlornly in the wind. Weeds grew tall in the back yard, and we could see a neighbor's pig, probably Vintner Gibbes's, rooting contentedly amongst the growth.

We walked around to the back of the house. There was a rear entrance and I pushed against it, but it proved to be locked. Another shutter hung loosely from one window, and I pried at its mate. It proved easy to loosen. An empty rain barrel stood at one corner of the house.

"We can climb in through here," I announced to Phillip. He nodded. We rolled the barrel over and stood it up on end below the window. I climbed up and wriggled my way through the opening. Phillip Woode followed me.

I looked around. We were in the hall, an old-style hall with a large fireplace at one end and columns spaced here and there, supporting the vaulted ceiling beams. A trestle table and some benches stood in the center of the room. Old rushes still lay on the floor and a little light came through the opened window. A thick layer of dust covered everything, along with some pigeon droppings. It appeared some birds had gotten in and roosted there.

"Phew," Phillip exclaimed, brushing dust from his cotehardie. He sneezed. "The place looks deserted."

"Yes," I agreed. A door from the hall led to the smaller rooms in the cross-wing. I walked over and pushed the door open as my eyes adjusted to the dim light. There was a solar, with faded wall paintings, and another room behind. Two chairs and a wooden trunk still sat in the solar but the other room held no furniture. In the farther room was a wooden staircase, somewhat fallen down, that led to the upper chambers. Carefully I climbed up, avoiding the missing boards.

Upstairs were three smaller rooms. One had a sagging bedstead and another a fine big bed with moth-eaten curtains. The third room had a small table and chair situated before the window. It must have been in this room that the merchant, or whoever had lived here, had conducted his business.

Phillip shrugged. "Well, there's nothing to be seen here after all," he said sadly.

I nodded. Indeed, there seemed nothing here.

"Mariota!" I called out on impulse, but of course there was no answer. We turned to go and made our way carefully down the treacherous stairway and back into the hall. We moved the bench over and climbed back out the way we had entered.

We poked around the outbuildings for a second time, but again our search yielded nothing. Thoroughly discouraged, we made our way back toward town. The sun was already sinking in the west and the air growing chill. Donald had returned to the widow's house for supper but I found I had no appetite.

"Phillip," I said, "let us go into town, to The Green Man. I'm thirsty."

I had not drunk as much, these past months, married to Mariota and savoring our new happiness. But that evening, my despair was such that I could not stand it and could not stand my own awareness of the lack of her in my life. I did not know what to do with the fear that had taken root and now grew inside my heart, the fear that I might never see Mariota or hold her again in my arms. I thought to drown my discomfort with some strong drink. Although *uisghebeatha,* which I would greatly have preferred, was not to be found here in England, I hoped perhaps some brandy wine might serve my purpose.

Phillip also, I think, felt morose. He agreed readily enough, and we entered the town walls through Smithgate and made our way down Catte Street and west on High Street to The Green Man. There was a pleasant fire on the wide hearth and as we pushed open the door, the air inside felt warm after the chill outside.

Abraham Jakeson presided over the tavern that evening. He nodded brusquely and his wife looked questioningly at us as we took seats on a vacant bench near the side wall. It seemed she and her husband had heard of the search that day.

"Nothing. We found nothing," Phillip informed her as she brought us a jug of claret and two leathern cups. The woman's face fell and she turned away. I downed my first mug of drink with great speed, barely tasting the wine. The second drink also.

The smoky atmosphere and wine had taken the sharpest edge of my pain away. I set the drink down after draining the third glass when the door opened again, and Delacey and his young protégée entered the room. They did not see us but took seats closer to the fire.

I did not think Julian Delacey had anything to do with Mariota's disappearance, but he could well have killed Master Clarkson. He had, after all, been alone in his room, with no one to vouch for him, as Berwyk had spent that fateful night with Torvilda. As the drink took hold of me I grew certain, with that false confidence that often comes with spirits, that Ivo had not done that thing. I pulled my mantle over my head a bit and sank back against the wall, into the shadows. I nudged Phillip and whispered to him. "Phillip, let us watch them both and see what transpires."

Woode pulled his hood up and also slumped against the wall. But we hardly needed to bother. Delacey and DeVyse seemed oblivious to the others in the room, laughing together at some private jest. They shared one drink, and then another; then I saw Richard throw some coins on the table and they rose to leave.

I poked Phillip. "Let us follow them."

Phillip looked surprised but acquiesced. Julian Delacey was his superior, after all, yet the drink was in Phillip and perhaps he did not mind too much. We quickly paid our fee and left The Green Man. The cold air outside went a fair way to sharpening my wits and helped shake the wine fumes from my mind. The streets were dark and we had no lantern, but up ahead it was not too hard to make out the figures of Delacey and his student, heading up High Street toward Northgate Street. They went up that street and through the city gate, as did we, passing through the greater darkness, at this hour, of the long tunnel that snaked under the Boccardo and out into the suburbs.

"I am surprised that young DeVyse did not go the other direction, to his lodgings on Catte Street," I whispered to Phillip at a distance from the pair. The two neared the gates of Balliol and entered the court. I saw Delacey push the door open and the two men entered the hall.

"I shall follow them in," Phillip declared in low tones.

"I'll go with you." I had an uncomfortable suspicion and wanted to know if there was basis for my thought. We waited a few moments, and then we walked up to the hall and entered. The downstairs rooms were silent and deserted. We walked up the wooden stairs leading to the next floor. Delacey must have lit a candle in the room he had shared with Berwyk; I could see light streaming out from below the door, and I heard murmured voices from within the chamber.

Phillip rapped on the door.

"Who is it?" came Delacey's voice.

"Phillip Woode."

"I've retired. Leave me in peace."

"But I must see you—"

The door opened a crack.

"What is all this about?" Delacey's face grew choleric when he saw the both of us standing on the stairway. I stepped forward boldly and pushed the door open more and saw young DeVyse, clad only in his shirt while Delacey had on only his braies.

Phillip and I turned to face each other a moment, as the full import of the situation struck us. Julian Delacey looked at us, ashen, for an instant and then his face flushed a choleric ruddy hue. "This is not what it seems—"

"What is it, then?" I asked. "It seems clear enough to me. The lad is your paramour."

"No, no," Julian protested, "the lad's cotehardie was wet with the rain. We but seek to dry it off."

That clearly was a feeble attempt to explain the situation and I told him so.

"So," I continued, "perhaps this explanation will be more sensible. You killed Clarkson when he learned of your sodomy. Perhaps he threatened you with disclosure or expulsion. You would not want that on your record, not a doctor of canon law."

"Indeed, that is not the case," Delacey protested, his face once again red with rage. "Clarkson never knew of it. No one knew of it."

"What of Berwyk, your roommate? You are saying he never

knew of it either? That strains belief."

Delacey shook his head. "The man was too often with that slut Torvilda. He knew not what I did, and he cared less. Ralph was not a man to judge others."

"So you lied about his whereabouts the night Clarkson was slain. You claimed he was here, when he was really on Pennyfarthing Street with Mistress Bonefey."

Delacey nodded. "Aye. Dickon was here with me, and I thought it best to hide that. And Ralph did not want his liaison with Torvilda common knowledge. But I swear I did not slay Clarkson. You must believe me."

This plea seemed odd, coming from the blustering advocate. I let that pass.

"So you heard nothing that night? Your room is close to Clarkson's chamber."

"Neither of us heard anything. Did we, Dickon?"

DeVyse, who had been silent while Delacey spoke, struggling to unobtrusively put his cotehardie back on, nodded his head. "I heard nothing that night. But we were here the whole time."

"And when did you leave? You were certainly not here that morning."

"Before Matins. I slipped out and went to my ordinary lecture. Julian let me out."

"And you saw nothing untoward?"

Both men swore they had not.

"What will you do?" Delacey demanded, with some return to his usual pugnacious nature.

"Nothing, for the now."

"So you do believe me?"

"My job is not to punish sodomists. But this gives you a powerful reason to have slain Master Clarkson, and Berwyk as well, if he guessed what you were about."

"He was with me the whole night," Richard DeVyse interjected with some shyness. The boy's cheeks flushed crimson. "We were here the whole night," he repeated. "We did not leave the chamber."

"But you would lie to protect him, would you not?"

The lad blushed again, like a maid. "You'll not tell my parents?"

"I have no idea who your parents are! And have no interest in telling them anything at all. But I might well speak to Grymbaud, and let him make sense of it all."

"I have benefit of clergy," Delacey interjected. "As does Dickon." He glanced at the lad's tonsure. "The authorities can do nothing."

"Not for sodomy," I retorted, "although perhaps the chancellors of the university may have something to say about it. But as for murder, Grymbaud may well have interest in that."

"But I did not kill Clarkson," Delacey protested. "Nor Berwyk. Ivo killed Clarkson, and that bookman stabbed Berwyk. They're imprisoned in the castle for it even now."

"Yet they swear they're innocent as well. No one admits to killing either man, but both are dead," I retorted.

"You have no proof," Delacey insisted, and in that he was right. So I left them, and Phillip Woode as well, in the old hall and returned to Widow Tanner's.

I found Donald, alone for once, in his room. Wonder of all wonders, he appeared to be studying, although the kitten had clambered on top of the desk and sat atop Donald's wax tablets. Donald rose as I entered the chamber. He picked the kitten up and put it on the floor.

"I wondered you did not come to supper," he said.

"I found I was not hungry," I replied shortly, not wanting to tell him all that had transpired with Delacey and DeVyse.

"I am sorry we found nothing today," Donald said awkwardly.

"Aye." But we had found something. I told Donald of Mariota's ring, which Phillip had found in the dirt of the road.

"That is passing strange, that we did not find it earlier," Donald commented.

"It was buried in the dirt of the road and easy to miss."

"Yes, but what if Phillip planted it there? To throw us off the track? He was questioned in Jonetta's disappearance, was he not? Perhaps he has something to do with Mariota's disappearance as well."

I grew annoyed with Donald's wild theories, although doubtless the lad just wanted to help. But he had initially cast suspicion on Phillip Woode, and seemed to be doing so again. I bade him good night and retired to my own chamber where the absence of my wife struck me again like a dagger wound.

Although exhausted, I did not sleep well that night, and when I did sleep I dreamed disturbing dreams. I saw Mariota, who called to me from some strange crystalline prison; she seemed imprisoned in a glass vessel. I could not hear her words, only see her lips moving. Julian Delacey and young DeVyse appeared, and Ralph Berwyk stood there also, holding something out to me, but I could not divine what it might be. Delacey threw Mariota, still within the strange vessel, into an ocean. At first the thing bobbed on the surface like a boat, but then roaring waves of a whirlpool washed over my wife and carried her away. In my dream, no matter what I tried to do I could not reach her, for my limbs felt heavy as lead and could not move freely. Still I tried desperately to throw Mariota something to grasp onto. A circle of gold glinted in the waters of the whirlpool and her ring followed my wife down to the depths of the sea.

I woke, my heart racing and a cold sweat on my back. It was an evil dream, I told myself. And that was all. But where was my wife, and what was she trying to tell me? What had I not heard?

A sudden movement on the bed caused me to startle, but it

was only the tabby kitten. It must have grown cold in the September night, for it came close to me and began kneading at the blanket, in the way that women make bread. Despite my misery I found some comfort in the beast and stroked it as it began to purr, until it finally curled up and slept under my arm. But I could sleep no more that night. I lay there, listening to the creak of the wooden shutters in the wind while the dark hours slowly passed.

It must have been close to Matins when I heard stirring in Donald's chamber and a few moments later he stuck his head in my door. "I'm off to my early lecture, Muirteach."

"Well enough," I muttered, although I might normally have wondered at this industry on my charge's part.

"What are you going to do this day?"

I sat up on the bed and wearily reached for my hose. "Keep searching for Mariota, I suppose. In the woods near where Phillip found her ring. Perhaps we overlooked something yesterday."

Donald nodded. "I'll seek you there, then, and join you after my lecture." I nodded assent and Donald left my chamber. I heard the sound of his steps down the stairway and the noise of the door closing behind him. I remained on the bed and heard the noises of the servants about their early morning duties and smelled the faint smoke of the kitchen fire. Then, finally, I roused myself and finished dressing. I threw my mantle on over my clothes and went downstairs, thinking to get something to break my fast. From not having eaten the night before, I found to my surprise I was hungry.

The door to the house swung open again, and Donald burst back inside. "Muirteach, you must come, and quickly," he cried before I could question him. "Anthony has been attacked!"

# CHAPTER 19

I heard Avice, who had come into the hall to see what was amiss, give a wail and run from the room as I followed Donald out the door and into the cold morning.

The sun was just cresting the rooftops and the blue haze of morning fires hung in the chill air like a blanket. I shivered and pulled my mantle more closely about my shoulders.

"Where is he?" I questioned. "What happened?"

"He was found on Catte Street, just near here," Donald answered as we entered the town walls through Smithgate. "He's been carried to his tenement. Someone struck him from behind. He's sore hurt but not dead."

"Thank the saints for that," I replied. "But who would wish to hurt Anthony? He's but a lad."

I might have expected Donald to bristle at this reference to his friend's youth, but he did not take offense at my speech. "I know. Anthony means harm to no one."

"And Crispin? Where is he?"

"He had not gone to the lecture this morning, so Anthony was walking alone. I saw a crowd as I neared School Street and found that it was Anthony. They made to carry him home and I left to fetch you. But Crispin should be with him now."

"Does he wake?" I remembered another time when someone struck from behind had slept for weeks, and that had a bad ending. My relief was great when Donald replied that Anthony had spoken to him before his litter-bearers carried him away.

"Let us see where it took place, and then let us go and speak with Anthony."

When we got to the location of the crime, there was not much to be seen. A narrow alley opened off Catte Street, barely wide enough to admit one person. It was there that Anthony's attacker must have waited for the boy. I could see a bit of blood still on the street, where the lad had fallen, but the growing morning light revealed nothing else in the alley. Whoever this madman might be, he showed no qualms about attacking folk from behind and I liked him the less for that.

"What of the bailiffs? Did they come? Or Grymbaud?"

"The town watch came by. They thought it just a student dispute and did nothing when it became clear that Anthony would live."

"Well, let us go and see him." We left that spot and walked back out through Smithgate and back down Canditch to the tenement where Anthony and Crispin lodged, midway between the Widow Tanner's house and Balliol. Inside was a great chamber, a dormitory, where close to twelve lads lodged on pallet beds. Some small tables under the windows served as desks. The room was near empty with most of the youths at their lectures, but at the far end we saw Crispin and someone lying on one of the beds—Anthony.

We walked closer and I felt great gladness to see the lad's eyes were open. He had a bandage tied haphazardly around his head and on the back of it I could see some blood that had seeped through. The lad's face was white beneath his freckles but he looked alert.

"Anthony," I greeted him. "Donald brought me news of your mischance. What happened?"

"I do not know, rightly," Anthony admitted. "I've a powerful pain in my head."

"Rest a moment. Then tell us what you do remember," I suggested. "Perhaps it will be of help."

Anthony relaxed against the bolster a moment, then gathered his strength and spoke. "I was walking down Catte Street. I hurried, as it had grown late and most students were already in the halls. There were not many folk about, I think." He closed his eyes briefly.

"And then?" I prompted.

"I had just passed that alleyway and was looking for the pie man who sometimes is selling by the farther corner. I had a farthing and thought to buy one to eat on my way to class. But I did not see him, and then came the blow. Or that must have been the way it happened, for that is the last I remember." Anthony moved his head a little, and then winced.

"It is not so bad," I said, hoping to reassure him. "Just a bump on the noggin."

"Indeed, you probably gave me worse that first fight we had," Donald said. "In that tavern."

Anthony smiled, and my heart began to feel a little lighter. "Still," I pressed, "you know of nothing to identify your attacker?"

Anthony started to shake his head, then must have thought better of it. "No," he replied slowly. "I did not see him. You can see he hit me from behind." He turned his head slowly so we could see the lump under the bloody bandage.

"You'll have a sore pate for a time," I repeated.

"But why would anyone want to attack Anthony?" Crispin wondered. And I wondered that as well. "You're not a threat to anyone. Now I would have seen the bastard coming."

"Oh, now Crispin, you know what a brigand Anthony is," Donald rejoined. "He's a fierce one, indeed. A threat to the peace of Oxford town, indeed, he is."

Anthony grinned, then winced again.

"What were you doing yesterday?" I asked. "Perhaps you offended someone, to cause them to lie in wait for you."

"I did nothing out of the ordinary," Anthony replied. "Well, I studied a time, after the lectures were over. And I went to the booksellers. I needed some ink and parchment."

"Adam Bookman's?" I asked. "Is he not in prison still?"

"Yes, but his wife runs the stall now. I heard you were searching the backlands, with the castle dogs. Are they as fierce as they say?"

"They are scenting hounds, not mastiffs," I replied, thinking again of my dog in Scotland. "So they are not so fierce. But they are large, with big slavering jowls. How did you learn of that?"

"Donald told me, after supper. We played some ball behind the widow's. You were not there."

"No, I was with Phillip Woode," I admitted. "Did others play with you?"

"Just some boys from here. And that lad that Delacey tutors. But he left before the game finished."

"I can well believe that to be so," I replied. "You look as though some rest would not be amiss."

I thought a moment. The attack on the lad had unnerved me. Anthony might be safer at the widow's, where more people were about during the day and I could keep watch over him. *As well as you watched over your wife*, a guilty voice inside my head nagged at me, but I ignored it for once. "Perhaps you should come and stay at the Widow Tanner's, until your head heals," I offered. "Crispin can come too. I am sure Avice would nurse you."

Anthony's face brightened considerably at this and Crispin smiled broadly. "The widow's a fine cook," he said, "and Avice . . ."

"You'll treat her with respect or you can stay here."

Crispin nodded, a little sullenly.

"You can sleep in Donald's chamber," I added, and watched Donald's face fall a bit. "There's plenty of room there. I will just go on ahead and speak with our landlady, to ensure she accepts this plan," I added. "Perhaps Donald can stay here with you until I send word."

I left the lads and walked down Canditch to Widow Tanner's. She agreed, although I did say I'd pay her a bit for her trouble, and I went back to Anthony's lodging. It did not take too long to get him carried back to the widow's house and installed into Donald's chamber. Within a short time he was tucked into Donald's bed while Widow Tanner fussed with his bandage and a poultice and Avice stood at the chamber door with some hot pottage. The tabby kitten amused itself by kneading affectionately at the lad's blanket and I saw Anthony fondling the beast. I sighed with some relief. Anthony would be safe enough here. All I had to do was tolerate Crispin.

I left the lads and went into town in search of Grymbaud. I continued to Oxford Castle, where I ran him to ground in his office. I told him of the attack on Anthony.

"And you're not thinking it was just a student dispute?"

"The lad was attacked from behind. Most student fights happen in taverns, after too much drink. Not in the early morning."

"Did the boy have enemies?" Grymbaud asked, idly scratching at the stubble on his chin.

"He is a pleasant enough lad. He actually spends some time at his studies. His family is not overly wealthy and he is grateful for the chance to get an education. No, I do not think Anthony had enemies. Certainly none to warrant this attack."

"Could he have angered some merchant?"

"I think not. He did say he had purchased parchment yesterday, however. I'll go and speak with Adam Bookman's wife and see if she has anything to say of the matter."

"Indeed, do so, Muirteach." Grymbaud paused a second and took a swig from the mug of ale that sat on his desk. "You may find the woman distraught. The date for the assizes is set. They will be held at the end of this week. Both Bookman and the gardener from Balliol will be brought to justice. It does not look good for either man."

"I do not think either man is guilty," I protested. "But I've found nothing as yet to prove their innocence. However, I did find something interesting last night." I told the undersheriff of finding Delacey and Richard DeVyse.

"Those academics are all perverted. It does not surprise me. But there is no evidence that the little braggart slew Berwyk or Clarkson. And he'd just plead benefit of clergy and no doubt get off lightly, even if there was evidence. But I'll set a man to watch the swine. Bring me some incontrovertible proof, Muirteach, and perhaps I can do something."

"I've had other matters on my mind these past days."

"Indeed. Your wife. I am sorry about that, Muirteach. You do not think she's run off? Women are foolish creatures, you know, easily tempted and led astray."

"Sir, you do not know my wife." I said nothing more, but bit my tongue and held my jaw clenched shut. I was sure that if it did move I would drive my fist into Grymbaud's face, which I did not think would help my cause. So instead I glared at the undersheriff and waited, my muscles tense and the hairs prickling on the back of my neck, while the man drank more of his ale.

At length he set his mug down, noticed my expression and spoke again. "Perhaps not your wife, though. She was of help when Berwyk was stabbed. And she did seem a person of sense, rare in such an attractive woman." For a brief moment I wondered if the undersheriff was married, and decided that, if he was, the union must not be a happy one. "We will keep searching for her," Grymbaud continued, "although if the ly-mers found nothing I doubt anything else will manifest. I am sorry."

"As am I," I retorted and turned on my heels and left Oxford Castle, pacing down Castle Street and back toward the bulk of Northgate, wanting to put as much space between myself and Grymbaud as I could. As I walked down the crowded, muddy street I heard the noise of the street hawkers, the townsfolk about their business and I dodged a pig rooting in a pile of refuse by a narrow side alley. My stomach turned at the crowded mayhem that passed for town life, and I feared I would retch.

Or perhaps my panic rose from the fear that I would never see my wife again. I could smell the terror from the sweat on my skin, and I hopelessly admitted to myself that I did not know where else to search, or what to do to find Mariota. My actions seemed futile, my search as blind as the alley I had just passed.

I cursed the Lord of the Isles and his son under my breath, fluently, in Gaelic. If it were not for him, both Mariota and myself would have been peacefully home on Islay. She would never have dressed as a man, never have attended medical lectures. She would have been safe. *As safe as you've kept her in the past,* an inner voice mockingly told me, and I cursed again, even more eloquently. For it was true that Mariota had often been in danger, and neither she nor I seemed to learn from it at all, at all.

As this last bitter realization sank in, I raised my head and looked about me. I had been walking without thought through the town but discovered I had now reached High Street. The shop of Adam Bookman stood not so distant. Perhaps, since I was so close, I might stop by and speak with his wife, as I had originally intended before my fury took ahold of me.

As I walked up the street a woman looked out from the open

shutters of Adam Bookman's shop, behind the street display of books, parchment and ink. She was young, with a thin face, a pinched look about her mouth and fair-lashed eyes, now red-rimmed. A few strands of pale hair escaped from a tidy coif, and I guessed her to be Adam Bookman's wife.

I had not met her before. Which might be a good thing, as she could not immediately blame me for her husband's imprisonment. I wrapped my *brat* a bit closer about my shoulders, feeling the chill in the air as the faint Oxford sun disappeared behind a cloud, and approached the shop.

"May I be of help?" the woman asked.

I picked up a book, a fair copy of *Sir Orfeo*. I opened it and looked at the story, a fine-looking tale of knights and their ladies. On some other day it would have intrigued me. I closed the book and looked at the woman. "I am not seeking books, today, Mistress. I need some information."

"Oh?" Mistress Bookman gave me a guarded look.

"Yesterday a young student bought some parchment and ink from you. A young lad, with reddish hair."

"Yes, I remember the boy. What of it?"

"What did he purchase, exactly?"

"What is it to you?"

"The lad was accosted this morning and badly hurt."

"It's nothing to me if students brawl. They are always at blows over something or another."

"This was not a student brawl, Mistress. The lad was attacked by someone who hit him from behind." I exaggerated a bit. "He lies near dead now."

"Well, I am sorry to hear of it. He was a well-spoken boy and had better manners than many. Respectful, and thanked me for his purchase. But what has all that to do with me?"

"Could you not tell me what the lad bought?"

"Yes, but it was nothing of import. Some old parchments and

ink. The cheapest ink I had. Soot ink, not gall."

"He is not a rich lad. What of the parchments he bought? Were they used?"

"Yes, they were from an old pile my husband had bought from one of the colleges."

"They were written on?"

"It's little enough work to clean them."

"Have you any left, or did the lad buy all of them?"

"There are some. You wish to see them?"

I nodded assent and the woman disappeared in the interior of the shop, then returned a few moments later with a pile of parchments.

"Here they are. Do you wish to purchase them?"

I examined the sheets. Covered with Latin writing, the parchments looked similar to the ones Donald and I had purchased here a few weeks earlier, the parchments that had been stolen from our lodging. Although these did not look to be the same exact sheets.

"Where did you get these?"

Mistress Bookman shrugged her shoulders. "My husband procured them. I am not sure from where. He had them put away, but times are hard. My husband is now held in the castle."

I nodded. "I had heard that. I am sorry for it."

"He is innocent. He did not stab that master."

I said nothing, and eventually the woman turned back to the parchments. "I thought to sell them and get the lot of them out of here."

"Well, I shall buy these remaining ones, if I may."

Mistress Bookman agreed, and we settled on a price. I gathered up the sheets and prepared to go. "Has anyone else been seeking these?" I asked as I bundled the sheets into my scrip.

"My husband's business is that of a stationer, sir," Mistress

Bookman returned. "I sell a fair number of old parchments. Students are always seeking them, to clean and reuse." So it seemed the answer to that question was yes.

"Who else has purchased them?" I persisted, badgering the woman. "That you remember?"

Mistress Bookman pursed her lips as she thought. "Students, the most of them were. Poor students, looking to reuse the sheets."

"And did you sell many to them?"

"No, for I just found them yesterday. My husband had tucked them away under a pile of other manuscripts. But there be no reason they can't be sold and be of some good to me. I have children to feed."

I felt a moment of guilt that her man might go to the scaffold for the death of Berwyk, if he indeed had not committed the crime. He swore he was innocent, but any murderer would lie to save himself.

"Could you describe the folk that bought them? Please?"

"Well, that red-haired boy. The one you said had been assaulted. He bought the most. And a yellow-haired student, with a short red-haired man, he bought a few sheets."

"Anyone else?"

Mistress Bookman shook her head in the negative. "That was all. As I said, I just found them yesterday."

# CHAPTER 20

I gave the woman some extra farthings for her trouble and her memory, sheepishly glad she had not connected me with her husband's arrest, and left the stationer's thinking over this new information. The fair lad and red-haired man could well have been Delacey and his bum-boy Richard. As I walked down the crowded street I passed Brother Eusebius coming from the opposite direction.

I turned, buying a pie from a vendor, and stood in the shadows of an overhanging building watching him as he approached the stationer's shop. Too far from me to hear the conversation, I saw Mistress Bookman shake her head as she spoke with the master. She disappeared into the shop and returned a bit later with a bottle of ink and some quills. I watched Eusebius pay her and turn back up the street.

I dropped most of my uneaten pie on the ground, where a dog snatched it up to the frustrated cries of a one-legged beggar who was not fast enough to grab it. Eusebius had just passed me and I fell in step close behind him, following him as he passed School Street and then turned up Catte Street walking north to Smithgate. I quickened my steps and caught up with him a bit further up the way.

"Brother Eusebius," I greeted him.

Eusebius turned and looked at me with an odd absent-minded glare, as if I had just interrupted some priceless and fleeting jewel of philosophical thought.

"Ah yes, Muirteach." He blinked those odd protuberant blue eyes at me. "From the north," he added, whether for his own edification or mine I did not know. "What brings you into town this day?"

"I am seeking my wife," I replied curtly.

"Oh yes, the medical woman. Who vanished."

"Yes, that would be my wife. Do you know aught of such things?"

Eusebius shook his head. "I am but a poor scholar, a seeker after arcane knowledge. I regret that I know nothing of your wife."

Well, I had not really thought he knew anything. It had been a wild throw, and it had missed. "Did you hear about young Anthony? The red-haired student from Lincolnshire?"

"What of him?"

"The poor lad was attacked this morning on his way to the early lectures."

"A sad and lawless act. What happened to the boy? Is he dead?"

"He survived and will doubtless be aright within a few days."

"Young boys have tough skulls." Eusebius looked distracted a moment. "Well, I regret I know nothing of your wife. I must away, I have been called elsewhere."

"We are walking the same direction, no doubt. Are you not headed toward the old hall?"

Eusebius swallowed a moment and I watched his Adam's apple move on his scrawny neck. "Indeed. That is where I was headed."

"I'll accompany you. I seek Master Delacey, and am thinking he might be found there."

"I believe he has a lecture at Sexte. In town."

"Perhaps he does. Or he may be tutoring." I thought sarcastically of poor Dickon. "Still, I shall accompany you to Balliol to seek him there."

When we reached the hall the new gatekeeper let us in with a surly look. This man did not look as though he would be amenable to opening the gate for drunken graduate students after hours. He was a burly man, with thick dark brows over piggy brown eyes and several days' growth of dark beard on his face, clad in a russet overkirtle and hood. I had not seen him before.

"Where did he come from?" I asked Eusebius.

"I am not sure," the master answered. "This is his first day, I believe. I do not recollect seeing him before."

I privately thought that perhaps Eusebius had just neglected to notice the man but said nothing.

We entered the old hall, and Eusebius excused himself and went to his chamber, while I went in search of Delacey. The man was not within his chamber and I saw no sign of his catamite either. Somewhat disheartened, I turned to leave and nearly ran into Phillip Woode on the landing.

Phillip was clearly excited, somewhat flushed. "Muirteach—I just heard of the poor lad Anthony."

"Who told you?'

"The students in my later lecture this morning could speak of little else. Will the boy be all right?"

"Yes, he is alert and able to speak some. I'm thinking the lad will do well enough."

"That is a blessing." Phillip crossed himself. "There has been too much violence of late."

"Where are you off to?"

"I just returned from my lecture," said Phillip as he followed me down the narrow staircase. "I could do with a bite to eat. And you? What brings you here?"

"I thought to find Delacey here."

Phillip laughed. "The man hasn't looked me in the face since

I saw him last night. He scuttled sidewise by me like some loathsome crab this morning on the stairs. I'm sure he's in fear that we will denounce him. We should watch our backs, you know."

"Aye. Perhaps we should take care. Do you think Delacey killed Clarkson and Berwyk?"

"It is indeed a powerful reason to kill. If Clarkson knew of his liaison, it would put an end to his chances for preferment. Delacey is nothing if not ambitious. And Berwyk could well have known of it also."

"Well, Grymbaud claims he'll set a watch on the man."

"That's good. If Delacey doesn't knife us first." Woode laughed without much mirth. "Or perhaps the men on his tail will see him do it and he'll hang for our murders at the least." He threw his cloak over his cotehardie. "Are you hungry, Muirteach? I'm going into town to get a bit to eat."

I had no appetite and did not regret having thrown away that pie. But I did not know where to search or where to go. "Aye, I'll accompany you," I heard myself say. "And perhaps then seek out Delacey."

"What are you wanting him for?"

I told him of the parchment and how Mistress Bookman had said that DeVyse had purchased some of the pages the previous day.

"It might be nothing," Phillip mused. "Perhaps the lad just needed some old parchment."

"Perhaps." I pulled one of the pieces I had purchased from my scrip and looked at it. The sheet had the same crabbed hand on it as the sheets we had found earlier.

"Do you think these are palimpsests as well?" asked Phillip.

"I do not know. They look similar. After we eat I'll take it back to the widow's, check on Anthony and perhaps the lads will clean them and see. No doubt Crispin will be happy to do so, looking for more naked women."

Phillip laughed and this time the sound was happier. "I've no doubt of that."

We left Balliol yard, passing the new gatekeeper.

"Who's your friend?" I asked Phillip. "The new man?"

Phillip raised his eyebrows. "I've no idea. My guess is Delacey hired him. From where, I don't know. The Boccardo, most likely. He is called Hodge."

We made our way into the town, passing through the dark length of the Northgate tunnel that ran under the Boccardo, the town gaol where thieves and such were imprisoned. I spared a thought for Adam Bookman and Ivo, both held at the castle for the more serious crime of murder. The assizes were to be held in four days, and their fates would be decided. I thought of old Ivo's bent frame as I had last seen him in his cell and I shuddered violently.

"What's that?" Phillip asked as we emerged into the daylight and the bustle of Northgate Street. "Did a goose walk over your grave?"

"I hope not."

"You look done in, Muirteach. When did you last eat properly?"

"I can't remember," I answered.

Phillip made a disapproving sound. "You'll never find your wife if you faint from hunger. Come on, man, let's get you some food."

We stopped at a tavern that sold good meals and, truth to tell, I did feel somewhat better after eating some savory roasted fowl and cabbages in pottage. Or perhaps the ale, which was well made and slid easily down my throat, helped. At any rate, after our meal I felt more in command of myself, stronger and less taken by fancies.

"What now?" asked Phillip as he sucked on the last wing bone.

"I'd best check on the lads at the widow's. And then perhaps return to the area north of town, where you found Mariota's ring yesterday, to search some more."

"And Delacey?"

"I'll seek him at the college hall in the evening. I've wasted too much of the day as it is."

"Well enough," Phillip agreed. "I'll keep an eye out for him at Balliol this afternoon."

"Phillip," I asked him, "Do you recall any arguments between Clarkson and the other masters over heresy?"

"I don't attend Wycliffe's lectures," Phillip said with a laugh, "although he did study at Balliol."

"No, I am not speaking of the Lollards. Mistress Jakeson told me of an argument amongst the masters last summer, at The Green Man. She said Clarkson argued with the other masters, Delacey nearly pulled a knife, and it came near to being an ugly scene. Were you there?"

"I am often at The Green Man, although at that time I may have been attending more to Jonetta than to philosophical discussions. But I do recall one evening, in high summer. I'm thinking it was Eusebius who was ranting about something—he is a difficult man to follow at times. Something to do with the divine essence—I could not follow it, and neither could Clarkson, apparently. Everyone was in their cups that night, even Clarkson, which was not usual for him. But it was hot, and summer, the break between terms."

"So what happened?"

"Eusebius was speaking of some tangent, and Delacey grew impatient. It was Eusebius he threatened, not Clarkson. Mistress Jakeson must have misinterpreted what she saw."

"Was there talk of heresy?"

"Not that I recall. Or perhaps Clarkson laughingly said something. No one can quite follow Brother Eusebius's ramblings, once he gets started."

"Yet he is a master of the college."

"Yes, and none so bad a teacher, when he sticks to the topic assigned him. But, by all the saints, please don't get him started on natural philosophy. He idolizes that Friar Bacon, the one that was imprisoned for heresy a hundred years past. Perhaps that is what Clarkson meant."

"And there was no bad blood between any of the masters after that evening?"

Phillip shook his head. "None whatsoever that I noted."

I pushed the bench away from the trestle table and stood up. "I'm away, then."

"And I too, Muirteach. No, don't worry for it," said Phillip as I reached for my purse. "This meal is my treat."

"I thought you had no funds."

"Not so many, but I can well afford this."

I thanked him and he paid the tavern keeper. We left, walking up Catte Street and back into the suburbs through Smithgate.

After we crossed Smithgate I left Phillip and returned to the widow's. I found Anthony still lying abed, while Crispin and Donald sat in my chamber playing the lute. This, apparently, had not overly disturbed Anthony, who slept, snoring gently. The kitten was nowhere in sight. No doubt it misliked the boys playing, as did I.

I dumped my scrip, full of parchments, on my bed.

"Here, I've something else for you lads to do," I said, pulling out the parchments. "See if you can clean these off. Perhaps there's some more mysterious writing under these."

"Where did they come from?" asked Donald, putting aside his lute.

"The stationer's, the same one Anthony visited yesterday.

Adam Bookman's wife said she found them put aside, but thought to sell them and get them out of the way."

Crispin picked up one and looked at it through narrowed eyes. "They do look similar to the ones you had, Donald," he said. "I'll go fetch water to soak them." Crispin left with alacrity.

Donald grinned at me. "He's hoping for more naked women."

"As are you, no doubt."

"Aye, for *certes.*"

We heard Crispin's somewhat heavy tread as he climbed the stairs to our chambers with a bucket of water. "Here it is. Where's the basin?"

The boys started to soak the parchments and I peeked in the other chamber. Anthony had stopped snoring and had his eyes open.

"How are you feeling?" I asked him.

"Better. I think."

"Widow Tanner's poultice must have helped." I looked at the back of Anthony's head and fancied the swelling looked diminished, although the lump still had a deep purple hue.

"Anthony, where did you go yesterday, after you bought those old parchments?"

"I attended one lecture in the afternoon, then Crispin and I stopped at The Red Cockerel and drank some ale. But we did not stay too long there. And then we were back to our lodgings, long before the gates closed.

"Did anyone see you at the bookman's?"

Anthony looked confused. "There are always folk about. It's High Street. I could not say who might have seen me. Why?"

"I'm thinking you were assaulted because of the parchments. Remember, the ones we had here were stolen. Where are the ones you bought yesterday?"

"Back at our lodgings, I would suppose. I left them in my satchel underneath my mattress. They should still be there."

"I'll send Crispin to get them."

Anthony nodded. "He'll know where they are."

Crispin appeared loath to stop washing the parchments we had, but agreed to return to their tenement and get the bag. "And Crispin," I cautioned him as he left, "Show some stealth. Be cautious. Don't let anyone see you with the parchments."

Crispin hooted. "There are ten other boys that share our room."

"You needn't tell them what you're getting, if you see anyone. Just say it is some things Anthony is needing."

Crispin nodded impatiently.

"Be careful," I added, but he was already out the door and down the stairs. I heard the main door slam shut as he left the house.

Anthony looked a little worried. "Will he be all right?"

"I think so. There are many folk about." I fancied Anthony still looked anxious and I felt guilty over sending Crispin out. "Here, now, I will just go outside and watch for him to come back up the street. It should not take too long for him to fetch the sheets."

Anthony looked relieved and lay back against the bolster on the bed. I returned to my own chamber and told Donald what I was about as I grabbed my *brat* and wrapped it around me. I passed Avice at the bottom of the stairs. She had a bowl of fragrant broth on a tray, beef I thought, and so it seemed that Anthony would be nourished in my absence.

Outside the afternoon sun was sinking in the sky. Canditch was crowded with folk about their errands, students and masters heading for their lodgings or to a last lecture. I saw some of the Austin Friars making their way back to their house around the corner as the shadows grew longer. A pie man had a stall across from the boys' tenement and I bought a beef pastry for a farthing, munching on it while I waited. Eusebius waved vaguely as he headed down the street, taking his usual evening walk. The minutes dragged by and I was heartened to see Crispin finally emerge from his lodging and head back toward the Widow Tanner's.

He scowled when he saw me. "What are you about, Muirteach? I've no need for a nursemaid."

I had heard similar phrases from young lads before and tried not to show my own annoyance. "Your friend was anxious for your sake. Don't act the churl over it. Did you find the satchel?"

Crispin nodded sullenly and I found myself wishing for an instant that he had been the lad knocked on the head, instead of Anthony. "Well, let us go, then," I said, glad Crispin was no mind-reader. "Here, I'll buy you a pie for your trouble."

Crispin brightened up a bit at this and devoured his treat while we walked back to the widow's. I saw Crispin safely to the door and then walked out on the road leading north, past the Benedictines' College and Vintner Gibbes's large house to the abandoned homes Phillip and I had searched the day before. I had intended to search this area, and although the day had come close to escaping me I could not abandon my quest.

I passed the houses by and entered into the woods we had searched with the lymers. I don't know what I hoped to find, some trace of my wife that we had overlooked before. But I found nothing, just hazel twigs and the first fallen oak leaves lying on the ground among the grasses and the bracken. The sun disappeared behind the trees and it got too dark to see anything. Disconsolate, I found my way back to the road and started the walk back to our lodgings.

The fading twilight gave a faint light to the road. It had grown chill; I wrapped my mantle more closely about me and shivered. A movement caught my eye, and I hung back in the shadows to watch. Most likely it was the vintner's pig, I thought, gotten loose again. I could barely make out the shape, blacker against the growing darkness. As I strained my eyes it seemed that the shape was too tall to be a pig or other animal. A human, then, but doing what in the darkness?

The figure reached the road. I saw it turn and survey the road behind, as if it did not want to be observed. I sank back into the shadow of a beech tree and watched as the person, apparently satisfied, turned again and started down the way toward the town. I considered whether to approach or not, and decided instead to follow and see where he led. It might, after all, be something entirely without consequence: the vintner looking for his pig, a lover parting from a sweetheart, or some such thing. But I would follow, in any case.

I stayed well back in the shadows but the figure, which I could now make out, wore a hood and cloak. He seemed satisfied he was alone and strode rapidly down the street, turning right when he reached Canditch. Here there were more folk about, and light spilled out from open doorways and unshuttered windows. The figure continued down the street and I strove to keep up while he passed the boys' lodgings and the other tenements. As we reached the corner of St. Giles's Street, the yowl of a cat broke the silence of the night. I turned to look, despite myself, and when I looked ahead again the mysterious figure had vanished.

# CHAPTER 21

I combed the street, walking up and down Canditch to North-gate and then back to the widow's several times. Thinking the mysterious figure must have ducked into a tavern, I also poked my nose into the few taverns in this neighborhood, but none of the patrons looked remotely like the mysterious figure I had followed. Then I walked up St. Giles's Street until I reached the open fields but saw no one. Finally, I abandoned the search, disgusted with my moment's inattention and myself.

The person I'd seen could have been totally innocent, I told myself. A lover returning from a tryst. Or, I added, more cynically, a housebreaker. The figure probably had no import to my search for Mariota. Still, I wondered, and resolved to search that area again on the morrow as I made my discouraged way home through the darkness of a deserted street to the widow's.

I could see a candle burning through the upper window of the chamber I had shared with Mariota and I judged that perhaps the lads were still working on the parchments. At least, thankfully, I heard no sounds of the lute. I opened the door onto the welcome light and warmth of the widow's hall and shut the door on the blackness outside.

"Oh, there you be," said Widow Tanner, looking up from some sewing she worked on by the firelight. "We've saved some pottage for you in the kitchens, thinking you'd be hungry once you returned. You must eat, sir, you are wasting away."

"Aye," I replied, "thank you for that."

The widow sent Avice to the kitchen for the food and then put her sewing aside and busied herself pulling up a stool to the table. "You're wearing yourself down as thin as an over-scraped parchment," she observed.

"And what would you have me do?" I asked, sounding as churlish as Crispin. "I'm going upstairs to check on the lads. I shall be back in a moment."

The widow's comment was meant kindly, I told myself as I wearily climbed the stairs. But that did nothing to help my mood. I entered my chamber and saw Donald and Crispin bent over at the desk Mariota had used. Anthony had joined them and lay on my bed with the tabby kitten pouncing on his toes under the blanket. Several wet parchments also lay on the bed, drying out.

"And so are you having success?" I asked.

Donald and Crispin looked up. "Aye," Donald replied, reverting to Gaelic in his eagerness to tell me. "All the parchments will be having some of that strange writing on them. And some are having the drawings on them as well."

He showed me the faint image of a strange circular object with crenellations somewhat resembling battlements around the edge of it.

"There are no naked women," Crispin interjected. "I've searched and searched and have not found a one."

"Aye, I'm sure you have," I said, wishing I could give the lad a clout. Instead, I turned to Anthony. "And you, sir, are you feeling better?"

"Yes, thank you, sir. Much better. I slept quite a time, and then was hungry. Avice brought pottage."

"And the other two of you, did you eat as well?"

The boys nodded.

"And you thanked your hostess? Widow Tanner is going to some extra trouble to have you all here."

"We are not knaves, Muirteach," Donald retorted. "We thanked her properly."

I nodded. "Good."

"Muirteach," asked Donald, "did you find anything?"

"Nothing," I replied, and leaving the lads to their labors I made my way downstairs.

The table was set with a wooden bowl of hot soup and some fresh bread. Widow Tanner was nowhere in sight. Although I had thought I had no hunger in me, the soup smelled tasty and I ate all of it, and some of the loaf. Avice came in to take away the dishes. I noticed she looked plumper in the belly; the babe was beginning to show.

"Anthony does much better," I observed. "You must be a fine nurse."

The lass flushed as she picked up the empty soup bowl. "I am glad of that, sir." She stood there awkwardly, shifting her weight from one foot to the other. "Sir," she finally asked, "how does my father? Have you seen him? I heard in the market today that the assizes have been called."

"I have heard that as well," I answered. "I have not seen your father in a few days but he is safe enough for now."

"But what if he is hanged after the assizes?"

"He swears he is innocent and I think he is. Let us hope the jurors find him so." I sounded stuffy even to myself, and I knew little of English practices of justice. In my homeland, even if he was guilty, the man could have paid an honor price and that would have been the end of it.

"Then who murdered Master Clarkson?"

I could not answer the lass's question and so said nothing. Avice finally left, leaving her question hanging in the air behind her, and I sat for a time, watching the flames in the fireplace flicker lower until I nodded off. I came awake with a jerk and nearly fell off my stool when Widow Tanner came in to bank the fire. I thanked her for dinner and for feeding the boys, and dragged myself upstairs.

Donald and Crispin were still working on the parchments while Anthony snored on my bed. I left them to it and went into Donald's room, collapsed on top of the bed without even removing my outer clothes and again fell into slumber.

I woke in the morning with a start. Again I had dreamed of Mariota, adrift in some strange vessel. I struggled to remember, but it was all confused. Mariota in some large glass vessel, or mayhap it was one of Vintner Gibbes's abandoned casks, adrift in the sea. I gave up and rubbed at my eyes, trying to push fragments of my unpleasant dreams from my mind.

The sun was full up and beside me on the bed Donald lay, snoring with his mouth open. I stood up, rearranged my disordered attire and peered into the other chamber. Both Anthony and Crispin still slept, looking like little angels in a stained-glass window, although I very well knew them to be no such thing. The kitten lay wedged between them, also asleep, stretched out on its back with its four paws in the air. None of them looked as though they would wake anytime soon.

I glanced at the metal candlestick on the table and saw that the candle had entirely burned away. On the desk next to the candlestick lay a pile of the cleaned parchments. I bent to look at them and picked up the top sheet, the drawing of the strange crenellated orb. The next page had a similar drawing. The third sheet was full of the same writing I recognized from the previous parchments, that strange script in an unrecognizable language.

Since the attack on Anthony I felt increasingly certain that these parchments had something to do with the murders. Clarkson had sold them to Bookman, I recalled. Perhaps they had some value, and Berwyk had seen them and recognized that as well, and for that reason Bookman had stabbed Master Berwyk. I gathered a few of the cleaned parchments together, bundled them up in my scrip and scribbled a note to the lads, then left the house.

As I walked down Canditch I saw the undersheriff near the pie-man's stall. "Muirteach," he hailed me as he paid the vendor, "I've news."

"Yes?"

"We've finally found that Walter of York. The chapman?"

"Was Jonetta with him?" I prayed that the lass had been found safe, but the man's next words dashed my hopes.

Grymbaud shook his grizzled head. "No. The man denies she was ever with him." He bit into his pie.

"Where was he found?"

Grymbaud chewed awhile, then answered. "Well out of Oxfordshire, on his way home, in the village of Heptonstall. Close to home, he was. We've checked out his story and folk in the villages he visited remember him passing through, alone. No one remembers seeing the girl with him."

"So either he is telling the truth—" I said.

"Or he's slain the poor girl and secreted her body away close to town here."

I shuddered.

"Did you find anything from Mistress Bookman yesterday?" asked Grymbaud, changing the subject before he took another bite.

"Nothing of import. I think the attack on the lad had to do with these." I pulled one of the parchments out of my bag and showed it to the undersheriff, who took it with his free hand. "If they have value it might have been a reason for Bookman to slay Berwyk."

The undersheriff squinted at the parchment, holding it upside down. "Gibberish, it looks like."

"We've made no sense of them. But Bookman had them secreted away, so it's possible they're of some value. His wife found them and thought to sell them."

"And do you know where Bookman got them?"

"He got them from Clarkson."

The undersheriff grunted and wiped at his mouth with the parchment. "So perhaps Berwyk killed Clarkson over the parchments, and then Bookman slew Berwyk in turn. But I don't see much use of this parchment except for an arse-wipe."

"What of Delacey?"

Grymbaud made a face. "I questioned him but the braggart swore he had benefit of clergy and that he was innocent besides that. And it's true, the little turd. That's the worst of it. We've no evidence or witnesses to say he did the murder, and he does have benefit of clergy. A great mess of stinking perverts, all these damned scholars. And their parchments."

"Here," I interjected before Grymbaud could throw the parchment away on the muddy street, "let me keep this for a time."

"Well enough, Muirteach. Well enough."

"And what of Walter of York?"

"We've got him here in the castle gaol. Until we can find what happened to that girl or find her body. What might be left of it, if the crows and wolves have left any trace. We've the evidence of that master that the chapman was seen leaving town with Jonetta."

"Mistress Jakeson will take this hard," I observed.

"Indeed," the undersheriff answered. "It's no easy thing to lose a child. I lost three in the pestilence. My eldest would have been well grown by now."

"I am sorry," I said awkwardly.

Grymbaud shrugged. "Most all of us lost someone. The saints turned a blind eye to our prayers. They did us no good."

I knew, for I had lost my mother as a lad to the plague as well.

The undersheriff continued. "But this lass was not killed by the pestilence. If she's dead, it's by man's work. And a man will hang for it."

I could not even argue with him that Jonetta might still live. It did not seem likely.

I bade Grymbaud farewell and left him, still scratching at his beard. I continued on my way down the street. It was in my mind to visit Balliol and seek out Delacey. Mistress Bookman had told me she had sold parchments to a couple that resembled Delacey and DeVyse.

When I reached Balliol, the new gatekeeper glowered at me but let me in when I gave him half a farthing. I surmised he was doing well enough at his new post, and thought Ivo had not taken such advantage of his position in the past. The assizes were to be held the next day and as of yet I had done nothing to help the old man. I pushed the thought out of my mind guiltily as I opened the wooden door to the old hall.

At table in the central room I spied Delacey finishing up his breakfast, some bread and white cheese along with a mug of ale. His face flushed unpleasantly as he saw me enter the room.

"What is it you are wanting, Muirteach? Are you not satisfied at having set Grymbaud on me?"

"You yourself told him there's no evidence against you. And you've benefit of clergy, as you also pointed out. You're safe enough, no doubt. I came to ask you something." I sat down, uninvited, at an empty bench opposite the table from Delacey. He said nothing but waited, his mug set down on the table and his arms crossed over his chest.

"Where is Brother Eusebius?"

"At his early lecture, I presume. What's that to do with me?"

"Nothing. I want to know what you had to do with some

240

parchments you bought, the day before yesterday it was, at Adam Bookman's stall."

"Parchments . . . oh, those. Dickon bought them, not I."

"Perhaps. Mistress Bookman remembers seeing the both of you there."

"What of that?"

"Why did you purchase them?"

"Dickon needed some parchments. It's easy enough to soak and clean these."

"Is that all?"

"What else should it be?"

I noticed there was an empty mug on the table and poured myself some ale from the pitcher, ignoring Delacey's irritated expression.

"Do you remember that parchment that the lads gave to Berwyk?"

"Aye. The one in code, that Ralph showed us?"

"When your Dickon cleans the ones he bought I'm thinking he'll find these are the same."

"What of it?"

I grew disgusted with Delacey's bravado and stood up to leave. "I'm thinking that these palimpsests are tied somehow to the murders. Ours were stolen. If your Dickon values his parchments then I'd advise him to hide them well. And to watch his back. The lad Anthony was attacked over the sheets he owned." With that I left the room and the hall.

I walked rapidly up Canditch and passed the widow's, wondering briefly if the lads were awake yet. The little dog Rufous came bounding toward me in the street, barking, but he quieted when he smelled my hand. I decided I'd not mind the company, missing Somerled, and let the dog tag along beside me. I turned up the street that led north and passed the walls of the Austin Friars' on the right, walking rapidly with Rufous up the street. I passed the Benedictines' college on the left, then Vintner Gibbes's house, until I reached the area where Phillip had found Mariota's ring in the mud. With the dog by my side I turned off the road and into the yard of the abandoned house. It looked as I had left it, the loose shutter still flapping in the breeze. I looked about for the barrel but did not see it. Perhaps Vintner Gibbes had come and fetched it back.

I found a log in the back and rolled it over under the window, with Rufous yapping at my heels in excitement. Standing on the log I was able to hoist the dog up and push him through the window, then make my own way through after him. The dog barked excitedly while I awkwardly wriggled in. The bench still stood below the window where Phillip and I had left it and I landed on it with a thump.

The empty hall looked just as it had before and the house seemed undisturbed. But Rufous ran through the dusty rushes barking wildly until he came to the side room where he nosed excitedly about the trunk. My heart sank as I looked at it—a large wooden chest with a complex iron lock. I pushed at it and jiggled it, but the lock stayed stubbornly shut tight. The little dog kept yapping.

The lock was somewhat rusted, old, and I surmised that perhaps I could break it if I could just find a mallet or some such tool. I walked back into the main hall but saw nothing of use. So I climbed the bench, wormed my way through the window again, my bad leg quivering with the strain, and searched around outside the house until I found a large rock near the back edge of the yard, close to the woods, that might serve as a hammer. Then I repeated the somewhat laborious process of climbing back into the house, my leg now starting to ache in earnest.

Rufous yipped, glad to see me, as I landed heavily once again on the bench. I sat up, brushed myself off and walked back into the side room with the chest. The lock looked still sturdy, the rust not too far advanced. I pounded at it for some time, my arms aching while Rufous sat by, watching attentively, one ear cocked up. Finally, the lock cracked and the lid opened a little, and I was able to pry it up, smashing my knuckles in the process.

The old leather hinges creaked as I raised the lid. I peered inside while my heart hammered in my breast. But all I saw was empty space. The trunk held nothing.

Discouraged, I collapsed on the floor against it. I am not sure what I had expected to find, perhaps some putrid remains. I felt relief, at least, that it had not been what I'd feared the most. Slumped against the trunk, I leaned my back against its bulk and closed my eyes a moment, the empty chest sliding a little from my weight. I felt a furry warmth in my lap and a wet tongue and realized Rufous had crawled in my lap and was licking at my ear. I patted the dog absently a moment before I opened my eyes, pushed the dog out of my lap and made to stand up, leaning my hand on the trunk as I levered my body up.

Rufous barked again and I bent down to pat him some more when I spied something in the floor—a joint in the wood planks that looked overly wide. Curious, I shoved the chest further aside and saw a wooden trap door with an iron ring for a handle on it.

I tugged at the ring and with effort was able to pull the door up and open. I peered down into the blackness. A wooden ladder descended into the undercroft, dimly lit by the light from the upstairs room. Rufous continued to yap. I took a deep breath and began to climb down the ladder.

The undercroft was a large room. I stood on the packed dirt floor and looked around. A faint light filtered down from the open trap door. As my eyes adjusted to the dim light I realized the cellar was not empty. Some large vats sat on the floor and in the further recesses of the space I saw a table and what looked like wooden coops of some kind.

A scent in the room teased at my nostrils. Something foul, like waste, and perhaps the acrid scent of fear. From above, the little dog still barked and I found I was glad of the companionship.

I walked closer, feeling my way past the vats and over to a table. A lantern stood there with a rush light lying nearby. I placed it in the holder and found flint and tinder there and struck a light. As the rush light caught and flickered, lightening the darkness, I saw a pile of parchments on the table. I picked one up and recognized the script and figures. Ink, quills, and pots of colors sat on the table as well.

A rustle from the corner startled me and I glanced up, peering into the darkness. In the furthest recess of the undercroft—I judged it to be under the furthest end of the great hall—I realized one of the strange coop-like structures held a white form and my heart began to pound frantically.

"Mariota!" I called, my throat tight. I thought I heard a faint cry and my heart began to pound like some wild thing.

I raced across the floor to the structures. The scent grew stronger, the scent of despair and fear. There were two of them, rough cages built of wooden sticks, closed with iron padlocks. And in one of them I found my wife.

# CHAPTER 22

"Mariota!" I cried and the figure in the cage turned and looked at me. I held my breath, not knowing what to expect, and my heart bounded with joy when I saw recognition in her eyes.

"Muirteach." She smiled a little, her voice faint. "You've come for me at last."

I fumbled with the padlock, but although it was not too complex, it was strong iron and I could not get it open. I reached in through the wooden bars and grabbed my wife's hand, tight. I had feared I would never hold it again.

"*Mo chridhe,* you're alive. You're alive," I repeated like some fool.

"Aye, I am," my wife replied with some of her old spirit, "but I'd like to get out of here. Muirteach, get me out and away from this place."

The coop was a small thing, and there was barely room for my wife to crouch in it. Surely she could not stand upright. She wore a linen shirt and nothing else, and her face was wan and frightened.

"Who put you here, *mo chridhe,*" I asked, loath to release the warmth of her hand in order to get tools to break her out.

"Eusebius," she answered. "And I am not alone here." She turned her head to the structure next to her and I saw that coop also held a human figure, crouching and staring at me with large silent eyes. "See," my wife said, "it is Jonetta."

I felt at my belt for my knife. "Just a wee moment, *mo chridhe,* and I will be getting the both of you out of here and away from this place. But I may need to be leaving you a moment to do it."

I let go of my wife's hand and turned to the woman in the other cage. "Mistress Jonetta, I am a friend."

Jonetta said nothing. The rush light fell on her white face in the darkness. She huddled there, unresponsive, clad only in her linen smock.

I pushed the rush light in through the bars of the cage to my wife. "*Mo chridhe,* I will just be going up to get a tool to break these bars and get you out of this place. I am not going far, just up the ladder."

Mariota nodded tautly and I sprinted through the darkness of the cellar to the ladder. Above, the little dog still stood guard, ears cocked. I climbed the ladder and reached for the rock and grabbed the dog as well, then made my way back down again into that hell-like cavern. When my feet were firmly on the floor, I set the little dog down and made my way back to the horrid cages at the far corner, followed by Rufous.

"Now, we will be just getting the both of you out of here." The padlocks looked hopeless. I hacked at the wooden bars with my dagger and was able to weaken them in two spots. Then I smashed at the weakened bars with the rock, until finally I made an opening in my wife's prison. Rufous whined and yapped while I worked.

"It won't be long, now, white love, and you'll be away from this. And that will be time enough to find out how you came to be here."

"It was Eusebius," my wife repeated. "He accosted me that morning—how many days has it been, Muirteach? I've no way of knowing. *Och,* Muirteach, he may be back, he will be back—you must be swift."

"I am trying to be," I muttered as I knocked in the last of the wooden bars. The splintering sound provided some satisfaction. "Now, my love, let's get you out."

I took the rush light and set it on the floor, then grabbed my wife and helped her out. Mariota could not stand but collapsed on the earthen floor, shivering. I took off my mantle and wrapped it around her, but she still shook violently, I do not think from the cold. Rufous jumped in her lap and she held on to the squirming dog tightly while I turned my attention to Jonetta's cage.

"This will not take too long," I said, hoping my voice would reassure the silent figure. "Your parents will be aye glad to see you, Mistress Jakeson. Folk had near given up hope, yet here you are."

I looked at Jonetta's face and thought I saw a tear trickle down her cheek. Encouraged, I kept babbling while I sawed at the wooden bars of the cage. Finally, I judged them weak enough to begin battering at them with my makeshift mallet, and my relief was great when I heard them begin to crack. "It will not be long now, Miss Jonetta," and with that the bars gave way. "Now we must get you out. You must help me, if you can."

With some effort, I extricated the tavern keeper's daughter from her hateful cage. It was more like moving a large doll or poppet as she passively let me move her. Yet I was relieved to see her free from that prison. Jonetta could not stand at first and sank against me. I held her and lowered her to sit on the dank floor.

"Now, ladies, we must get you out and away from this place. But to do that you must stand and walk. Can you?"

Mariota nodded assent, pushed herself up with my help, and then shook free the mantle, glancing at Jonetta. I wrapped it around the lass and chafed at her body, seeking to warm her and get her upright. Finally, Jonetta also stood. She looked at me and I began to find hope the girl had not gone mad from her ordeal.

"Come then, let us be away from here."

We made our laborious way across the dimly lit cavern to the ladder. "Mariota, can you climb?"

My wife nodded and began making her grim way up the wooden rungs. Jonetta also seemed able to climb and began the ascent. Although the ladder was only a few feet tall, the way seemed endless as I watched the women. Finally, assured they were safe, I grabbed Rufous and climbed up myself, emerging finally into the little room off of the great hall.

The two women stood blinking in the light, clad only in their linen shifts. Jonetta held my brat over her head; I surmised the light hurt her eyes after her long confinement. Mariota held her hands over her own eyes to shield them from the daylight, while Rufous, calm for once, sat expectantly at their feet.

I had neither food nor drink with me to give them and sorely wished I did. Yet I grabbed my wife and embraced her tenderly, holding her close and feeling her heart beat against mine for a moment.

"I am all right, Muirteach," she said after an instant. "But we must be away from here. He may be coming back."

"Eusebius?"

She nodded. "He came at odd times. At least, in that darkness we had no way of telling when he would come, or how long he would stay. Oh, please, let us be away from this horrid place."

And so we left.

We quit that place through the window. I bundled the two women up with my brat wrapped around the both of them, and we made our way down the street to the Widow Tanner's, Rufous trailing at our heels. We ignored for the most part the curi-

ous looks of the few passersby. We did not see Brother Euse-
bius, which may have been a good thing, as I would have knifed
him on the spot. When we got to safety I sent Crispin to the
Jakesons' with word to come quickly and sent Donald to tell
Grymbaud what I had found, while Anthony was put back in
Donald's chamber.

The widow gave orders for a bath to be prepared and after a
short time, despite all my protests, she banished me to the front
hall while she and Avice bathed and fussed over the two women.
When she finally allowed me to return, both women were looking somewhat better. Widow Tanner had found clothes for
Jonetta while Mariota was back in her own garb. While the
widow left to fetch a warm posset I finally had a better chance
to speak with the women and, although Jonetta had little to say,
my wife was in full possession of her wits and all too eager to
talk.

"And so what happened?" I asked.

"It was that morning—how many days ago was it?"

"Four days," I said. "*Mo chridhe*, it has been four days."

"Is that all? It feels like I have lived a life in Hell since that
time."

I took my wife's hand again and sat down next to her on the
bed. Jonetta lay near us, covered with blankets, but I paid her
little mind, intent on Mariota who continued speaking.

"I had left the lecture and was nearly home, thinking to
change and meet you at Berwyk's funeral mass as we'd planned.
And I was nearly home, when I realized Eusebius was following
me. He stopped me, speaking to me as if I was William of Uist,
and spoke of some experiment in natural science he wished to
show me."

"And you went with him?" It was on the tip of my tongue to
call my wife a fool but she shook her head before I could utter
the words, which was no doubt a good thing.

"No, I said I had another lecture to attend and must be on my way. But he grabbed me, very persistent, and then I felt a knife at my side. And he told me to come quietly and not to scream, or the sound would be my last. And so I went with him then, for I did not want to die."

I shuddered.

"He pulled my hood over my face so I could not rightly see where he led me. I knew it could not be far and saw from the dirt when he led me off the street. I tried to lose my ring, as a sign—I do not think he saw that but then he struck me on the head and I do not remember what came after. When I came back to myself I was as you saw me, in that little coop. But there was no light and Eusebius had gone."

"And Jonetta?"

"It was all blackness, and I could not see a thing. It was only when Eusebius returned, later, with a light, that I knew she was there."

"Why did you not cry out?"

"I did, Muirteach, but no one came. And there was one time we heard noises, as though someone was in the house, and I did cry out, but no one heard us."

I thought of the day when Phillip and I had explored the ruined house, and how close we had come, and cursed that we had not found her then. But at least she was now free.

"And when he did come," I said, hesitant.

"He did not mistreat us. And he fed us a little, some stale bread. And would leave a light, but that burned out quickly, and then it would be all dark. Muirteach, the man is mad. He would make notes on those parchments of his, and brought vats in, trying to assemble something—conduits of some kind and the vats—all the while muttering to himself about the feminine essence. I do not know what exactly he planned but I thank the Blessed Mother you found us before he had all ready. For I do not know what he would have done with us, in the end."

Just then we heard the front door of the house open and the widow's voice, speaking to the undersheriff. His heavy tread came up the stairs, and the door to our chamber opened.

"And so you have found them both. Well done, Muirteach, indeed."

I nodded, and we told the story to the undersheriff.

"And the girl's parents?" asked Grymbaud.

"Are on their way, no doubt. I sent Crispin for them."

Just then we heard more commotion downstairs and a moment later the door opened again, and Jonetta was reunited with her parents. At which point the girl, stoic until now, burst into floods of tears and I began to pray she had not lost her wits entirely. But after a time, when things had settled and our little chamber was quite crowded, she managed to find the voice to tell her own story, not all that different from my wife's. Jonetta had been at the market when she had felt a knife against her side and was cautioned to come quietly or she would die. And she also had gone with Eusebius.

"And you also were not assaulted?" the undersheriff asked. "No violence was done to your body."

"No sir, but I was made to stay in that coop, in the blackness. I thought I would go mad indeed, from the lack of light and the fear."

"Brave girl," said Grymbaud, patting her awkwardly on the shoulder while Mistress Jakeson fussed over her daughter and sat next to her on our now very crowded bed, and her father swore vengeance to the undersheriff.

"We must make plans, I think," said Grymbaud, and both Master Jakeson and myself were well inclined to agree. "Not many folk saw you return?"

"There were not so many folk about."

"Well, perhaps Eusebius does not yet know his birds have

flown. So we will catch him in his own nest," said the under-sheriff as he scratched at his beard. And so we plotted. The afternoon sun was not yet far to the west, and I remembered Eusebius's evening rambles. We made haste to set our trap before the day was over.

I was loath to part from my wife again, but the thought of vengeance lured me away from her company. The widow gave her a sedative draft, and the Jakesons agreed, once we had settled on a course of action, to leave Jonetta at the widow's and put out the story that Crispin's fetching them earlier in the day had been but some false alarm. For we did not want our quarry to learn of what had transpired.

Mistress Jakeson remained with her daughter while Master Jakeson, Donald, Crispin, and I, along with Grymbaud and some of his men, made our way to the abandoned house.

"Well, Walter of York, at the least, will be happy of this day's work," Grymbaud remarked to me in an undertone as we approached the building. "He will be a free man."

We made our way into the house through the broken window and hid ourselves in the house, waiting while the sun sank lower in the sky. Grymbaud had some of his men positioned down in the undercroft with shuttered lanterns while the rest of us hid in some of the side rooms off the hall. Then we waited, silent, for our quarry.

The light had mostly faded from the sky and we rested in the hall in growing darkness. My nerves were taut and my eyes strained in the twilight as I stood immobile. After what seemed like an eternity in Purgatory I heard footsteps approaching the house and a key in the lock, which sounded well oiled and turned easily. We heard the door open and footsteps cross the hall to the room with the trap door.

The sound of the chest scraping the floor as it was pushed aside came next, then the raising of the trap door. A scuffing

sound told us that our quarry had descended into the undercroft.

I felt Grymbaud next to me give the signal and we followed
Eusebius to the cellar, going down after him. The undersheriff's
men had unshuttered their lanterns and we saw Eusebius standing in the middle of the undercroft, looking back and forth at
the armed men and then at us, behind him at the foot of the
ladder. The flickering light from the lanterns—his and our
own—illuminated his tall frame and pale face, and I fancied he
looked confused.

"Where are they?" he roared as he approached his cages and
realized they were empty. "Where are they?"

"The women, you mean?" asked Grymbaud, advancing with
his sword drawn. "They're gone, safe now. And you will be
coming with me."

"No, no, I cannot," cried Eusebius, crossing to the table piled
high with parchments and attempting to gather them up. "You
don't understand—my work, my studies—I must continue. The
voices will it."

Grymbaud gave me a speaking look as if to say the man was
mad. And indeed he seemed so, ignoring the armed men and
scrabbling desperately at his papers, like a rat, I thought. The
sound of his voice sent chills down my back.

"I must find new subjects, the feminine essence must be
distilled, the secret of immortality . . ."

What the man was saying made no sense to me, or to Grymbaud. He signaled his men to approach and take hold of the
Franciscan, and I thought for a moment the man might come
quietly. But Eusebius proved me wrong.

As the guards laid hands on him, Eusebius threw his arms
up, pushing them away. His lantern overturned and I smelled
scorching as the parchments caught, the upset candle licking at
them with a hungry tongue of fire. He screamed in anguish,

almost as though his own flesh burned and began to hit at the parchments, attempting to smother the flames. The men went after him again, but Grymbaud motioned them to stop.

"You must come with us. You can take these parchments with you, if you must," he said, speaking as if to a child.

"They will be lost, all lost," cried Eusebius. "Clarkson tried to stop my work, they all tried but it must continue. I alone have the knowledge, the guidance to do so—the work must not be lost."

"No, now, it shall not be. They're here," said Grymbaud, placatingly. "The most of them. Come quietly now, come with us."

"But there is too much work yet to do—I cannot leave it undone, I must finish—the voices command it."

I could see Grymbaud's dark eyebrows rise as he rolled his eyes at me and I saw one of the men cross himself. Brother Eusebius did not notice, so intent was he on extinguishing the last smoldering flames on the scorched parchments.

"Come, gather them together and let us go," I said, approaching him. The guards stood back in the dimly lit undercroft.

"But the feminine essence—it is all lost," cried Eusebius, looking again at the empty cages that stood, broken doors open, in the corner darkness.

"No, now," I repeated, "it is all safe." And I thanked God indeed that that was so. "We will take you someplace where you can continue your studies in safety. Come along with us."

And to my great surprise, Eusebius complied.

# CHAPTER 23

"We can take him to the castle temporarily, at least for the night," Grymbaud muttered to me as we walked Eusebius, now compliant and quiet, through the dark streets, "but when the chancellor gets wind of this there'll be trouble. The man has benefit of clergy; we can't hang him for kidnapping, no matter how perverse a bastard he is."

"The man is mad, I think," I observed.

"Indeed, possessed by some demon more likely, and how did he gain access to that house?" Grymbaud wondered. "And what was it he said about Clarkson? The assizes are tomorrow, and the old man is to be tried for that murder."

As if I was not well aware of that fact. "This changes things, does it not? Perhaps we can make some sense from his ravings."

Grymbaud shrugged grimly in the light from his lantern. "Good luck with that, Muirteach."

We reached the castle and installed Eusebius in a cell under guard. He only seemed concerned for his parchments and then, like a child, quieted when he had them nearby. Although a light was denied him when we left him, he was holding them close to his face, studying them, as though he could see in the dark, like some cat or wild beast.

I sent word to the widow's that Eusebius had been captured and thought to send word to Balliol as well, but Grymbaud forestalled me.

"Let us wait on that, Muirteach. As soon as those university men catch wind of this, they'll be all for releasing the bastard. Wait until we know more." With that he called for some supper to be served and I found I had an appetite for the first time in days, knowing that my wife was safe at home. I ate with relish, although I found the meat tough and stringy and the bread stale.

After we had eaten I judged it time to speak again with Eusebius. It had grown late but the stairs leading down to the cell were lit with torches, giving off a resinous scent. I took a lantern, and the guard unlocked the iron lock and pushed the cell door open with a creak.

"Has he been quiet?" I asked.

"He's raving." The door slammed shut behind me and I faced the man who had abducted my wife.

I wanted to take his head and slam it against the rock walls of the cell until his face was nothing but a bloody pulp. But I managed to hold back, thinking of Ivo and even Adam Bookman. I told myself that I'd find out what I could before giving myself the pleasure of such actions.

I looked at my adversary. He did not look so dangerous now. Eusebius sat on the dirty straw surrounded by his piles of parchments. He stared up at me with those strangely protuberant blue eyes.

"You see, it's of such import," he said, all in a rush of agitation. "This is divinely inspired. Clarkson didn't believe me, when he found my work—he swore it to be heresy. But it is not, the voices tell me what to write and how to write it. It is the tongue of the angels. I must have ink, though. The knowledge will be lost; I must get it down. They speak so quickly, you see. You must help me, get me ink, and a quill."

"Perhaps later. I need some information first from you."

Eusebius smiled. "You comprehend, then. Information, you see, that is what this is all about. You understand, do you not?

The knowledge, the divine intelligence that speaks to me; it gives such vast quantities of information and none of it must be lost."

"How did you gain access to the house?"

"The angels willed it. My uncle owned it, but he died, you see. In the plague. I inherited the key. The angels willed that he leave me the house, wanting to help in my work."

"And what of the women? My wife, whom you abducted? And the other, the tavern maid?"

"I was upset at first," Eusebius admitted with disarming frankness. "After they were discovered. But now I understand. They are of little import. I had hoped to prove the divinely inspired intelligence, the theory—you do understand, do you not?" he repeated. "It is the angels speaking directly to me. And I was wrong to doubt it, to think it needed proof. Ergo, the women were freed. They were not necessary—but I must have ink and paper."

"And Clarkson? Was he not necessary?"

"He thought all of this heresy. But it is not, you see."

"Indeed."

"He found my parchments and took them, sullied my work and wrote upon them. Saying that they were ravings only, and heretical. That they should be destroyed. That they were the work of a madman. I am not mad, the writing not heresy. They are not ravings—it is so very clear, divinely inspired. Inspired by my voices—the voices of the angels."

"And so you struck Clarkson, in his chambers."

"He'd have betrayed me. It was needful. The voices spoke to me of it, they said it was no sin."

I sighed in relief. At least Ivo would not hang on the morrow.

"You comprehend, do you not?" Eusebius repeated. "Ah yes, I can see that you do. For you have brought me light, so that I can continue my work. But where is the ink?"

"I've brought no ink. What of Berwyk? Did you slay him as well?"

"He had my parchment, and showed it as a novelty. A novelty! He did not understand its import. And would have shown it to all, as a curiosity. It is far too sacred for that, it must be kept in secret until mankind is ready."

"Thus the code?"

"I told you, it is the angels' own speech. And they told me how to slay Berwyk. I had to be crafty, sly. I led us into the town, for there was no messenger—or was it an angel at the door? And the melee, a divine opportunity, don't you see?"

"So you knifed him in the church?"

"The angels ordained that I followed behind him, when we ran to safety. And divine assistance made it easy. You see," he lowered his voice, "this work will not be tampered with, it will not be stopped."

"You broke into the Widow Tanner's and stole the parchments."

"Once I learned where Berwyk's sheet came from, I had to reclaim them."

"And attacked the lad as well. Anthony."

"He is but a puling youth. His eyes should not see such holy information; he has not the wisdom for that. You see, these parchments contain the secret of the eternal union with the divine." Eusebius paused, with a listening look on his face.

"Hurry, you must help me, get me parchment, and ink—they are giving me more to write, I cannot remember all of it, I must write. Quick man, where is the ink? You have brought ink; did you not say you would bring me ink? And quill—no matter, I can use the straw for quills, but ink I will have. Ink I must have."

I showed him my empty hands. "I have no ink."

Eusebius listened again, but not to me. "Yes, yes, I understand." He stood, approaching me. "Ah, but you have brought me ink—it is your own blood that you have brought me, and I can write with that very well."

I stepped back, but the lunatic lunged at me and grabbed my wrist, trying to bite at it. I yelled for the guard while Eusebius reached for my dagger, but in that he was unsuccessful and I satisfied my urge to slam the man's head against the wall. The guard came just in time.

"You are right, he's raving," I told the guard. "But he's confessed to two murders."

As I ascended the steps to the main floor of the castle I could still hear Eusebius screaming for ink in the darkness of his cell.

The next morning I was back at the castle for the assizes. Mariota, looking much better, also wished to attend, although her evidence was not required in these cases. The trials were short, as both men's innocence was proved by my own testimony. Eusebius was not in any shape to speak. He had been found that morning, having bitten at his own wrist for blood, writing busily on the walls of the cell with his finger in that strange cipher of his. The daylight revealed the stonework covered with coded gibberish and strange diagrams, and Eusebius himself, although weak from loss of blood, was not yet dead when he was discovered.

Delacey had been summoned, and the situation explained to him. Pompous as ever, he conferred with the university chancellors and they quickly made arrangements for Eusebius to be transported under guard and cared for in a secluded monastery far to the north—Yorkshire, I think it was.

"Benefit of clergy, bah," Grymbaud swore, as the rolls from the assizes were completed and Ivo and Bookman released. I spied Mistress Bookman embracing her husband in the crowd, as well as Avice with her father, and was thankful that they at least were not mourning their kin that day. "That lunatic should hang for what he did."

I tended to agree with the undersheriff. But perhaps Eusebius lived in his own hell now, before going on to that of Our Lord at his death.

# EPILOGUE

Mariota and I remained in Oxford through the winter, although my wife refrained from attending more lectures dressed in men's garb. She seemed subdued by her ordeal and I feared she would once again panic and grow ill, but she spent her time reading medical texts and Rudolf of Salerno agreed to tutor her privately. I escorted her and slept through their discussions. Ivo joined Avice in service at Widow Tanner's, for neither felt inclined to return to Balliol.

Delacey, not surprisingly, won election as the next master of Balliol and Phillip Woode at length passed his dissertation. So Phillip proved not fated to teach eight-year-olds their letters in the parish school, but could remain in Oxford, completing his studies and flirting with Jonetta. Although from what I observed on my visits to The Green Man, their relations might soon surpass mere flirting and move on to more serious courtship.

Donald actually made some progress in his studies that winter. Perhaps the excitement of the first portion of the term allowed him to settle later into a somewhat more studious bent, although neither his lute nor the taverns were altogether neglected, to my regret. And finally, much to my relief, the Lord of the Isles felt his son well enough established in the south that he called me and my wife back home, and sent a groom and another manservant down to keep watch over his son.

So it was that on a raw March day, Mariota and I, along with one half-grown tabby cat shut up in a wicker basket and a small reddish-brown dog, a final gift of Widow Tanner's, thankfully left the gates of Oxford behind us and started our journey back to the Isles along the north road. As for what it was that His Lordship wanted of me, and his reasons for calling us home, that is another tale.

# ABOUT THE AUTHOR

**Susan McDuffie** has been a fan of historical fiction and mysteries since childhood, spending such vast amounts of time reading historical fiction that she wondered if she was mistakenly born in the wrong century.

*A Mass for the Dead,* Susan's first historical mystery novel, introduced Muirteach MacPhee, the bastard son of a medieval prior. Muirteach continues his adventures in *The Faerie Hills* (awarded the New Mexico Book Awards "Best Historical Novel 2011") and now in *The Study of Murder.*

Susan has lived in New Mexico since 1982 and shares her life with a Cochiti Pueblo artist and four rambunctious cats. She is currently working on Muirteach's next case. Susan loves to hear from readers and can be contacted at s.mcduffie@att.net or via her website at www.SusanMcDuffie.net.